He lay back and fixed his eyes on a small crack in the smooth ceiling. They were bedroom eyes—two vibrant explosions of color, with green and gold flecks of starlight shimmering in a pair of glistening blue universes. The eyes had either caused the crack or were trying to mend it. Behind them was soothing music that washed over and through him. His muscles ached, sore and raw from an abusive workout—a good pain that reminded him he was not only alive but being well and getting stronger. Draped in the light of a single lamp, which, on the lowest setting, colored his ruffled sheets and the piled furniture of the room with a yellow whisper of illumination, with the sky outside a long band of post-sunset gray, not yet black, he ruminated. This was the final evening of a very familiar era of his life—a fact he was fully conscious of as his mind reeled, as his feet waited on the precipice of what came next.

A few blocks away, on a Pacific beach, several rhythmic drum circles joined together and gave their collective percussive offering to the dusk, and the gathered groups danced and pounded their drums and pulled the shade closed as the day dissipated into its ongoing, starlit conclusion.

In the morning, before dawn, he would be moving on.

MUSIC MADE BY BEARS

Other books by Daniel Donatelli

JIBBA AND JIBBA

OH, TITLE!

Music Made By Bears

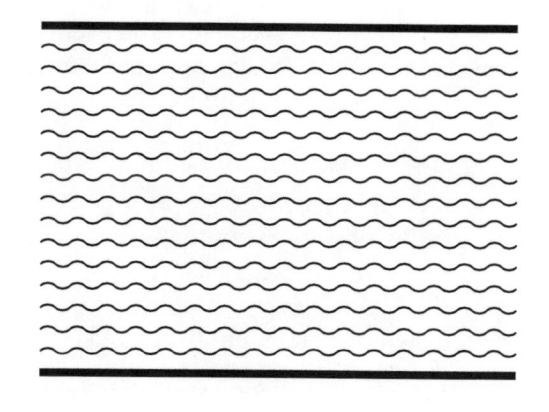

Daniel Donatelli

H.H.B. Publishing, LLC

Copyright © 2011 by Daniel Donatelli

All rights reserved. No part of this publication may be reproduced, stored in a retrieval system, or transmitted in any form or by any means, electronic, mechanical, photocopying, recording, or otherwise, without the prior written permission of the publisher.

This is a work of fiction; all characters and events in this novel—even those based on real people and real events—are entirely fictional.

Paperback ISBN: 978-1-937648-00-8
EPUB ISBN: 978-1-937648-01-5
Kindle ISBN: 978-1-937648-02-2
PDF ISBN: 978-1-937648-03-9

Published by H.H.B. Publishing, LLC
Henderson, Nevada

Design and layout by M. Wang

Manufactured in the United States of America

www.hhbpublishing.com

"In the dark woods, on the sodden ground,
I found my way only by the whiteness of his collar."
—*Franz Kafka*

PROLOGUE

NATHAN CAMERON
AN INTRODUCTION

His parents were born and raised their family in the small town of Winston, Pennsylvania. The bricklayer and the hairdresser met in high school, married in their early twenties, and had their only two children before they were thirty.

The first child inherited the father's massive frame—with each man looking more like a war machine than a human being—and received a formal education from the town school system before going to a local university on an athletics scholarship, where he studied for the masonry business that he would also inherit from his father.

Nathan Cameron was born two years after his brother. Inheriting his mother's slight frame, Nathan looked like a human archetype: thin, yet exaggerated; Caucasian, yet swarthy; quiet, yet explosively present. He received an informal education from his brother, a formal education from the same local school, and a hodgepodge post-high-school education that spanned the breadth of the North American continent.

The two brothers were considered some of the finest athletes their town ever produced. They both excelled at baseball—their sport of choice, and the town's—but both petered out of their respective systems in favor of Something New. For the elder brother, it was the business of bricklaying; for Nathan, the early markers for what would transpire after he left his hometown can be found in a poem he wrote in one of his school notebooks. It read:

From childhood's hour I've always been
As others were; I've always seen

> *As others saw; I always bring*
> *My passions from a common spring.*

A diametric departure from the opening quatrain of the Edgar Allen Poe piece from which it was copied and altered, the name of the boy's poem was the same as Poe's: "Alone."

Alone.

He grew up a minor legend in his hometown and a source of quiet admiration among those who knew him. People he met and befriended walked away from their initial meeting with the comfortable feeling that the two shared a special bond, which made Nathan profoundly popular and beloved even by people with whom he wasn't acquainted—people who found themselves already charmed by all the fine things everyone else had to say about him.

His reputation was massive, yet he himself was quiet and approachable.

His friendships spanned the social spectrum, though his allies in each social group had certain traits in common. Objectively, his friends appeared to be those who had exploitable assets, and those friendships, it seemed, could shift by the day, or, as the situation dictated, by the moment, or, within the time it takes to twinkle an eye as hand meets hand.

It was a cold March afternoon, and Nathan was in fifth grade. Two of Nathan's schoolmates were talking to each other about a recent snowboarding trip when young Nathan approached them bearing a couple thin cans of a supercaffeinated energy drink, which he'd smuggled into school after stealing them from a local convenience store.

"Hey, you guys want these?" he asked as he approached them confidently. "I just chugged one, and I'm too wired to drink the rest."

"Sure," one of the friends said immediately. If pure, caffeinated energy crystals could be liquefied in a spoon and injected directly into the heart, this was the sort of kid who wouldn't hesitate before tearing his shirt open.

"Uh, sure," the other one said, and they both popped the

tab and began guzzling.

The three knew each other, at least in passing, because they were in the same grade, and, in that school, you were in the same classes as everyone in your grade. This was the first time, however, that Nathan had approached the friends, who were social outcasts—snowboarders. The two snowboarder friends had known Nathan as the quiet kid whose older brother was a bullying legend at their elementary school.

"I like to drink this stuff before I go boarding," Nathan said.

"Oh, yeah?" one asked.

"Yeah," Nathan said. "It sucks there's nowhere around here that's any good, though. This place blows."

"Yeah," the two friends agreed simultaneously.

The bond was set.

In truth, Nathan had never been snowboarding before. But his plan had worked.

Eight months later, the three boys, now close friends, stood together on top of Mt. Hood, in Oregon, with Nathan's new friends beaming for the camera while Nathan stared off into the distance with a stone face, like his father.

A few months after that, the three boys chugged energy drinks and warmed their hands by a fireplace in Canada after a long day of snowboarding—painfully exhausted yet bubbling over with the effervescence of youth and a jolting-caffeine-blood shock.

The three seemed to be inseparable, except in the summer. Nathan, like his brother before him, was an exceptional baseball player. He had been invited to play on the city all-star team.

His snowboarding friends tended to metaphorically shrug their shoulders each spring as they watched Nathan become someone else for the next four months. They didn't play baseball, and, because of that, it seemed to them impossible to be Nathan's friend during those months. They would sometimes head up to the baseball fields to cheer him on (there was very little else to do in town), but Nathan always seemed distracted. Almost distant. Almost uncomfortable with them being there.

But they didn't care that much. They enjoyed hanging out with Nathan, but he didn't add any sort of irreplaceable element to their boyhood adventures, so, in the summer, they moved on. The snowboarders built and did tricks on crappy skateboard ramps in their driveways, and Nathan Cameron went off on baseball trips with baseball people.

And then autumn would fall, and when the cold weather returned, they would inevitably receive an invitation to Nathan Cameron's birthday party, and the three would be friends again.

Just in time for the friends' annual Thanksgiving ski trip.

SNOWBOARDING WAS great, but the snowboarders weren't exactly known for their prowess with the girls of Winston. In fact, they were downright awkward.

As young Nathan matured from boy to near-man, growing on the horizon of his hopes and plans for conquest were no longer the literal snowcapped mountains of his youth but rather the fleshy mountains growing exponentially under the warm sweaters of all the young ladies in his high school classes. And in Winston, there has never been a shortage of excited girls around the baseball fields.

Looking down on the town from a helicopter or airplane, one could briefly describe what he or she saw as a hastily thrown together, unimaginative neighborhood containing rows and rows of doppelganger houses broken up, now and then, like a grateful reprieve, by a few verdant parks and baseball fields.

Whether it was because of the shortage of cultural/entertainment alternatives or because of Winston's tradition of producing legitimate baseball talent, all-star baseball players were Winston's rock stars, and Nathan Cameron was about to reap the many resulting corollary benefits of that culture.

Over time, Nathan's allegiance with the snowboarders incrementally decreased—a friend-gap that was filled readily by the community of baseball extremists with whom he had become allied.

Whatever practice Nathan had with his chameleonic transformations was only sharpened by his new emergence as what could essentially be described as being the lead guitarist in the town's rock band. All doors were opened to him, particularly the door of his newest best friend—a fellow popular baseball star.

The two changed from rivals to friends when both of them made the varsity baseball team as freshmen.

During his rare times with his old snowboarder friends, when the topic came up, Nathan would typically deride the baseball star and his wealthy family: how they were stuck-up, disrespectful, just not his type of people. But, he openly admitted to the snowboarders, he remained in the friendship because the all-star also typically had a line of girls around his house waiting to go swimming in the pool out back—girls who often changed or otherwise got naked in the adjacent pool house.

The snowboarders never even bothered asking whether they could go swimming there sometime. The answer was so obvious it was almost embarrassing to think about for them.

Nathan and his new friend soon took on an even deeper local celebrity than their athletic successes alone would have warranted, mainly because of a number of lucky factors, including their good looks and the aforementioned pool, but, possibly most important of all, Nathan's new friend's parents were a well-to-do power couple who spent most weekends on business trips. To combine a parent-free house, a large pool, a legal guardian who was rarely there (and who didn't really care what her decade-younger siblings did), and the molting sexual inhibitions of popular, confident teenagers meant one thing: the social structure of Winston soon turned an invitation to hang out at the all-star's pool into a sort of Rite of Passage for the young beauties in town. At such tender and curious ages, these girls, spanning a sexual spectrum from fifteen to twenty-six, experienced many new and exciting things either in the heated pool or on one of the large couches in the pool house.

While the two snowboarders were making loud explosions using plastic bottles, dry ice, and water, their friend Nathan was making one small step for mankind and one giant leap for young men under the strained metal and satin of many willing girls' unclasped bras. These were girls the two snowboarders would have considered the ultimate culmination of their sexual lives, while Nathan and his new friend considered them Tuesday and had forgotten them by Wednesday.

But what's curious about all of this is that a comparison between the snowboarders and the baseball star reveals that the "friends" Nathan shared only had one thing in common: obstinate wealth. The snowboarders watched and quoted Monty Python in hysterics; the all-star watched action movies and sports. The snowboarders were both working by the time they were fourteen; the all-star, to this day, has yet to earn a legitimate income. The snowboarders skillfully mocked anyone who made stupid decisions; the all-star mocked anyone who wasn't Nathan Cameron.

There were other differences, but the young man's fungible spectrum of friendships was established. Nathan was someone who could be friends with two "losers" like the snowboarders (being a snowboarder in the plains of Pennsylvania makes you about as cool as being a devout Catholic in Hollywood), with all their inside jokes, Monty Python quotations, and benign battles against boredom, and he could also be friends with someone as popular as the all-star and his friends, whose sense of humor centered squarely and unabashedly on schadenfreude.

Nathan walked that line, and he was rewarded for it—all the way from Jackson Hole to a local swimming hole filmed over with various bodily fluids.

NATHAN GRADUATED high school with a baseball scholarship to a small Division I school a few states over. In August, having just turned nineteen, he packed up his things and drove with his parents and brother to the new school, where he would establish the next phase of his life.

As things turned out in this new world, Nathan was miserable. Daily depression. Long afternoons and evenings in a muted dorm room. The shades drawn. Somber music climbing the walls. Nathan slumped in his desk chair, more alone than he'd ever been at any point before.

As alone as he'd ever be.

The school he briefly attended had fatal shortages of Nathan's two friend-based commodities: it had no money, and it had no wit. It was essentially a commuter school with a good baseball program. The students were less than exemplary, and his teammates were less than insightful. And it being a commuter school, there was a much thinner band of baseball groupies than there would have been at a larger university. The result was a perfect storm of misery and loathing for Nathan Cameron. He was a tornado without an atmosphere, a cell without a mitochondrion, a shark on the moon. The only thing he had left there was baseball.

But Nathan, as good as he was, did not make it into a larger, better school. As described before, had he his father's figure, he probably would have played professionally, and this book might not have been written. But he inherited his mother's slight frame, and as Nathan got further and further into Elite Baseball Competition, he soon found himself being far and away the smallest player on the field.

Halfway through his freshman season, he tweaked his elbow while warming up before practice. It would require about a month of mild rehab.

Instead, he dropped out of school.

DURING NATHAN'S sophomore year of high school, a new student moved to Winston from overseas. The young man had a sad past: he had lived with his mother until just after the ninth grade, when her psychological problems forced the boy to move to America to live with his father. But this immigrant boy was surprisingly intelligent for also being known around the area as a top-level athlete. He got through the first day's awkwardness and quickly became a member of the Winston Elite.

The new kid had his own ideas on life, but they were in

many ways and at many times contradictory. One minute he was studying arduously for a math exam, the next he was skipping history class to drive a pretty girl to a local restaurant for some one-on-one time at lunch, and the next going to the weight room to work out with some friends.

Some friends that included Nathan Cameron. Not all the time, but Nathan had kept this smart, athletic, now-popular new kid in his social sphere since a few days into his arrival at the school.

Someone once described the new kid as a big gun with a silencer. He barely ever made a sound, but when he did, it was fatal. There would be blood.

Nathan learned a lot from him.

Three years later, the alliance paid off yet again.

Sadly, the summer after high school ended, the new kid's father passed away, leaving him the house in Winston.

The new kid received an athletic/scholastic scholarship from an Ivy League school, but something happened there—the details are still unclear—and shortly after that, without parental or scholarship backing, he was forced to move home and live alone while studying at a local college for ambitions undetermined.

Nathan Cameron, as mentioned before, got depressed and injured and then dropped out of school. He moved back to Winston; nevertheless, having tasted the sweet life of independence from his parents, he couldn't move back in with his family. Well, he could have, and he did try, for a few weeks, but he soon realized he didn't have to stay, because he discovered that the new kid had an empty bedroom and a need for company and monthly mortgage money.

In the time he lived there, Nathan continued his hedonism with a growing and younger group of girls from the local high school. The all-star had moved on and was "studying" at a baseball-factory school in the South, and the legendary pool had lost all of the romantic charm it once had—a romantic charm that disappeared from the town until it reemerged in the upstairs of the new kid's house, where literally dozens of girls from Winston and nearby neighborhoods began or continued their sexual lives.

The parties were legendary for their salacious simplicity. A girl knew exactly what she was getting into, and what would be getting into her, the moment she heard that a Cameron party was happening and that her friends were getting ready. There would be drinking and mild socializing until the music grew too loud, and then they would dance. They would shed their sobriety, and in turn their inhibitions, and, given enough time and pleasurable friction, their clothes.

This happened three times a week—the Winston Elite and Winston's Sweetest Treats, together again.

But it didn't last long. Eventually, Nathan Cameron felt he was compelled to move out of the house and travel all the way to California. This time, unlike college, he would go with a friend in tow—a friend the opposite of Nathan Cameron in many ways.

But, most importantly, a friend.

Someone.

AND THEN there was something else entirely. A catalyst. Or crystallization. As Nathan arrived in California, led there by the memory of a trip he took to Mammoth Mountain with the snowboarders when he was fourteen, as well as because of the guiding force of his desperation to get away from a town that had become stale to him, he discovered a fresh, dynamic world and a seminal text.

First, the California he found was an everyworld. You could be anything you wanted to be, and most likely you were, even if you had to do it for free. This was one of the charming aspects of the California culture for Nathan—that it was a land where the possibilities of rebirth were as evident and abundant as the sunlight and all its glinting reflections. In every moment, the air crackles with the possibility of turning it all around, making a sudden and massive shift in direction, and heading for a better port under somehow-bluer skies.

Nathan's traveling companion and friend moved to California to test out the wings his parents had been clipping since he was a boy. Here was a free spirit among free spirits. Here was a mind and body already transcending its Winstonian limitations before it even arrived in the land where limitations are virtually nonexistent, where change is one of the only consistencies, and where people with the right mindset can become one with the pan-dimensional universe or end up homeless (or both).

Nathan, until this trip, had always been known as a player. He could play women, and he could play ball, but none of it really worked as far as making a living was concerned.

So he enrolled at a local university, where he began studying art.

It would be wise to note how radical a departure this was for Nathan. While in his youth he had fallen in with a few melancholy poets like Poe and Plath, his eyes had always fallen on the living art of the women and other people around him—human art. Nathan was terrified of being alone, and there is nothing more alone than an artist at work. Art cannot be created by committee. Brainstorming, certainly, but the creation itself is both Artist Versus Artist and Artist Versus the Universe.

But there Nathan was, taking classes in art, going for an undergraduate degree after dropping out of the two previous schools he attended. It was an intriguing development, but shortly he would drop out of that school, too.

Nathan found common ground within a book given to him by an old friend. The book was essentially a neo-Machiavellian historical study that detailed the lives of various unheralded-yet-influential people throughout history and how they had used their position and understanding of those who held power to improve their own station. It seemed to solidify a point that Nathan had begun to learn on his own when he handed those cans of supercaffeinated energy drink to the snowboarders and then reaped the benefits of their friendship: it is not as important to have wealth and intelligence as it is to have influence over those with wealth and intelligence. If you can do that, you can do anything and never be accountable for any of it.

Nathan took to the book with vigor. Never having been much of a reader, he was surprised at how eager he was to take big bites out of it during those inevitable, inexplicable occasions when he found himself momentarily alone and listless.

It would become the blueprint for what he would continually build and destroy.

Nathan spent several years in Southern California. It was there he completed his transformation from athlete, to lover, to drifting art student, to all three: the indelible, chameleonic Nathan Cameron.

At that point, when he had finally blossomed in the opposite direction his friend and traveling companion had blossomed, Nathan once again raised the stakes of his life and set off to live with a woman with whom he found a new and unique attraction.

An artist named Victoria, from a small town in the woods.

PART ONE
MANTA

1

AROUND MIDMORNING, after heaping five shovelfuls of corn silage into a rusty wheelbarrow, the old man stepped through the creaky silo door, into the day's blast of light and heat, and as his eyes readjusted to the glaring brightness, they settled on the peculiar sight of a young man walking down the road.

Curious, the man parked the wheelbarrow by the open door, waved his arms, and flagged the traveler down. Having spent the previous evening in a long, emotionally painful conversation with his wife—about their stillborn child, dead two weeks prior—the old man was in no mood to talk. His wife was still pale, grieving, unwell, and the old man was worried about her, because she seemed to be blaming herself for one of those things that just seemed to happen to people, good or bad, particularly at their age. He had talked and talked, and he was all talked out today.

But he'd never seen anyone walk down that road before.

The old man continued toward the road, the young man headed toward the farm, and they met at the fence.

"Mornin'."

"Good morning, sir."

"You lost, son?"

"No, sir."

"Where ya headed?"

"North—a town called Manta."

The man asked himself, *Who in the hell is this kid?*

"You sure about that?"

"Yes, sir."

The man studied the strange boy.

It was the boy's turn to ask the man a question.

"Can I get a ride? I have money."

The old man could see that the boy was determined. But he sure didn't look like he belonged in Manta. The man further noted that it didn't look like the boy was *from* anywhere at all—unusual. The boy was dressed in clothes that transcended any generation: blue jeans and a white T-shirt, work boots worn with age and use, a plain blue baseball cap with the bill pulled low on his forehead. The bags he carried were old and looked to have been purchased secondhand, or his father was in the armed services twenty years ago. The hands that held the bags were strong, but the fingers were delicate.

"What the hell—sure," the old man said.

As he gestured toward his truck and walked in that direction, he realized he was only giving the boy a ride so he could try to figure out what was going on here.

"I'M SORRY, son, but if you know Manta, then you know this is just about as far as I'm comfortable going. Them folk give me the heeber-jeebers, so you're on your own from here. Is that okay?"

"Yes, sir," the young man said with a nervous smirk. "You've been very kind."

"You sure about this?" the man asked. He felt obligated to ask when he saw the small metal sign—**Manta 7 miles**—and felt another chill. *This boy does not belong there*, he thought.

The boy placed a more-than-fair share of money on the dashboard and walked to the back of the truck to grab his bags.

"I already told you that you don't owe me anything," the farmer said, holding out the money as the boy walked away.

"It's yours," the boy said to the man. "Thank you again, sir. I hope you find peace with whatever it is that's troubling you."

The farmer, mildly surprised by the boy's observation, looked up at the sign again and then back at the boy.

"You, too."

The driver honked twice and drove off, watching his rearview mirror until he reached a gradual bend in the road and made off on his own route back to his home, wife, and grief.

THE BOY collected himself.

It was savagely hot, and the surface of the road was thirty degrees hotter than the now-lifeless air. The atmosphere under the canopy of the forest on either side of the road, however, was significantly cooler than the pavement under his feet—where the midsummer sun cooked the sunning, black, serpentine path of the road.

The surrounding foliage, a thick northern forest shooting the vertical shafts of trees into the horizon like a camouflaged army of massive standing soldiers, was pockmarked with brilliant sun puddles—pools of light waxing and waning from the soft breeze teasing the golden-green leaves above. The trees were tall and old. Not ancient, as this land had been cleared out for farming about two-hundred years ago, but soon thereafter the markets went dry. Most inhabitants left their modest plots and headed elsewhere, and of course the forest rushes in where human markets fear to tread. Or, in this case, where human markets just happened to become unremarkable and forgotten.

The road was long, and the adjacent forest was thick, quiet, and teeming with tiny life scuttling through the brown earth, where piles of dead leaves and needles continued disintegrating back into the nurturing dirt in which their father trees were born and from which their children trees will spring.

The boy—if we can continue calling a twenty-one-year-old such a thing, but the description having a certain accuracy in the events as they unfold—took a seat on his stacked green bags and leaned his body into the full heat of the day. He thought back to being told by his high-school guidance counselor that he had been rejected from the only university to which he'd applied.

He'd received the bad news in the parking lot outside of school. The counselor walked away, and the boy's eyes unconsciously pored over the concrete as he considered what to do next.

The way the sunlight hit his face on that quiet road took him back to that moment.

After graduation, the young man lived in his parents' basement for three years while he worked as a janitor in his hometown's high school, in order to save money to finance his future plans—three years he had to endure being a part-time shadow and full-time laughingstock in his neighborhood, three years he had spent in a cocoon of thought and self-education and social exile, three years that were over now, with today beginning bright and wide as the world outside.

He reached into his pocket and pulled out a magazine clipping, the creases weak from age and wear, the filaments of pulp and ink flaking on the abused bends, and he read the opening line, which he had first read when he was twelve years old, sick in bed.

"A former professor of mine was fond of saying that the best things in life cost the most."

He continued reading.

"But he wasn't limiting this observation to the concept of money, as some might have mistakenly believed. This professor held that even money bears a heavy cost, because, he would argue, the only currency that we ever really own is ourselves, and by extension, our time in this life. For most people, making a lot of money, besides winning the lottery or an inheritance, requires a lot of effort, concentration, and as a corollary to that, time. So while you may end up rich, he suggested, you had actually been owned that whole time by your devotion to the score.

"You had traded your currency for a different currency, and, he would argue, both currencies were based on the philosophical need for personal freedom.

"Now my former professor is retired and supposedly lives alone in the woods. Nobody knows how to reach him except a few intransigently tightlipped friends. Which, I suppose, is right, particularly for a man who so owns his own life."

The article continued, but it was those paragraphs that struck the boy deepest, and it was those paragraphs he had read and reread over the years.

While bedridden with a childhood disease, the young man had grown to appreciate the concept of his time, and though only a child during this epiphany, he himself had grown to think of time as a form of currency that is a part of the market of life—a form of currency, possibly due to his many ailments, he felt certain was in short supply. Of course, back then he wasn't able to put it in the same wording as his retired hermetic inspiration could, but the seed was there, and those opening paragraphs fertilized the concept and grew it into the active theme of his life.

Later, when he had broken the shackles of disease and found himself back in the realm of the healthy self, the theme took on an even greater meaning and instilled in him a need.

It took him years of avid research before he discovered where the inspirational thinker might be, and, oddly enough, or fittingly enough, he found the lead he was following now within the dusty pages of an obscure religious periodical called *Chant*.

There was an old article in the magazine written by a now-deceased journalist about "The Odd Light in the Forest." The writer had discovered the "ghastly glow" and "tremendously emotional and beautiful musical offerings" of a secluded religious community that had effectively cut itself off from the outside world and had chosen a thickly forested town in which to establish its own bubble. "The seclusion," the writer said, "is self-inflicted, and outsiders are as unwelcome as disease."

The young man could feel the gloriously hot sun on his skin. He looked around and basked in the sensuous symphony of the forest. He breathed deeply. The air was a floral bouquet. Eventually, he noticed that in the distance, between the trunks of the many trees to his right, he could see a thin, gleaming slice of moving water. Though the sun's rays were stiflingly hot, the uncertain sight of the running river cooled him immediately. He looked up the road in the direction from which he'd arrived, and he gazed back thoughtfully.

The clue to the professor's whereabouts came near the end of the article.

"If you're hunting for more mysteries than the residents of this xenophobic community, sometimes there are odd rumors that float to the surface here, including those about an old man haunting the woods outside of town—a ghost whose presence here casts yet another shadow or shroud or fog. Although his actual home in the forest has never been seen, his presence in the area looms, and the townspeople talk about him the way most people talk about something they all agree is disagreeable."

An inexplicable anti-neighbor haunting a secluded religious community—surely this was the home of the great Halo Kilgore.

The young man pocketed the clippings and picked up his bags. He took a breath, turned to the north, and walked.

To the town of Manta.

2

THE FRONT and back of his shirt were wet with sweat, producing an inkblot-like image of hip-bone X-rays (front) and a tornadic cloud system (back), and with sweat dripping from his hands onto the heavy cloth of the bags he carried, the young man saw, after a few miles of cogitative walking, a break in the forest. The green forest shade, broken only by a few quivering yellow sun puddles, suddenly gave way to a towering, vibrant, blue wall of light.

The forest opened to a large, plowed field—dead, golden, and waving in the sunny breeze. To his right was a busted tractor littered with broken bottles, brown with age, battered from long use, and now in rusty rest. Ahead of him was a wide band of open land, and then the first buildings of a small town poked their noses into the field where a craggy old road met this sunbaked new road, and the town of Manta officially began.

The air was hot and stirred lazily. The only sounds besides the sough of the soft breeze were the soft taps of windswept plants as they were breezily pushed into and tickled each other. Occasionally, the young man would hear a bird's poo-tee-weet or an insect's droning buzz, and with each step forward he heard the gravelly crunch of his boots cracking pebbles on the pavement.

"Hello there," a voice called from behind him.

Before the young man could turn around, he felt a generous licking at his sweat-salty left hand.

He looked down and saw a black Labrador with what he could swear was an actual smile on its face, its tail awag. Finishing the turn, he faced a gentleman in his early sixties. Tall, bald, slow in movement, the man had a stern, hard face and warm green eyes.

"Hello," the young man said.

"I bet you're as surprised to see me as I was to see you," the older man said.

"Safe bet, sir."

"So, do you mind if I ask who you are and what you're doing walking through this field with those bags?"

"Not at all," the boy said as he set his bags on the ground and gave the welcoming dog a good pet. Its tail doubled pace, and the Labrador panted intensely in the heat and rubbed its ears and head against the boy's inner forearms.

"My name is Dalton Hughes," he said, extending his hand after wiping sweat and dog hair from it.

"Clem Lemon," the older man said as they shook hands.

"Nice to meet you, sir," Dalton said. "I'm moving here. I know about this place, and it seems like where I belong now."

"*Hm*," the man grunted. "You got a family?"

"Yes and no," Dalton said, not meeting his eyes. "It's . . . complicated."

Clem studied the boy, not unlike the driver had studied him earlier. Neither older man was sure what to make of this kid.

"What do you do?" Clem asked.

"I can do everything except lie, sir," Dalton said, smiling. "My professional interest is journalism. My plan is to work for the paper."

"You'll be looking for Quentin, then," Clem said.

"Yes, I believe that's his name," the boy said. "Mr. Hancock."

"What do you know about that town?" Clem asked, gesturing toward Manta.

"I know it's the home of a religious sect known as the Luminarians, of which, despite a lot of research, I know very little other than they've only been attacked by law-enforcement agents once."

Clem chuckled.

"Other than that, I also know it's situated in some—" Dalton looked around. "Well, just look at this place!"

Clem had a good look around.

"It's awful pretty, ain't it?"

"It's *tree*-mendous," Dalton said. "Do you mind if I ask a little about yourself?"

"That's fair," Clem said.

"What're you doing out here?" the young man asked. "The town's a few miles up ahead."

"I'm retired," Clem said. "I can still take long walks with Hunter here, so that's what I do. I like to get out in this, what did you call it, 'tree-mendous' country."

"Retired from what?"

"Almost everything," Clem said and smiled with a certain charming finality. "Well, Hunter and I are about to head to our favorite spot. You should go ahead and make friends with the town."

After a moment he added, "I'm sure they'll be very interested in meeting you."

3

THE TOWN records—admittedly some very sparse and nearly useless documents—showed that no new buildings had been erected in the city of Manta for more than fifty years. Not a single new home, office building, or even public toilet.

Despite that, it had a charm of its own. But much like some young men's first taste of beer, it was an acquired charm that was initially slightly repulsing, at least to Dalton, on both accounts (beer and Manta). Like anyone who needs to become inured to something new, Dalton choked it down with a sense of bitterness and hopeful maturation.

There seemed to be a thick coat of dust in every corner, in every exposed nook and cranny, across every flat plane of space. Filmed over with a general filth that the people of Manta considered part of its rustic charm, the town looked like a "before" picture or an "after" picture—depending on the makeover or calamity in question.

Dalton walked, duffel bags in sweaty hands, to the middle of Manta around two o'clock in the afternoon. The center of town contained a small park with a few weathered picnic tables on it. The grass was brown and dead and dry as tinder. He turned in a circle, to take in the town. On both sides of the park, running parallel to each other, were two long rows of adjacent business offices with brick-and-mortar facades that had been sun-baked in parts to a light pink and which had been weather-worn in parts to a fecal brown—producing an effect that Dalton had never seen before, of two different kinds of age and neglect amplifying each other's more charmless qualities. The glass fronts of these buildings, most of which were out of business—their empty faces staring straight ahead, blank-eyed—were streaked with long horizontal lines of some white residue, like dust, but lighter and seemingly more permanent, producing an effect not unlike the clouded-over eyes of old men with cataracts. To the north was a large white church with a glinting, gilded steeple, which was topped not with a cross but with an open, golden ring. To the south was the rest of the main road, which led back to the open field where Dalton had met the old man, Clem, and his dog, Hunter.

The effect of the overall spin, for Dalton, was like stepping into an alternate reality. It felt literally unreal and (therefore) terribly intriguing. It felt like, at any moment, the screen of his consciousness would tear open, like if someone were to cut his way through a movie screen and step through the projection.

He couldn't seem to shake this impression until he heard the church's bell begin to toll and ring out across the whole town and field and forest, and he could feel the peals ringing through himself as well, and he was brought back to the moment.

It was Friday, August fourth—a Luminarian holiday known as the Feast of the Exodus. For many years, August fourth was simply known as The Feast and was a celebration of the early harvest, but that all changed when, during the celebration several decades ago, law-enforcement agents swarmed into the Luminarians' previous encampment—Bovary, Ohio—and effectively drove the unwanted sect out of the state. The faithful Luminarians had not been prepared for the attack, and consequently they now celebrated the conjoined anniversaries each year as a reminder to appreciate life's harvest while always being prepared to defend it from those who might wish to take it from them.

Three Luminarians died in the exchange, as did two police officers who'd been killed by gun-toting believers. One state agent was severely injured by a young, overzealous Luminarian who'd seen his father arrested—the boy had almost cut off the agent's arm with a butcher's knife.

The case made national news due to the officers' deaths and the bizarre nature of the unannounced siege, which had come under the dark of night, as the agents themselves, wishing to blend into the black, hadn't worn identification, which was required by law. The Luminarians won the case because of this—a landmark victory for a judicial system that was known to favor heavily on the side of law enforcement—and saw no arrests of their people and were given a large sum in compensation.

The attack had been instigated by a jealous governor who had no real criminal records on which to base his siege. The governor had been jealous because the leader of the Luminarians at the time—a larger-than-life man named Kevin Mustain—had succeeded in winning a number of religious converts within the governor's own office. The governor had previously declared the Luminarians "a heretical menace to the common good" (for what appears to be the simple reason that there just can't be two alpha dogs), and yet his face had turned red with rage and embarrassment when he found out his own chief of staff had converted to Luminarianism after—"*After!*"—the "menace" speech.

That night, after the attack had ended and the dead believers were collected and buried, the entire Luminarian community packed up and moved off. By the time the sun rose over the squalid city of Bovary, still smelling of gunpowder and covered with Luminarian soot, it rose over a ghost town, nearly half of which had been set ablaze by the fleeing owners. Ninety percent of its inhabitants had left the town forever—screen doors open, children's tire swings rocking gently in the new, seemingly post-apocalyptic silence and morning light.

The town of Manta appeared much like that very town as Dalton looked around—not one person in sight. The spiderweb of his senses didn't catch a single human sensation. The wind whistled around hard corners of tomb-silent buildings.

The houses all followed the same general design. Same with the commercial buildings and offices—each building was designed and built for function, with all elements of form sacrificed, leaving only what was necessary. But this was not the sleekness of some modern architecture. These were the austere houses and buildings of ascetics. And then, eclipsing all of the architecture in town, was the towering, gleaming-white church. It was directly north of Dalton, its steeple-top golden ring lustrous in the hot August sun.

Behind him he heard a door click shut and two feet scuffle across a wooden porch. He turned to see a plump young woman, around his age, hurrying past him. She gave him and his bags an odd look as she hustled by.

"Hey!" Dalton called out. "Where is everyone?"

Without talking, the girl turned and motioned for him to follow.

He followed.

They walked past offices and houses and stores, all shabby, dusty, and worn down with age. They walked past a quaint park and a small public pool, gleaming blue in the white-light sun.

And soon they were approaching a magnificently manicured lawn, sixty yards square, lush and green and singing with life, which, thanks to subtle pushings of the wind, coaxed the two, like all the blades of grass, forward across it and toward the large church in front of which the lawn pooled.

Then Dalton was inside a large room packed to the walls with people, their heads bowed in an eerie silence. It was completely dark but for five candles spaced intermittently about eight feet above the gathered attendants. The air was as still as the inside of a coffin, and the lack of any windows or conditioning provided the attendees with a heavy sweat that left the room also smelling like the inside of a coffin.

Dalton seemed to be the only one who noticed.

Silent and still and . . . .

Dalton couldn't quite put his finger on it.

The young woman he followed had quickly kneeled at the nearest open spot and was soon as still and silent as everything and everyone else. Even the candlelight stood motionless.

He waited. And waited. Their eyes were shut fiercely. Their hands were clasped together in front of themselves with a sort of white-knuckled desperation. Their shoulders were tense, their foreheads stern, with only their mouths making only the slightest, repeated, whispered movements.

This was prayer.

And it continued for a full half-hour of remarkable-though-chilling silence. With his back still pressed against the door, Dalton could hear the muffled chirps of birds and buzz of bugs and the wind's wisps that pressed into the gap between the two large wooden doors and whistled softly.

And then the otherwise silence was broken by the light jangling of a few handheld bells. One-two-three. One-two-three. One-two-three. Clapped hands joined the rhythm. One-two-three. One-two-three.

A piano entered the score, riffing lightly on the beat.

Then a low, mournful, held note, from the saxophone of the man on the altar. The one-two-three, one-two-three always there, and the low note giving rise to a lifted, vibrating tone, leaping playfully into reverberating pools of sound before falling back down to rest in the rocking arms of the rhythm from which it had sprung.

A sincere, sonorous, holistic improvisation. The congregation shaking keys one-two-three. Clapping one-two-three. Jingled bells, low humming, all contributing.

And then a voice, as mellifluous and booming as any Dalton had ever heard:

Peace is a united effort for the coordinated soul.
Peace is the will of the people and the will of the land.
With peace, we can move ahead—together.
We want you to join us this afternoon in this universal prayer.
This universal prayer for peace,
For every man.

All you've got to do is clap your hands.
One-two-three.
One-two-three.
One-two-three.

Hum, Lorrah—hum, Lorrah—hum, Lorrah.
Hum, Lorrah, yay yay, hum, Lorrah—hum, Lorrah.

Lorrah, please, won't you hear our plea?
And bring your bells and feast?
Let loving never cease.
Lorrah, please, won't you hear our plea,
And bring your bells and feast?
Let loving never cease.
Hum, Lorrah, yay yay, hum, Lorrah.

One-two-three. One-two-three.

At the front of the altar, the speaker picked up the saxophone again, which seemed to hold a holy aspect as it gently glowed in the candlelight, and he fitted the piece to his mouth. In reverence, the saxophone's mellow bellow, itself a joyous prayer, filled the air like unseen incense.

The gathered crowd chanted along with the music: "Hum, Lorrah—hum, Lorrah."

One-two-three.

One-two-three.

The song continued: a solemn sonorous tribute to the Lorrah. The piano, under so many layers of rhythm, maintaining its light play, contrasted with the bloody music dripping from the sax. The song, bouncing off the walls, rebounding under rows of people, through the still stink and sweat, created a musical offering—an affectation of god-love.

Dalton stayed for as long as he felt safe, intoxicated by the intricacy and beauty of the multilayered music. But he noticed he was gathering the attention of those around him who had now opened their eyes to join in the melody—to see it all happening—so he quickly slipped out the door and headed toward the center of town, searching for the local newspaper.

The heavy door closed behind him, and he could hear nothing coming from within.

4

A FAT gray rain cloud had floated up the far horizon, and the air had cooled considerably since Dalton had gone inside the church. The rain would arrive within the hour, and he had much to do in that time.

He found his way back to the main road and scanned the names on the front of the few operational businesses, looking for the offices of the newspaper, where his future awaited. And then he found it.

The Radical Post

He was relatively well acquainted with the paper. It was mentioned in a few of the articles he was able to find concerning the town and its fanatical religion. The long and short of it was that the paper, though distributed among a largely homogenized readership, remained an unlikely profitable business. The *Post*, and its editor, had been established in the town years before the Bovary exodus, and thus preexisted the radical shift in the paper's readership.

When the young owner set out to name his enterprise, he recalled how in his vocabular youth he had grown fascinated with a relatively common word. The word, which had various definitions, and given the area in which he lived—surrounded by trees, loggers, and the ghosts of the town's history—eerily fitting ones at that, was Radical. Radical's meanings included "growing from the base of a stem," "designed to remove the root of a disease," "relating to the origin," as well as "tending or disposed to make extreme changes in existing views, habits, conditions, or institutions."

The "Post" part was easy. Journalism is the first draft of history. It's the facts after the fact. It's "post." To the fifteen-year-old who started the paper in his own bedroom, it was the perfect name—and decades later, he was still just as happy with it.

The Radical Post.

The Luminarians had of course tried to build and maintain their own newspaper, but *The Radical Post* had always won the paper wars. Even the most religious people in the community preferred its reporting. In an industry where catering to the audience is considered paramount, the *Post*'s departure from audience-coddling displayed the stubborn editor's idealistic intransigence, as well as the ways that a job well done can break almost any supposed barrier.

The owner, writer, editor, photographer, and publisher of the paper, who was now leaning over a small, cluttered desk, was a bespectacled and stoic sixty-year-old man named Quentin Hancock. He had a precise pen, an affable interviewing style, an insatiable curiosity, and the Zen facade of a self-made man who ran a self-made business effectively. Otherwise, people said he was like a rose bush: you could never get close to him without getting needled.

Hancock had moved to Manta with his family when he was a boy. His father sought work as a lumberman, and his mother sought work as a schoolmarm. Nevertheless, his father died young (a genetic enlarging of the heart muscle, which skipped a generation, as Quentin's perfect heart could attest), and his mother, with no money and nowhere to go, stayed. She taught young Quentin how to write, and at the age of fifteen he started his own little rag for the tiny lumberjack community.

Besides five years served in the armed forces, when he traveled to places like Korea, Holland, and the Antarctic, he'd been a Manta citizen all his life.

His father had come for the trees; the son had stayed for the paper.

"Who the hell are you?" the older man said, looking up from his desk at the young man standing just inside the door.

"My name is Dalton Hughes," he said. "I just moved here, and I would like a job."

"Moved here?" Hancock asked. "Why'd you move *here*?"

"This is where I belong," he said.

"You a Luminarian?" he asked, looking closer. "You don't look like one."

"I'm a journalism student, and I would like to continue my education here. I like this paper. It is well made."

"Is that so?"

"Yes, sir," he said.

"And how would you qualify that opinion?"

Hancock turned now and faced the boy, as if to welcome the challenge. He placed his glasses on the table and rubbed his eyes with his palms.

Dalton tossed one of the previous week's editions of the paper, which he'd been given by the farmer on the way into town, on Hancock's desk. There were a few red errata markings on the front page and every page thereafter.

"You're a good writer," Dalton said. "You could use my help, though."

Dalton faced Quentin soberly and added, "And I could use your help."

Quentin picked up the marked copy and read through some of the fixes. He didn't hear the last part; he was too busy looking at the little red audacities. A slight smirk curled at the corner of his mouth. He looked at the paper a good while.

"Tomorrow," he said finally. "You got anywhere to stay?"

"No, actually," Dalton said. "I just arrived."

Quentin wrote down an address and handed it to the boy. "This house is just outside of town. Ask for Jane. Tell her I sent you. She might have something."

"Thank you, Mr. Hancock," Dalton said and extended his hand.

Quentin looked at the hand for a moment and then turned back to his work.

"See you tomorrow, Mr. Hughes," he said.

5

AS DALTON approached the house that matched the address on the paper Quentin had handed him, he found himself wondering how such a structure could exist in such a place as this. The building was a work of art—a glass-and-concrete statue, a shining crown, a piece of engineering completely unlike the architecture of the rest of the area. He was supremely curious to meet its owner.

Jane.

He knocked on the front door and waited. It was a while before the smoky-glass door was pulled open by a paint-smocked woman of considerable size and grace.

Jane Jefferson greeted her visitor with a horizon-wide smile.

"You must be Mr. Dalton Hughes," she said, her smile growing in intensity as she saw the young man's confusion. "Quentin phoned ahead."

"Ah, yes," said a relieved Dalton. "Yes, I am Mr. Dalton Hughes, and—"

"You need a place to stay."

"Yes, ma'am."

Jane leaned against the door and observed the boy. "So you got past the guard dog, huh?"

"I'm sorry?" Dalton asked. "You mean Hunter?"

For a moment, Jane looked surprised by his response.

"Quentin," Jane said. "What did you say to him?"

"I asked him for a job."

"Mm-hmm," Jane said. "And?"

"I showed him some mistakes I found in his paper."

Jane had a big, shoulder-bouncing laugh at this.

"You're a brave young man," she said and continued chuckling.

At that, she made her decision.

"Let me show you where you'll be staying."

SOMEWHERE AT the far edges of the sky, there is a field where the particles that comprise the very upper reaches of Earth's atmosphere are sucked into the vacuum of outer space, and within that field is the imprecise line where the two different atmospheres press into each other.

And likewise, Manta. The area around Manta was on the imprecise line where the world of mountains meets the world of plains. From above, there were long, wide bands of flat land that were rippled, every so often, by the foothills of foothills.

Jane Jefferson's unusual house stood proud at the peak of one of those foothills, and down her house's particular hill— a long green sweep down to the curved spine of a running river—sat a small logwood cabin, which was also part of the estate.

The cabin was pleasantly simple—just three rooms and a porch. A small bathroom—white white white everything, and clean. A small bedroom—bed, dresser, nightstand, with walls paneled with wood like the rest of the cabin. And also a main room/kitchenette for everything else, with a fireplace.

Through the front door (the only door in or out) and

directly to the left was the kitchenette, comprising a refrigerator, oven, sink, some utensils, and some linoleum counter space. Straight ahead was the stunted hallway leading to the bathroom (left) and the bedroom (right). To the right of the doorway was a couch, a chair, a wall of books, and a sliding glass door leading out to a small, screened-in porch, just feet from the giggling trickle of the river. The porch glowed at night from a grimy yellow light in the ceiling that shined onto a small wooden table.

The wood-paneled walls were bare but for three framed pictures. The first was the architect's color-pencil drawing of the grounds as they would be built. The second was the front page of an old *Radical Post* bearing the headline A NEW DAY DAWNS over a photograph of a vast wagon train of Luminarians arriving from their Bovarian exodus. The third was a painting, which Dalton observed with interest.

It was a portrait of the heavy waters and light spray of an immense ocean ramming against a rocky cliff, and at the top of the cliff stood a man with his back to the water, facing a city blended with a forest—the city and forest winding into each other like a double helix. The sunrise, or sunset—but, to Dalton, and from the overall "feel" of the piece, a sunrise—provided a luminous golden outline for the standing man's contemplative, tall silhouette, and contrasted with the rows of dark plants and buildings surging from the ground. It was unsigned.

Jane Jefferson was a heavyset old woman who, when asked, would describe herself as "Afro-American." She was the kind of old woman who always had something on the oven—either cooking within or cooling atop. She lived alone, but she was not lonely. Among her friends, she was cherished as an easy laugh. It was a laugh that did to a roomful of people what butter does to a recipe. Her wide-ranging sense of humor indicated the breadth of her intelligence. Talking to her, one could almost hear the synapses in her brain as they synthesized the observer, his clothing, his bearing within the room, the content of his observations, and a myriad other factors most people would ignore while they tried to think of what to say next. Jane never had to think about what to say next; she had to think of where to stop.

"Well, Ms. Jefferson," Dalton said, looking around, "I really like this place."

"Thanks, honey," Jane said, comfortable with Dalton, dropping her charade of formalism. "I do, too. Haven't been back here in ages, though. No reason to anymore, I suppose. Quentin and I used to come back here to relax and listen to the river, but . . . ."

Dalton could sense some tension there, a bittersweet tension. *Things change*, he figured, *and most of the time it's beyond our control, and even when we do have some control we still make mistakes*, and he found himself looking at the painting again.

"I've never seen a painting like this," he said, and that's all he said about it. The subsequent quiet, and the attention he put into closer observation of it, finished the unintentional compliment.

Jane didn't say anything. She watched him. If Dalton were waiting for a reply to his statement, he didn't look like it. He looked like he'd forgotten the comment he'd just offered.

"It was for an old friend," she said.

And evidently a new friend, Dalton thought.

Indeed, this was where he would be staying.

It was getting late—he could see the exhaustion in Jane's eyes—so they finalized the arrangement by shaking hands. She handed him the door key and turned to leave.

"Have a good night, darlin'," she said over her shoulder.

"Jane," Dalton said.

"Yes, child?" Jane said, turning back.

Dalton walked over to Jane and hugged himself into her deep, sweater-warm hug. "I am glad to have met you," he said.

He could feel himself rise and fall with the quake of her laughter. "You too, Mr. Hughes."

She wished him a good night and left.

Dalton sat down on the couch and fell asleep shortly after Jane clicked the door closed and made her way back up to her magnificent house—its windows warm with light amidst the ink-black night outside.

6

"He *came* into the *church*, Vee," Augustus snapped. He was standing near the fireplace, which cradled a small fire that was throwing light and shadows at his pant-legs, and which had been started despite the heat outside. "He came in with Marcia White."

"Who was late as usual," Phillip said, seated luxuriously in a deep brown leather chair angled toward Augustus and the fire.

"Is this something we really need to worry about right now?" Charlotte said, who had a habit of straightening up a room whenever she was nervous. Right now, she was plumping couch pillows that were already well plumped. "I mean, today *is* a holiday. We have a congregation to lead."

"Yes and no," Phillip said. "We should be with our brothers and sisters, yes, but this is most definitely something we need to worry about. We have people counting on us to look into this—to find out what's going on here . . . to protect them from it."

"Yeah," Augustus said. "I didn't like the look of him at all. Did you see his *face*?"

"I saw it," Vee said flatly. She was agreeing with him or mocking him.

"Gus, I want you to ask Marcia White how she knows our new friend. And Vee, I want you to meet this young man. Find out who he is and what he's doing here."

"Do you think maybe he knows Nathan?" Victoria asked. She was draped across the couch lazily, like a jacket thrown without a thought, and the aspect of her relaxed grace gave the impression of momentary formlessness.

"Nathan will be back in a week," Phillip said.

"No, I mean . . . fine," she said, standing.

The brother and sister left the room quietly as Phillip sat in contemplative silence in the back room of the church. His wife Charlotte rearranged the bottles of liquor on the table in the corner and then sat comfortably in his lap. Soon they too would stand and head out to join the celebration, but for now they had this new development to consider.

DALTON ARRIVED around forty-five minutes early for his first day at *The Radical Post*. Mr. Hancock arrived forty minutes early, and almost immediately the two fell into a sort of labor-harmony. A simple operation is not always simple, and a complex operation, like putting together and editing a twice-weekly regional periodical, is often only as simple as the minds conducting the work are complex. Quentin had been working at this for decades, and Dalton had been preparing for this for years.

Back in his hometown, when he was a custodian, Dalton had specifically requested the night shift. At night, there was hardly any work to do and lots of time to read in the library. About journalism. About grammar, syntax, etymology, and Flaubert's obsessive pursuit of *le mot juste* . . . About wild-eyed stories by gonzo journalists and professional jobs about boxing legends, new cars, weather patterns, gambling, the birth and death of the New Age . . . Religious treatises on faith, philosophical treatises on the triumphs and limits of reason, popular and unpopular fiction and nonfiction . . . Biographies of great men and women, scientific periodicals, the delicate poetry of the East, the life-trumpeting poetry of the West . . . Man landing on the moon, man machine-gunning waves of men on blood-soaked beaches, the best and worst of a very curious human history in a dark room under a single lamp.

Humorously enough, and ironically, Dalton found that his first responsibilities at *The Radical Post* involved custodial work.

Quentin's pre-Dalton decades had thrummed by to the steady percussion of his fingers plying a typewriter and the *clacketa-clack* of his small printing press operating against the wall in the other room, and consequently there materialized a sort of organized chaos in the cluttered office where Quentin Hancock daily cleared a path for himself between the front door, the typewriter, and the press. Anything in the way had been pushed aside like debris on a swollen riverbank.

Dalton's job was to make order of the aftermath of those years of organized chaos, something to which he had grown comfortably accustomed, both physically and mentally, over the course of his life.

So while Mr. Hancock (always "Mr. Hancock") was off covering a story about the recent Feast of the Exodus festivities, Dalton was granted the time and privilege of gaining intimate knowledge of the paper and, by extension, the town. Meanwhile, Mr. Hancock was acting as a sort of introductory diplomat on Dalton's behalf.

The School (as it was called—no namesake otherwise, nor a mascot, just, "Get yer butt to The School!") graduated approximately fifteen students per year and was provisionally accredited by the state only recently, though records indicate it had been graduating students for as long as the *Post* had been around.

The "Police Department" consisted of three men and a woman, who all worked for the Luminarian Church. They were Chief Artimus Blake and deputies Alan Thinne, Pete Brooks, and Lucy Hait. The "Police Blotter" was often devoid of any actual crimes and thus consisted of such stories as "Hawthorne Blvd.—Cat in tree" and "Domestic Dispute—Man/Wife, no injuries" (a juicy little story involving a broken dish). The "Police Station" was the back half of Artimus Blake's house, where there was a desk and a small, barred cell.

The *Post* featured a weekly editorial cartoon, the drafts of which Dalton had found here and there throughout the office. It was authored by a local Luminarian and Manta councilman named Wendell Pency. This week's bore a picture of a cat and a dog, with the dog saying to the cat, "I'm afraid I'm not even sure that we can agree to disagree."

The information on Luminarianism was abundant but

superficial. The current leader was an absolutely massive man named Phillip Hershey. He had been awarded the position by the Clergy of Twelve, who represented the highest Luminarian authorities, six years earlier, when the previous leader—a man named Alexander Bergstrom—had died of pancreatic cancer. Phillip had a wife (allowable in Luminarianism) named Charlotte (née Swallows), who was born in Manta. Together they had two children: Augustus (himself mammoth, brooding, the heir) and Victoria (Dalton had seen only one picture of her—a decade-old photograph of the young woman, very pretty). But beyond that, on the matters of what the faith actually stood for—beyond the trivia like the church-leader's name and such—there was very little information above the mention of important holidays and not-fully-understood references to their significance in the church. There wasn't much by way of objective edification regarding the actual spiritual/metaphysical beliefs of the town's devout faith. Dalton supposed that either the townspeople had enough of that everywhere else they went—at church or in quiet discussions at home—or Mr. Hancock simply found it either unimportant or uncouth and unnecessary for the pages of his paper. A division between dogma and press.

On the front page of a few very old copies of the paper, Dalton saw strange pictures of people with terrible sunburns being baptized into the church. They were adult males, and in most of the pictures they looked overwhelmed but were an outward projection of unencumbered, thoughtless bliss. Dalton scanned the ledes: "Glenn Hubrick returned late Wednesday night from his baptismal journey, and after visiting the doctors and Luminarian Head Pastor Hugh Whitney, his full conversion to the faith was announced to the community, and a large party took place afterwards on the church lawn."

One of the more interesting aspects of the town Dalton had seen so far was that the people of Manta refused to allow televisions anywhere at all. There was very little mention as to why this was, but Dalton had come across an article Mr. Hancock had written concerning a local dispute between some of the younger townspeople and the Clergy of Twelve regarding the television prohibition. Apparently, a teenage Luminarian named Andria Scott had been mailed a popular celebrity magazine by a well-meaning cousin. Had the mailman not refused, on religious grounds, to deliver it, the magazine would have given the young girl her first glimpse of the world far outside the quiet confines of their forest nest—a world declared by the clergy too dangerous for the minds of young believers. The magazine was confiscated, and Dalton never found any other references to Andria Scott. Which made him nervous. This was a small town, and the paper was littered with references to all sorts of people, repeatedly, and while there were plenty of articles about the Scott family, none ever mentioned Andria. In a twisted way, he hoped she'd learned her lesson and was keeping her head down, because the tone of the quotations he read from the town leaders made him worry about what happened to her after the fuss died down.

Dalton also discovered a map of the area.

The forest surrounding the town was thick and stretched for miles in all directions. Nevertheless, bisecting the forest in a serpentine wriggle was a watery gash. Known as the Crondura River to official atlases, there were also other names for it, much more demeaning and degrading, which referred to the people of Manta and their small faith-based community, but even the Mantanites, who seemed to rename everything around them, referred to it as the Crondura River.

The river approximately paralleled the same rarely traveled road the old farmer had taken Dalton down on his initial drive into town.

Given its name by the native Olwahapa tribe, its literal translation is lost—the tribe is extinct. The river first appeared on a Western map in the early 1700s. A well-read American explorer found that the name given to the river by the tribe happened to have linguistic connections to European languages. The Greek root "chron" means "time," and the Latin root "dura" means "long," "lasting," or "hard." Hard Time. Long Time.

White ice disappears, running,

> *A cleansing ghost, another blue beginning,*
> *A child and another child forever*
> *Makes and remakes the Crondura.*
>
> [translation of an old Olwahapa poem]

Otherwise noteworthy in the region was the steady encroachment of another local city, still some miles away, but expanding yearly by leaps—one of the fastest-growing cities in the region.

A place called Haverbrook.

7

DALTON SPENT a lot of time at the *Post*. The cleanup efforts had taken a few days, and his first noncustodial responsibilities for the paper were to edit copy for a local sports story (a Manta city youth baseball game: TIGERS DEFEAT LIONS!) and try to help Quentin complete his dimonthly original crossword puzzle. ("At my paper, Mr. Hughes," Quentin had said, "there is no tolerance for ambiguity, and thus, at the *Post*, 'bimonthly' means 'occurring every two months,' and 'dimonthly' means 'occurring twice per month,' got it?")

Dalton walked out just after the sun had dipped completely behind the town's arboreal horizon, as the smoldering red-and-purple embers of the sky were being incrementally extinguished by a yawn of wide gray, steadily to the cabin and to the starry black.

He walked through a town already well into rest for the night. There was one teenager in the little park, sitting rather still on a swing, and another, older man just outside a row of almost identical houses bearing large, dusty porches glowing yellow under their old lights. The teenager paid Dalton no mind; the older man exuded the sense that he knew exactly who Dalton was and that it would be wise if the young man just kept at his own pace and direction and left town right now.

It would be charitable to call the welcome Dalton received from the townspeople "warm." At best it had gone thus far without incident, but even that was something for which, fortunately or unfortunately, Dalton had been prepared to face: namely, the opposite of love—not hate, but indifference. Most of the people he met in town saw through him. Not that they saw his intentions and true self, but something in the way they were raised, perhaps only ever interacting with their own kind, had left them with the uncanny and truly awful ability to ignore Dalton as they ignored anything but themselves and each other. Nevertheless, perhaps this older man's subsurface animosity meant that that special power only worked for so long, and a reaction was coming.

All things considered, Dalton wasn't sure whether that was a good or a bad thing. Either way, he nodded at the old man as he walked by, quickening his pace for his own sake and for that of the man who began moving toward him.

He thought he heard footsteps following him as he reached Jane's house, but when he turned around he only saw the blue moon rising and the shiver of the green (though now eerily silver) trembling grass.

When he turned to face the cabin again, he saw a band of moonlight shining through one of his windows and illuminating a square of wood and grass at the bottom of the stairs leading up to the door. Sitting within that square was a pearl-white hand and the orange wink of a half-smoked cigarette.

Dalton stopped in his tracks and waited. The fiery eye jostled a bit as the fingers flicked some ash from the eye's crusted lid. He continued toward the cabin, and as he got closer, the hand added an arm, a torso, an X of legs, and then a blonde head of hair draped over a forearm resting on pulled-up knees.

"Is there something I can help you with, ma'am?"

The body jolted in surprise, and the face turned to Dalton. And what a face! It was almost devoid of emotion, but it wasn't robotic. Perhaps it was devoid of all negative emotion, but it was not smiling. It was angular, rounded, symmetrical, and unlike any face he'd seen around town before, though it bore an odd resemblance to an old photograph he'd seen of Head Pastor Phillip Hershey's daughter on a dusty *Post* front page. In the picture he saw, however, the little girl was about ten years old—cute, but not beautiful like this.

"Hello, Dalton," she said. "I'm sorry if I startled you by being here."

"Not at all. Good evening, ma'am."

"I've heard a lot about you and wanted to meet you," she said. "My name is Victoria. Hershey. Victoria Hershey."

Dalton extended his hand to shake, but Victoria made no reciprocal movement.

"I'm not allowed to shake your hand," she said.

"Right," he said.

"It's not just you, though," she said. "We're not allowed to shake anyone's hand who isn't a believer."

"Who says I'm not a believer?"

"My father, and Quentin. And Jane."

"Ah, not a believer in your specific ideas, yes. So I guess asking you to come inside and take a load off would be a waste of time, right?"

"Right," she said. "I'm sorry to have to ask you this so bluntly, Dalton, but my father would like to know what you are doing here."

"I have a job at *The Radical Post*."

"Then obviously you aspire to be a journalist," she said.

"I aspire," Dalton said lightly. "I have lots of aspirations."

"Okay, that's fair. So you came to Manta to learn from a one-man paper in the middle of nowhere?"

"I don't have any credentials. I didn't go to college."

After a brief moment, he added, "And I like Mr. Hancock's paper. I read everything, and I know I can learn a lot from him."

Victoria felt the truth in this and said, "Good. I like that."

"So . . . what's it going to be then, eh? We've met. You're Victoria. I'm Dalton. You live here; I'm just an unqualified worker trying to build a life. You're very pretty, by the way."

Victoria frowned subtly and took another drag from her cigarette. This too seemed to confirm something for her.

"Thank you, Dalton."

"Listen, this is weird. If there's anything you want to know right now, please ask. I'm really tired, and I feel like I'm supposed to be careful around you if I want to be able to do my job."

"It is weird, and you do need to be careful around me," she said. "Good intuition. Is that why you complimented me?"

"It was an observation."

"Right."

"I don't mean to be rude, but if you don't mind, I'm very tired," Dalton said.

"Yes, of course," she replied. "My father simply wanted me to meet you. You're the first new person to arrive in our community uninvited in many years. We were all worried, after what happened last time."

"You're right to be worried," Dalton said with sarcastically sinister tented fingers.

Victoria laughed.

"Have a good night, Victoria Hershey. Nice to meet you. It's good to finally talk to someone else around here."

"I agree," Victoria said. "That reminds me: my boyfriend Nathan is returning to Manta soon. I think you would enjoy talking with him. He's not from here, either."

She took a drag from her cigarette. When she exhaled, she added, "Though he was invited."

Dalton listened but did not reply.

"Good night, Dalton."

Victoria stood. She was taller than he'd expected, exactly his height, but on the first step she was eight inches taller than he. As she stood, bright moonlight beamed through the cabin window and glinted off the platinum curls of her hair and slid down the silky sweep of her cheek, darkening further the dark corner of her lips.

The two stood there for a moment, observing each other. Not a look of flirtation and not a stare between two prize fighters before a match—just a sort of interested observation in curious light.

"Oh, I nearly forgot," she said, taking up her purse. "This is for you."

She handed him a small box with a bow on it. He took it from her and observed it—turning it over in his hand.

"What is it?"

"A welcoming gift," she said. "Welcome to Manta, Dalton."

She stepped past him and glided across the grass, her feet submerging and emerging between delicate, tiny waves in a silver sea.

8

EARLY THE next morning Dalton awoke to the sound of three soft kicks against the cabin door. It was Jane. She had two mountains of breakfast in her hands and something on her mind.

She and Dalton sat at the small table on the porch as the cool morning air invigorated them both awake. The water outside the wire mesh windows lapped slickly against the muddy rocks and sediment and made a constant sort of trickling giggle that affected a feeling of moving forward into the day for them both. Despite that, the mornings on the porch also gave Dalton the feeling of timelessness. The colorful air of dawn felt surreal, like he was sitting within a liquid, down in some sunken block of boat at the bottom of a light, breathable, golden ocean.

Manta and Jane had converted Dalton to a morning man.

"Mr. Dalton Hughes had a visitor last night," Jane said.

"Yes, indeed," Dalton said between massive bites of the mouth-melting deliciousness of Jane's peanut-butter pancakes (soaked in syrup). After chewing through another mouthful, he added, "But it felt more like a dispatch between two foreign diplomats than the introduction of two, you know

". . . people."

"Well, that makes sense," Jane said. "That's what it was. Or did you expect these people to just start high-fiving you on your way to work?"

Dalton laughed.

"Now I assume she gave you your welcoming gift . . . ."

"Yes," Dalton said, still chewing. "A small box with a key in it. Kind of funny, actually."

"Well that's not exactly the reaction I was expecting, but what kind of reaction should I expect from The Stranger Boy?" Jane asked jokingly and rhetorically, referring to the nickname some of the townspeople had given Dalton. "What makes it kind of funny?"

"It's a long story, ma'am," Dalton said. "And it's not even mine."

"For goodness' sake, Dalton," Jane said. "I keep telling you not to call me that. What century are you from, anyway?"

Dalton smiled introspectively. "Sorry."

"Care to tell me this long story?"

"I'll do you one better," he said, standing. He walked to the living room and scanned the wall of books, searching amongst the few volumes he'd brought with him and added to the collection. He pulled one out and brought it back with him, setting it on the table as he found his seat again and dug back into the mountain of sugary goodness.

Jane picked up the book and examined the cover, trying to suppress a laugh as she found the author's name.

"*Lock and Key* by Halo Kilgore?" Jane laughed again. "I didn't even know this was still in print."

"It's not," Dalton said. "You've heard of it?"

"I've actually never read it," Jane said. "I asked him about this book once, but he said he didn't think I would enjoy it as much as some of his others."

And then Dalton's head went fuzzy with a flash of adrenaline, and his fork clanged against the plate, which, to Jane, had the effect of humorous melodrama.

"You know Halo Kilgore?" Dalton asked.

"Sure," Jane said, suppressing another smile, which made

her smile all the more.

Dalton sat back in his chair, beamed, shook his head, and said, "Of course you do."

"Is that why you moved here?" Jane asked.

"I could answer that question, Jane, but I'd have to give you the rest of my books."

Jane giggled.

"What's he like?" Dalton asked.

Jane thought about it for a moment. She took a contemplative sip of her ultra-strong coffee and replied, "He's like . . . he's old now . . . but he used to be like getting a hug . . . from a loving tidal wave. In fact, I saw a movie once where a crazy man said something that immediately made me think of Halo. 'Pardon me,' the guy said. 'I don't mean to impose, but I am the ocean.'"

"That's beautiful," Dalton said. "And it sounds about right."

"It's been a long time since I saw him, though," Jane added. "He left a while back."

"Everything okay?"

"I'm sure he's fine," Jane said, gathering their plates. "He sent a few postcards, most of them from somewhere in Utah. Says he's getting along, feeling old, misses my pancakes."

"Is that a euphemism?" Dalton asked with a smirk.

Jane laughed again.

"Kids," she said and gathered her other things. "You're both kids."

"Thank you for breakfast, Jane, you weird woman."

"You're very welcome, Dalton, you strange little man."

9

MARCIA WHITE felt like she'd begun falling through open space as she watched the towering figure of Augustus Hershey fill the frame of her kitchen doorway, and she almost immediately doubled over from nausea, fear, and vertigo.

In the back room, baby Shelly began to cry loudly.

"Augustus, please . . ." she said, already pleading and backing away. "Shelly was being fussy and wouldn't take her bottle. I'm so sorry about being late. *Believe me!*"

Augustus laughed to himself and gestured for the young woman to sit down. "Marcia, my dear, please do relax. We've had this talk before. If it's not Shelly, it's a plumbing problem. If it's not one thing, it's another. But what's the one constant?"

"I know, Augustus, I—"

Marcia's heart was racing as she looked up at Augustus, at the eyes that judged, at the smug curl on the corner of the mouth, at the face otherwise frightfully expressionless. A mouth carved out of cold granite, and, now, as malleable. One day earlier, that mouth had brought sweet life to a silent saxophone.

"The one constant is tardiness. To me: an obvious disrespect for the church and your value to the church. And this time your disrespectful truancy bore a heavy cost, Marcia."

"If this is about that new newspaper guy, he wanted to know where everyone was, and Exodus being a big holiday for us, I thought he might have been a prodigal, or a pilgrim. He looked familiar. I don't know! Please stop looking at me like that."

"It's not I who's looking at you like that, Marcia," Augustus said. "It's you."

Marcia's eyes dropped back to the floor, which, though just at her feet, seemed a thousand miles away.

"It's you who is projecting your awful guilt onto my countenance," Augustus said. "Why, just this morning Lucy Hait said she loved the way I looked at her, but I wasn't doing anything then, either. We were just talking."

A dead silence spoke for both of them. But Augustus wasn't satisfied. He continued.

"She has a clean soul, Marcia," he said. "Her heart buries no guilt between its toil. Every beat rings for the Lorrah."

Marcia's hands were shaking, cold. Her breath was shallow. He hadn't threatened her—never shown her a glimpse of animosity or animus—but she was immobilized to the point of animation: shaking, quivering, weak.

"I'm going to talk to my father about this," he said and plucked an apple from the counter. "We have to begin preparing for Nathan's return, but we will figure out what to do about this disrespect of yours—believe me."

He chomped into the apple. Then he turned and walked out of the house—the hard soles of his shoes thudding heavily on the old wooden floor. When the back door clicked shut, Marcia put her head in her arms and wept long, shuddering sobs. In the next room, her child also cried, and the sound of it multiplied Marcia's fear and sadness.

Little Shelly.

10

FOR THE past week, Victoria Hershey's new boyfriend, Nathan Cameron, had been away from the town of Manta. In order to become formally accepted into the Luminarian community, Nathan had been sent to the desert, to find his spiritual core.

Nathan wrote the following passage in his trip journal, "The Neophyte's Journey," which detailed his time before returning to Manta. It is a tome written by the soon-to-be-baptized, if they are accepted to join the Luminarian faith as adults.

Despite Quentin's research, it is still not completely understood why Nathan or all converts must write their Neophyte's Journey passages in the third-person voice.

A few of Nathan's journal entries were later posted on the door of the church, by the Hersheys themselves.

"Nathan could feel the white hot sun scalding tiny nerves in his back and the back of his neck and down the length of his

arms while the sand beneath his legs cut into his raw skin. The sun above him a microwave light, virulent and relentless. His exterior was burnt to a tone darker than even his usually dark face had ever shaded. Motionless sweat offered no cooling relief in the total absence of a breeze as it beaded and became currents cut down the grooves of his muscular torso and powerful legs. This was day three. No water. No food. No movement save sitting and lying and trembling. Three days baking in the furnace of a Utah desert and freezing under a matrix of stars so deep the layers produce nauseous vertigo. His stomach clawed at his insides. His blue-white eyes on a blue-white sky ablaze with the peripheral tracers of a swelling, dehydrated brain's desperate cries for shelter and water.

"Normally most at home amongst a group Nathan's wretched loneliness was barely made endurable by the constant companion of his ever changing pain. Two more days until he would stand and walk to the all-terrain vehicle he'd driven here that was now resting a thousand paces from where he sat—this all a pain payment for having so long neglected his begotten faith. A pain payment due to prove to Head Pastor Hershey that the world from whence Nathan came was a nightmare from which he was now finally and fully awakening.

"He had felt one night a scorpion delicately climb his arm and walk across his torso and that terror had been part of the payment. He had heard coyotes howling with delight just over the bluff where he lie shivering his feet and hands throbbing from atrophy and ache, and that too was part of the payment. Before a child can be baptized it must be born. Sometimes a soul is born twice: once into a living hell of godless plurality, and then, when the fool's veil has been lifted, again in the land of damned sand, where the Lorrah's searing glare is a blessing."

That was what Nathan Cameron wrote in his journal on the day young Dalton Hughes arrived in the town of Manta, which Nathan would soon also call home.

11

Under the dingy yellow light of the porch, near the tiptoeing feet of the Crondura River, screened in from the bugs that tapped every few seconds against the thin wire mesh, Dalton and Jane sat conversing at the wooden table, sharing a marijuana cigarette after a long day of work.

Dalton had become well versed with this drug as a janitor. The head custodian at the school, a man named Carl Buddy, recommended that everyone on his staff "puff enough to keep their heads" and often supplied them when they ran low. He grew it in a far corner of the school furnace room, where everyone else was afraid to go.

"So, Jane, can you explain to me this key they gave me?" Dalton asked after a long, pleasant break in their talk. It was dark, and they had been listening to the water and the wind and the insects—the night outside.

"Honey, I can tell you this: you'll never see that key hit lock."

"What lock?"

"A Luminarian is an absolute follower of the dictates of the Lorrah as interpreted by the Head Pastor, the Clergy of Twelve, and the Voice. That's capital-V Voice."

"What's the capital-V Voice?"

"'The things that happen,' or so they say."

"Meaning existence?"

"Who the hell knows?" Jane said.

Dalton laughed. "Right."

Jane continued, "Part of that luminary faith, you see, involves giving yourself over to the church and the Voice absolutely."

"This is the key to a box where I'm supposed to put all of my money and possessions?"

"Right, right."

"Ha!" Dalton coughed out a dry laugh. "I wonder if Victoria was being serious."

"She was," Jane said. "That's the tradition."

"They do realize that my possessions comprise half-a-duffel-bag of books, some clothes, and hardly any money at all, don't they?"

"Hardly any money is still more than no money. Those people gotta eat, too."

"Yeah, I got something they could eat."

Jane, who after she made her point had taken a big drag off the joint, started coughing and laughing when he said this.

She coughed and laughed for a while.

"Did you ever read that book I gave you?" Dalton asked.

"Halfway through it. I think I see what you were getting at."

"Did you get to the speech yet?"

"No. No speeches yet."

"If you think you see now, just wait. That man is a goddam genius."

They drifted again into a pleasant quiet and let the Voice tell its dark story. The black afghan fully descended, and the insects found themselves drawn to the little yellow light on the screened-in porch by the river, and while the army of insects repeatedly smacked into the screen, the water outside kept moving, like time, seen or unseen, down a line forever, to the point where it itself runs out into something bigger.

12

ON A surprisingly chilly, rainy morning later that week, with the sky an unbroken gray-black from horizon to horizon, billions of raindrops bombed against the windows of the buildings and the first hard, curled brown-and-yellow leaves lying lifelessly on the soft wet grass, and Quentin Hancock found that his knees didn't agree with making the walk to the City

Hall, so he sent Dalton instead. This would be Dalton Hughes' first ever official piece of reportage.

Quentin knew both the Luminarian and Manta city calendars, and he figured the bimonthly budgetary meeting would be insipid enough to be perfect for the occasion. He sent the anxious reporter out with the mission to "run your fingers through this baboon's fur and see what kind of ticks you can eat."

Dalton arrived inside the city hall shaking out his umbrella. He also had with him a tape recorder, a pen, and a notebook. After a thorough and unnecessary investigation of his possessions by Police Chief Artimus Blake—standing, or, rather, leaning guard just inside the main door—he was allowed to enter a medium-sized civic room.

At the front of the room, the only decoration on any of the walls was the Manta city crest, which was featured behind the long, brown half-wall that separated the city council from the citizens.

A small group of Mantanites gathered in front of the two rows of set-up collapsible chairs in order to fulfill what they considered their religious/civic duty, by venting or by simply acting as witnesses and private journalists. Or they were just hanging around to see what other people were up to, attempting to add meaning to their existence by standing in the middle of the green-lit streets of other people's lives.

When Dalton entered the room, the various conversations among the citizens fell to need-to-know whispers, and all backs turned. Little placards were set up in front of each empty chair behind the half-wall. Dalton busied himself by writing down the correct spellings of the names, along with their titles, in his notebook.

Councilman Ross Jeffries
Councilman Joe O'Brien
Councilman Whalen McCray
Mayor Tony Capps
Councilwoman Paula Sneed
Councilman Pete Brooks

Councilman Wendell Pency
City Controller Charlotte Hershey

A little girl, no more than five years old, was playing with an extraordinarily ordinary doll (a blocky wooden female-ish shape wearing a white dress, with an expressionless face staring straight into nothing) in the corner, humming to herself. This happened to be the corner Dalton chose to sit in. It gave him the widest angle to take in both the aspects of the council as well as the reactions of the citizens. The girl's father—Dalton could tell by their faces and long necks—was involved in a particularly heated discussion with two other men; otherwise, certainly he would have gotten his daughter away from Dalton a hell of a lot sooner.

But he didn't, and the girl, still humming to herself, began to take notice of Dalton, who was, for the moment, oblivious to being observed by her.

At some point the sheer nervous excitement of his first journalism assignment overwhelmed his nerves, and he had to take a deep breath and run his hands through his hair to relax. The little girl must have found this weird private exercise funny, because she giggled at him.

Dalton snapped out of his introversion and saw a little girl still giggling into the coarse hair of her doll. Dalton smiled and waved, and the little one reciprocated. She liked him. He didn't look like the other people in town. He sure was funny looking, though.

"Hi," she said.

"Hi."

"Who are you?" she asked.

"I'm a reporter," he said. "My name is Dalton. Who are you?"

"Shannon," she said.

"Shannon is a very pretty name," he said. "So you here to talk to the mayor about a new civic plan or something?"

Shannon tittered and said, "*Noooo!*"

One of the men talking with the girl's father noticed this happy, italicized refusal and nudged the father, who turned and frowned. He excused himself from his conversation, walked over to his daughter, picked her up, and carried her away, without acknowledging Dalton whatsoever.

Dalton wrote in his notebook, "Shannon not here to address mayor/civic plan" and laughed to himself.

His laugh was interrupted by the air-moving rush of large wooden doors being thrown open and the march of the city council members entering the chamber and making their way to their respective seats.

The game was on.

"AND YOU say this is the first story you've ever done?" Quentin asked.

"Yes."

"It's good. Plenty good enough."

"Thank you."

"I mean, it's not that great, and you missed a few details, like you forgot to ask Charlotte about the secondary funding efforts, but I can get a quote from her and round out your story. Overall, though, Mr. Hughes, I think you did a fine job."

"Thank you, Mr. Hancock."

A merciful wave of warmth washed through Dalton. He'd been so nervous to hear what Quentin thought of his story that his hands had turned white and clammy. He hadn't eaten all day, and all of a sudden, now that things had gone well, he felt his delayed hunger surge into him.

"Who's this Shannon in your notes?"

"Oh, that's some little girl who was at the meeting. She was playing near me, and I took that note as a joke."

"Shannon Penrose?"

"I believe so, yes."

"Cute kid."

"Yes, sir."

"It's a shame about her mother."

"Her mother?"

"Died last year."

"Oh," Dalton said. He found he had to know, despite the fact that it looked like Quentin didn't want to talk about it.

"Of what?"

"Brain hemorrhage, in her sleep—they say."

"'They say,' huh?"

Quentin sucked a long, thoughtful toke from his tobacco pipe. "I thought it was fishy, but I'm just a paranoid old bastard."

"What was fishy about it?"

Quentin looked at Dalton. The look again seemed to suggest that he wished he hadn't brought it up and that Dalton should just shut up about it.

"Hey, you're the one who brought up murder conspiracies, Mr. Hancock. Pardon my interest. I hear a nice woman with a young daughter dies under possibly mysterious circumstances, and I start asking questions. Isn't that our job?"

Quentin laughed out some smoke.

"There's a ritual the Luminarians do with children, kind of like Christian baptism, but more . . . unpleasant. More like circumcision, actually. Anyway, Patricia Penrose was strictly opposed to this ritual, and Phillip Hershey wasn't sure what to do about her. It was the height of contention around here, and I mean things got as ugly as they've been since I can remember. A good number of mothers came to Patricia's defense, and everyone else defended the church. And then one morning the church's so-called prayers were answered. Shannon's mom had died in her sleep, and Shannon's father went ahead and allowed the ritual."

"What's the ritual?"

Quentin pulled out a key and opened a locked drawer in his desk. "I guess it's about time I gave you this."

He handed Dalton a tattered notebook.

"The Luminarians don't have an actual religious text. Well, they do and they don't. Mainly, their sermons are conducted by Pastor Hershey and supposedly detail his conversations with their godhead, whom he and his fellow followers refer to as 'Lorrah' or 'the Lorrah.' This notebook contains my own written transcript of the rituals and prayers and general trivia concerning Luminarianism, or at least the stuff for which I was able to attain some kind of verifiability. It is the only such record I know of, so you need to be careful with this notebook, Mr. Hughes. It's important that you learn and understand this stuff, but it's even more important that nobody else knows you have it."

"What about Jane?"

"Fortunately for you, Jane already knows. She helped me gather some of the information, and she's one of the only other people who's read the entire contents before. She'll help you hide it and provide you with the decoder."

Dalton opened the notebook and saw an inscrutable code of numbers and letters, written in microscopic shorthand.

"I know these people are unusual, but a decoder—?"

"It's for the same reason I smelled fish when I heard Patricia Penrose had died in her sleep. I'm a paranoid old man. And these people have killed before. Anything's possible when you think you have God's permission."

13

NATHAN CAMERON opened the door of the Luminarian truck and sat in the shade of the cabin and gazed over the bright desert horizon, which danced in the heat.

He pulled out his journal around the same time Dalton, nearly two-thousand miles away, lying on the couch in Jane's cabin, turned open the first page of the decoded notebook and began reading.

Dalton read Mr. Hancock's notebook, "A Luminarian Study," and Nathan completed his "Neophyte's Journey."

"Nathan considered something Head Pastor Hershey had recited over him before his voyage to the desert.

"'At noon of the fifth day, you shall Awaken, and you are given to return, for we will be waiting to feast with our new brother. You will return to us to be born again with us.'"

"When a child is born, it is closed off at its openings, and even the Lorrah, the Great and Powerful, cannot breathe music into its soul."

"The skin of his head, torso, and legs was a flaking and pustulated sheet of brown-red. The backs of his hands scraped painfully against the now-coarse-feeling fabric of his shorts as he fished for the keys. His arms and legs throbbed with pain."

"And the Lorrah, all that is love and music, is deeply saddened by this, so the Lorrah commands our leaders to undertake a cleansing and opening, that we may all hear the majestic life to come—the music and its effects on our hearts and her world and all things."

"Unable to stand or walk any longer, Nathan sat in the shadow of the truck's cabin and thought about what had happened to him, or what he thought had happened. There had been another scorpion, and again the distant howling of hungry coyotes, and there had been other nightly insects scraping and scuttling along the sand,

"and there had been a light."

"A child is born without sin against the Lorrah, and is thus ready from the moment of birth to be cleansed of earthly detritus and tuned to perform in the Lorrah's Infinite Choir."

"The light had started at the far corner of his eye. Perhaps the winking blink on the wing of a passing plane. It grew and dashed before him almost immediately upon perception, and he, on his fifth straight day of absolute silence, was almost made to scream by the extraordinary sight, but the scream was quelled by the nature of the light itself. It exuded a cottony warmth, pressing heat against his face and chest—the shivering cold shooting through his twitching muscles being soothed to relaxation."

"And before the one-thousandth day of the child's life, when the medicians declare the body ready for its tuning, the Luminarian leaders take the child from its home and its parents, and the masters prepare the child for the music it will become. This, the Lorrah says, is necessary for the child and the parents. The child for preparation and the parents for the knowledge that theirs is the Lorrah's as the Lorrah's is theirs."

"The light circled for hours, a slow little dance on the stage-chest of his bare torso. He was no longer breathing, yet he was alive. The light was breathing for him, into him. The multitudes of stars in the sky collapsed to the floor like a dropped final curtain, and the light was all that remained, emitting a faint, soothing song, and dancing. Always dancing. Until the morning when he awoke and the light was gone—and the transformation was complete, and he prepared to finish the writing of his journal.
  "For inside him was the light."

"The child is returned to its biological parents after a performance with the master and a full review by the medicians, where its physical health shall be put on its way to matching the spiritual virility of its soul."

"For Nathan, his Luminarian self had been readied. It was time to return to Manta, to his brothers and sisters in faith."

"A man or woman joining the Community after the age of twelve must also be cleared of the carrion of its instrument and be readied to be fluted through the Lorrah. It is the Head Pastor's duty to prescribe each convert's cleansing ritual."

"The heat of the cabin in the car caused him to sweat, and the sheets of sweat coursed into his grotesquely burnt skin and sent spasms of itchy dread throughout Nathan's body, and there was no stopping it. Head Pastor Hershey had disabled the truck's air-conditioning. It would be hours before Nathan would find a shady breezy respite, and for what felt like an

eternity his weak hands white-knuckled the steering wheel as the salt in his sweat produced painful shudders that ran roughshod over his seared body."

IN THE following day's *Post*, Dalton's first ever published news story, about the town council meeting, was given the byline "By Quentin Hancock." At the end of the article, an italicized paragraph read, *"Additional reporting by Dalton Hughes."*

They both agreed it was for the best. After all, Dalton wasn't there for the "glory" of the byline, nor the notoriety. What exactly he was doing there was still a mystery to Quentin, but he liked the help, and he liked the boy, and he'd come to appreciate the working comfort between them—something nice that he hadn't felt in decades.

The first mention of Dalton's name in the paper might have caused a more disagreeable reaction if it weren't for the exciting news, in a banner article written by Quentin, that Nathan Cameron was returning to Manta, to join the Luminarian community, this time as an equal and brother and new instrument in the Lorrah's Infinite Choir.

14

VICTORIA WAS again awaiting at Dalton's cabin when he got home, this time earlier than the previous night, and Dalton was not surprised to see her. The following morning he was scheduled to head out with Augustus Hershey, to cover a story about the preparations for a big party the following evening.

Victoria was again sitting on the modest wooden steps leading to the door of the cabin. It was early evening, and the trees by the cabin threw long shadows across the lawn. Victoria had always loved twilight. It was that vulnerable phase when day meets night—the twice-daily clash between the force of light and the anti-force of darkness. As Dalton approached her, he remembered reading about how dawn and dusk are the times of day when most prey are seeking food, and most predators are seeking prey.

Dalton had been thinking about Victoria since they met. He recalled, quite often, the unusual beauty and paleness of her face and skin and the extraordinary life abounding in the waving locks of her thick, blonde hair. There was something about her overall effect that made him want to tear her clothes to shreds and have her to shards. But there was also something about her that was revolting. She was, after all, an important member of a religion based on beautiful music and, evidently, not much else. But that odd confluence of good and bad—her simple beauty and her complicated background—probably had something to do with the salacious torrents that ripped through him when he looked at her. He'd never encountered a woman who was all good, and he'd had a small number of exciting encounters with crazy women who were, in many ways, great, so as she sat before him, a mix of light and shadow, here in the gloaming of a cool evening, Victoria's attention left Dalton at a loss as to how to act and feel, which was so new to him that it made her all the more tantalizing.

"Hi," Victoria said.

"Hello, Victoria," Dalton said and, with both hands at his sides, bowed respectfully.

Victoria smirked and continued, "I hear you're heading out into the woods with my brother tomorrow."

"Yes," Dalton said. "Mr. Hancock's got me researching a story for some sort of upcoming celebration."

"My boyfriend is returning to be baptized."

"Ah, yes—him. A newbie like me, eh? How very exciting," Dalton said with the remotest trace of sarcasm. "So what are you doing here?"

"I came here to warn you about him."

"Your boyfriend?"

"My brother."

"Does he have a habit of strangling reporters in the woods?"

"Not exactly."

"Well, then—"

"He's very smart," Victoria said. "And manipulative. Just be careful."

"Noted." He looked at her. "Is that all?"

"No," Victoria said.

She stood up and approached him slowly, holding his eyes with hers as she split the distance between them. Dalton did not move, but waited for her to come to him. Soon she was standing within a few inches of his face, and she took him in. His eyes, his cheeks, his nose, the boundaries of his facial hair. She took him all in. They breathed the same air. The urge to grab her by the arm and bring her into his cabin had the force of nuclear energy, but Dalton was his own god and resisted the forces that roiled within.

After the longest and shortest few moments of Dalton's life, Victoria grinned to herself and walked past him and back toward the church. Over her shoulder she called out, "Good night, Mr. Hughes."

Dalton didn't reply.

"Be careful tomorrow."

He watched her leave and then walked into his cabin and feasted upon the dinner Jane had snuck in while he was at work. Next to the plate of food were the book she had borrowed and a scrap of paper. The paper read: *"For woman, lock—and man, her clueless key." —H.K.*

THE SUN had not yet risen, and outside it was black, silent, and cold.

Augustus Hershey awoke with an odd smile on his face. He dressed in the deep-woods clothing he had prepared the night before. He cooked himself a simple breakfast and loaded his gun—an old hunting rifle, his great friend.

His father had taught him to shoot when Augustus was a young boy. Everyone in the family could do it, even Victoria and Charlotte. Victoria deplored guns, and always had, but she learned their importance when she was twelve. She helped keep her family alive during a particularly disastrous winter by shooting rabbits and birds, when not setting traps.

The rest of the Hershey family slept as Augustus clicked the door closed behind him and thumped down the porch stairs, making his way across town toward the wide expanse of Jane Jefferson's large property and the cabin behind it.

When he arrived at the cabin, he found Dalton waiting for him outside.

"Hello, Mr. Hughes," Augustus said and extended his hand to Dalton, who responded with his own much smaller hand. The hands clasped confidently and returned to their respective owners.

"Hello, Mr. Hershey," Dalton said. "Nice gun."

Augustus was nine inches taller than Dalton, who was not very small himself. It was almost impossible for Dalton to see how this thing could be related to its sister.

"Today, you get to join me in experiencing a Luminarian tradition almost as old as the church herself."

They began walking toward the woods Dalton had emerged from so recently. On the eastern horizon, the darkness was letting up—a misty gray fog yawned over the treetops and between the dark wet trunks.

"Our church is a harmony of traditions, Mr. Hughes, so please try to keep up. I wouldn't want you to get further confused; it is difficult for most neophytes to understand the many layers that comprise our faith."

"I'll do my best," Dalton replied. "You said your name was Abraham, right?"

Augustus fought the urge to laugh.

They continued. Their feet crunched the dry brown leaves that blanketed the hard ground.

"So about these tradi—"

"Today, at around three in the afternoon, my sister's boyfriend Nathan will be returning from his baptismal journey, and tonight we will celebrate his conversion to our faith.

"You and I are going hunting for the main course at the festivities. It's a tradition we don't often get the chance to celebrate. Our remote location is a boon for our faith, but it . . . has certain limitations."

"And why not just have some food shipped here?"

"Do you have any beliefs, Mr. Hughes?"

"Off the record, I do. I have a religion, sure. Right now, however, as a reporter, not to sound corny, but my religion is The Truth," Dalton said.

"Mr. Objective, hm?" Augustus said and halfheartedly failed to suppress a giggle of condescension. "The Lorrah gave us our knowledge, tools, and skills for them to be exercised, not relegated to an inhuman, specialized market. A man is more than a chopping arm."

"So you hunt your dinner on special occasions to keep sharp the wits with which you were provided," Dalton said, both as a statement and a question.

Augustus walked on without reaction. Dalton took his lack of refutation as an agreement with his meaning, though it could have just as easily been an impatient indifference towards trying to translate his religion to a hopeless philistine.

Far beyond the scope of the forest before them, the unseen horizon unveiled the day's first bands of light, and their world again awoke.

It awoke to the sound of two men crunching through the woods, looking for something to kill.

"This really happened?" Quentin asked after reading the first draft of Dalton's story, which came in at just under five-thousand words—immense for a newspaper article.

"I have no reason to lie, Mr. Hancock," Dalton said. "Every word in there is as I remember it."

"Mr. Hughes, this is . . . profound. The story, I mean. Your writing is a bit scatterbrained, but in this piece it almost works."

"Thanks?"

"Shut up."

"It's too long, right?"

Quentin laughed. "It's much too long, and, I'm sorry to say, it's bullshit."

"I guess that's a good question from a young man such as

yourself," Augustus said. "It must be strange for someone from—"

"Elsewhere," Dalton replied.

Augustus couldn't help but enjoy Dalton's cryptic reply. "Right. For someone from Elsewhere. So what is it about this particular tradition puzzles you, Mr. Hughes?"

"From what little I know of Luminarianism, it seems to be a religion that takes place within the temple of the brain, not a very showy and ornamental religion—"

"*Shht*," Augustus hissed, staring at something in the distance. Dalton froze.

Trying to find where Augustus was looking, Dalton followed the older man's eyes to the other side of a hilly ravine, where two deer—what looked like a father and its deer-child equivalent of a toddler—were themselves staring down the funny monkeys tromping through their homeland. The air was perfectly clear, the ground, the tree bark, and the two deer were shades and shades of brown, and the yellow-white gunpowder explosion from Augustus's rifle marked the moment just before the smaller deer dropped to the ground, dead, with all the honor of a bag of sand. The bigger deer, with the grace of natural coordination and vital urgency, bounded over shrubs and under branches and off to an incredible distance, while the leg of its young kin shook with twitching final convulsions, and soon the little deer was motionless, and Augustus began walking toward the kill.

Dalton vomited.

"I guess they don't hunt deer Elsewhere," Augustus said, almost disgusted by Dalton's reaction.

Dalton coughed out a few bits of bile and turned to the towering figure. "We don't kill the cute ones, I guess."

Augustus chuckled. "Sometimes, Dalton, you need to do something distasteful for the sake of something bigger than the mere moment," he said. "It is one of the unpleasant realities of this life."

After a long moment, Dalton wiped at his mouth with the back of his hand and asked, "Why'd you kill the young one?"

Augustus stopped walking and turned. "You'll see."

He pulled a large knife from his belt and continued walking.

Dalton was instructed to hold the rifle while Augustus tied the deer to a strong branch.

"You see these brown rings around its eyes?" Augustus asked.

Dalton turned around and looked only where Augustus was motioning with the point of his knife. He saw the rings.

"Yeah."

"This deer has a disease that's been wiping them out in these woods the last few years."

Dalton turned back around. "I see."

"Sure you do," Augustus replied. Then Dalton heard a ripping sound, and then the spill of heavy liquid hitting dry leaves.

"So you guys are going to eat a diseased deer in celebration?" Dalton asked.

"The disease has no effect on people. In fact, if you ask me, I find that it tenderizes the meat beautifully. And this young thing's as tender as she comes."

Dalton just watched the blood pool on the ground.

"Lots of bears in these woods, and they can smell blood for miles," Augustus said. "You see a bear, you kill it. There are no second shots with bears. You agitate them, they kill you. You hear?"

"Yeah."

Over his shoulder, unable to look again at Augustus's efforts, Dalton asked, "Why are you cleaning it out here?"

"The Olwahapa are gone, Mr. Hughes. We don't use every bit of the deer. All we need is the meat and the heart. We'll leave the rest for the forest to consume and honor. The Lorrah sings in all things, even in the exposed remains of its sacrifices."

The work continued. The deer was robbed of its heartiest shanks of muscle, which were placed in a plastic bag and then a large backpack (Augustus's). Afterwards, Dalton saw a very sad and ugly sight, like something out of a childhood nightmare—a sawed-open animal carcass, bones and organs and blood falling out without any trace of the grace of life that had once inhabited them.

And then the two men headed farther into the woods, for the hunt was not over.

"What's bullshit about it?"

"Almost everything he said. For instance, does Augustus Hershey look like a veterinarian to you?"

"How do you know Augustus isn't just branching out from the dictations of his father? Preparing for the day he takes over? And I'm sure he knows some things about the animals of these woods."

Quentin thought about this. He'd known Augustus since the boy was a trouser-crapper. It was hard for him to see the boy as a man, as the man he had become.

"You might be right. For now, let's work through it as though Augustus were merely giving the new reporter a hard time, perhaps hoping to make him look foolish by writing what to others would be seen as a wholly inaccurate account of their beliefs and traditions. Because, Mr. Hughes, these people never tell anyone anything about their beliefs. It's a members-only club, and everything I know about them—everything in that notebook I gave you—is based on my decades of observation and extrapolation. I've never seen anyone, ever, speak this openly about Luminarian beliefs, particularly with a member of the media."

They came upon a babbling stream that was running clumsily over large rocks smoothed slick by years of erosion, and they sat down to eat the apples Augustus had brought—apples given to his family by a few members of the community who had liberated them from the White property.

"What do you think of your sister's boyfriend?"

"Are we off the record?"

"You tell me."

"Well, I think I like him enough. He seems to be respectful of my sister, but my father will be the last judge, whether he's satisfied with Nathan's trip to the desert."

"Care to tell me anything about this trip he's returning from?"

"I believe he'll be better able to tell you when he gets back. A man's journey is his own, is it not?"

"I'm not talking about the details of his specific trip; I'm referring to the philosophy behind it."

"And I'm saying that that's just not possible, and you'll have to ask him."

"Why is it not possible?"

Augustus drew in a deep breath and pushed it out in a controlled manner. He entered a momentary trance, and soon his eyes flashed open again and he looked at the young reporter.

"Growth is painful, Dalton."

Dalton took that down a bit confusedly and had a look around. It was midmorning, and the forest was wonderfully awake, swaying and whispering in the calm breeze. There was a reckless order to it, the dead leaves of yesteryear in piles, the ubiquitous trees, arcing their powerful backs and thrusting their massive hands to the sky—truly nature's cathedrals. Truly a holy land.

Because of its tremendous nature, the animal can smell an apple from miles away, and, because of that, as Dalton was looking around, he happened to notice that a hundred yards in front of them a large furry brown mass was making its way toward the babbling stream—a grizzly bear. Augustus noticed it too when the animal gave a low growl as it stepped over a fallen trunk.

Augustus stood sharply and shouldered his rifle, but he made no move beyond that, because the bear had stopped walking. It rummaged around a bush, swatting at a few leaves, hoping to find some berries, probably. And then its woolly neck flexed, and its head turned, and it saw the two funny monkeys, one standing fully erect, shouldering a powerful rifle, and the other still crouching, its jaw six inches underground.

This was Dalton's first encounter with a real-life bear in any situation. He'd never even been to a zoo, and the sight of a bear in their reckless, open situation, with no borders between them, and one manipulative maniac providing support, left Dalton in a lonely and terrified trench. He could do nothing more than stare at the powerful animal.

It began walking forward. That time of year, when autumn already had its poisonous talons dipped into the surrounding flora, was a time of feasting for bears, as they had to fatten up for their coming hibernation. Dalton's eyes flashed from the bear to Augustus and back and forth and back. Armed only with a set of quick legs (too slow to beat a bear, though) and a backup plan he'd seen in movies where people play dead, his dependence on Augustus and Augustus's practiced rifle was almost absolute.

Augustus himself seemed to sense this and for a moment broke visual contact with the bear to look down at what he would later describe to his friends and family as "the pitiful puddle of a reporter." Then he snapped back to the bear.

The bear continued its slow walk and was now within thirty yards of the two men.

"We are here too, animal," Augustus said in his deep, measured voice with a distinct tone of respect. With much less respect he turned and said, "Dalton, get up."

Faced with the prospect of a jaw-crunching death, Dalton's psyche reverted back four-million years, and he rose with primal fury. The warrior blood of his ancestors turned his muscles into cosmos—like an ape-man going wild in a hunt.

He stood and made himself appear as large and menacing as possible.

"You must go now, bear," Augustus said. "We will let you live today. But now you must go."

The bear made an auditory response, low and almost human-sounding. It took a step forward.

"LEAVE! NOW!" The echo of the cry reverberated through the forest. Augustus lowered his gun and pointed north. *"GO!"*

Dalton joined in pointing north, himself yawping a wild cry, mindless and guttural, fueled and amplified by adrenaline and terror.

In the disquieting silence after the echoes of the shouts, there was a moment when Dalton saw that Augustus and the bear appeared to be sizing each other up, both fearful and respectful.

Two hours later, the men emerged from the woods shouldering the food they had collected for the coming feast. Dalton, upon emerging, vomited once more. In their packs were the shanks of a deer, several rabbits, and many armfuls of wild berries.

Somewhere behind them, miles away, a brown bear foraged for berries out of those same bushes.

Quentin edited Dalton's article down to a brief, exciting story about the bear encounter, omitting nearly all quotations directly attributable to Augustus regarding Luminarian beliefs. Dalton's overall, larger story wasn't dead, however; Quentin wanted him to work on the full version, and this would continue for some time (writing and rewriting and rewriting until it was right). It served as a particularly useful pedagogical tool for Mr. Hancock's efforts at improving his young student's style and substance.

Dalton titled his article "The Predator Prays."

15

JANE JEFFERSON exploded into the cabin, crying without reservation, and not just crying, but heaving sobs, gasping, her shoulders bouncing up and down as she tried to vent her pent-up grief. This was the sound and sight Dalton woke up to, rubbing his eyes and pulling himself up off the couch in the main room of the cabin.

After his extraordinary morning, Dalton had been sent home to rest before the celebration that night. He had fallen asleep almost as soon as he walked through the door. He had dreamt of bears, and, for a very bizarre moment, when Jane came crashing in, he thought she was that wandering bear, still startled by her close encounter with Augustus and his world-changing rifle, saddened by the death of her unlikely friend—a child deer.

And then reality registered.

He stood up and walked over to Jane and gave her a hug. She was a big, wonderful woman, and he cherished the warmth between them. Then he pulled open the sliding glass door leading to the porch and gestured for her to join him out there in the dusky air, where they could talk about each and every sob in the glowing light of the early evening.

"First off, Jane," Dalton said as they sat down, "what the hell are you crying about?"

Jane didn't appear to feel the dark-humored needle in Dalton's question. For a moment, she didn't answer at all, but rather just stared at her own thoughts.

"I was offered a contract today that will make me a millionaire," she eventually said, dabbing at her tears with a bleached-white handkerchief.

Dalton suppressed a smile. "*Well, that sucks,*" he said, with sarcasm.

Jane couldn't suppress one of those crying laughs, but it didn't defeat her weeping as much as stun it.

"How about you give me a couple-hundred-thousand dollars and explain it to me?" he said and went out of his way to pleadingly nudge her arm with his elbow.

This time she vented a stifled laugh.

"You know that painting?" she said, gesturing toward the piece that Dalton still found himself staring at sometimes in the moments between his reading and writing.

Dalton looked at it and back at Jane.

"Have you ever wondered how I was able to afford this property?"

"I did initially, until I realized you painted that."

"I'm a big fraud," she said.

"You're a big *beautiful* fraud," Dalton said with a toothy smile, really laying it on thick. "I was just telling Quentin that's what I like about you—how you're a big fantastic two-

[72]

faced phony."

As expected, Jane gave Dalton one of her trademark "looks" before she explained.

"Have you ever heard of the sports-marketing campaign *But Is It Art?*"

"Sure. They were just about the only advertisements I could stomach back in the real world."

"'Back in the real world,'" Jane said, repeating Dalton's phrasing to herself. "I like that. Anyhow, *But Is It Art?* was me."

"What do you mean? You did it?"

"Two years ago I submitted a spec marketing campaign to one of the advertising world's biggest companies—this aromatic troop of slick monkeys in classy suits in New York called Prask Impressions Advertising, comma, L-L-C—and they liked my campaign ideas so much they hired me to freelance for them."

"That would normally be considered good news, Jane."

"Do you consider it good news?"

"No."

Jane had to give Dalton a second look, this time truly with incredulity: his opinions always seemed to surprise her.

"Why?"

Dalton gave her question a considerable amount of thought. Jane found herself fascinated by his extended, thoughtful silence. Apparently, the answer to that question was an army so big it took Dalton Hughes himself a considerable amount of time to organize it.

"Well, Jane, this is actually something I care about quite passionately, so I've been known to go off on the subject—I mean, I really hold forth. Are you sure you want to hear what I think?"

"'The unexamined life is not worth living,'" Jane said, quoting Socrates.

"Right," Dalton said. "Okay." He finished gathering his thoughts, took a breath, and began.

"I don't mind the occasional, simple advertisement that displays the who, what, where, when, and why of a new product—like a movie coming out or a new restaurant opening—but the ubiquity that commercialism has taken on in our culture is just . . . ugly . . . or . . . yeah, a favorite word of mine, *pernicious*. Not only are ninety percent of advertisements a replacement game where the unenlightened copywriter reminds you of something that is wrong in your life and then proposes a ridiculous solution—say, buying a new shaving razor in order to have sex with women who aren't attracted to you not because your face isn't shaved but rather because you're the type of person with so little self-confidence that you actually think a new razor is even close to being a useful solution. What's worse is that there's a sea of sharks playing this exact same game, so there's always blood in the water. There are millions and maybe even billions of messages out there centered on the negative aspects of existence and human life. The only positive message in those advertisements praises a commonplace and usually shabby product. I mean, after all, if the product were any good, word would get around on its own. All this only further serves to make cynical the very wide audience that is constantly being reminded that they don't have the girl, or the job, or the life they'd always dreamed of. A fake dreamed life that they constructed through the false and ridiculous images created in the minds of these hack copywriters. It's infuriating to me to see the mirrors-facing-each-other of self-loathing writers writing misguided thoughts for self-loathing consumers. And the people who do have the self-confidence to see beyond the outright bullshit are rewarded for this by cogitatively suffocating in a world littered with cheap, poorly-thought-out, forced education into crap they never cared about to begin with. It's—They're just awful. Even good advertisements contain the stink of some original sin.

"So we've covered the consumer side of things, but what about their creators? These are people who wanted to be artists. When they were children, they saw a piano and they heard Elton John and they wanted to make the world sing. They saw "Starry Night" or some other art print in their classroom and they wanted to paint the world beyond beauty.

They read words on a page that moved them emotionally and they wanted the masses to leap for joy in the streets upon the news of their latest release. And then the pianist grew up and wrote a jingle. The painter designed a goddam billboard. The writer started scripting radio advertisements. And this happened so slowly that they were able to reason with themselves that they were actual artists, despite being dreadful sellouts. And the guilt of that selling out, repressed as it may be, is evident in nearly every marketing campaign you've ever seen. Because it is the real original sin—the combined rejection of personal dignity and the importance of our reality."

Dalton finished. For a moment, he and Jane sat there in the brief conversational void left by the completion of his speech.

"Do I stink of some original sin?" Jane asked. She didn't realize how much she could be affected by a young man's wild rant. By now, her eyes were merely red, and she thought over the things Dalton had said, which she felt like she'd heard in her heart so many times.

"You stink of amazing, Jane," Dalton said. "But you might be feeling guilty for that sin, too. After all, why were you crying?"

They sat in thought.

"I have a counter for you," Jane said.

"Bring it on, crazy lady."

"What about the idea that that's what works? Bait-and-switch and other commercial sophism lead to consumption because they're the best and sometimes only way to make something new appealing. Keep in mind how 'well' most new things go over in all human cultures."

For a few moments, Dalton's brain scanned its archives for a reply.

"Wait a minute," Dalton said as he tried to come up with something.

He failed.

"Stupid brain," he said.

They both laughed.

"Did I ever tell you what happened when I had my first

showing in New York?" Jane asked.

"You mentioned it in passing once. It seemed like a sore subject, and I didn't want to follow it up at the time because we were getting along so well."

Jane pulled out one of her magic marijuana cigarettes and, handing it to Dalton, asked, "Would you like to hear a story?"

Dalton took it from her and grabbed a *Radical Post* matchbook from the table. (Dalton: "Why does our paper have matchbooks?" Quentin: "The first week the Luminarians were in town, they burned the stacks of papers I had placed on some of the street corners. The next week, I had these made and placed them on top of the pile.") Dalton gazed at the flame atop the match, held the orb of the flame to the joint, took a puff, and handed the joint to Jane, who began her sad story.

SEVERAL DECADES ago, a young woman living in New York City wanted to become a professional artist. She had made friends with some "known" people in the art community, but she wasn't sure whether that was the result of her talent or just because of the notoriously thin self-esteem most artists have, which leads to a dependency on anyone who proclaims to like their work. For all this young woman knew, these people only kept her around because they thought she thought they were talented.

At the time, this young woman had only begun to tap into her considerable artistic skills. She had spent a hard youth with two vicious parents—a famous singer and her husband/manager. In those days, the manager would smack the singer and the daughter around. The father ran the family like a cold business for the first twelve years of the young girl's life. She knew little of love other than the kind that just happens automatically with the words Mom and Dad, which isn't to say that that kind of love can never go away, because it can, and, unfortunately for the young woman, it did. Her mother tried to be loving and doting and devoted, but she was an entertainer and could not compromise her one love for the other, and in the end chose her "calling" over her daughter.

The mother eventually ended up resenting this cruel dichotomy, natural or unnatural as it was. When the young artist was twelve years old, her mother wrote a wretched note and ended her own life with an overdose of painkillers. During the height of her celebrity.

The father took to the bottle and projected all of the blame on the daughter, and he beat her good—good and plenty for a long time, until the bloody-lipped young woman disappeared from their home.

She ran away to stay with friends, and, while staying with those friends, she, despite being so young and so forgiving a child, was already thinking of mirroring her mother's fatal decision. After all, if her mother, such a strong and successful woman, could not outmaneuver the destructive impulses of her father and fix a necessary love-anchor into the world, then how could she? Her head was awash with terrible thoughts—about herself, and life, and whatever could be waiting for her before and after she closed her final eyes.

What got her started wasn't a painting or a sculpture or a photograph or some sort of unsolicited compliment on a doodle she had doodled; it was just that one day the young woman was so overrun with torrents of hate and suffocating desperation for life that she hit the bottom of her mind, her psychological foundation, and discovered that she had an important choice: to be, or not to be. But, in this process, she also found something else.

People are profound and carry a profound capacity, and with little reason to do so, she decided to live, and soon thereafter she began drawing pictures of the things that were happening in her mind. She thought it might work to either have them explode into the artistic ether and out of her brain or lead her on a path of discovery toward discerning whatever it was inside of her that wanted to live. Like maybe she could eventually infer an insight she couldn't consciously voice.

She was working on one of these sketches one day while sitting in Central Park when a man passing by offered to buy her piece right there on the spot. The man was not an art critic or even much of an art fan, but there was something, he said, that he just really liked about the way her sketch made him feel, and he thought he should ask to buy it.

She was sixteen by this point, still living with sundry friends and acquaintances. The man asked to see other works she'd done. The two met again at the same spot in the park the following week (she had no studio to bring him to, obviously), and he bought several more pieces—purchased them at such generous prices that she was able to pay back the friends and families to which she felt so deeply indebted.

She began to walk art galleries on the weekend when not working as a waitress or burning the midnight oil behind the counter at a dangerous convenience store (she was punched unconscious once by a masked gunman who robbed the store). She went to these galleries not because she particularly liked what she saw but because she wanted to be a part of this open world, which, the young artist soon discovered, wasn't difficult. What was difficult, however, was finding other artists with whom she could get along. She'd turned away, with unfriendly distaste, from so many artists she met at those galleries—frustratingly aloof people who'd anointed themselves as brilliant despite the fact that their "art" was often purposely convoluted to make up for a lack of any real artistic ability.

Then she met Simon Fisher.

He was a hard, older man, but not that much older, and not much harder than she was by that point. She was seventeen and he was twenty-five.

The son of a self-made man and a sensitive woman who died when the boy was young, Simon Fisher was raised around plumb-work (his father the owner of a small plumbing business) and under the careful and well-practiced eye of a father who essentially sacrificed himself for his work and his child—a man who had faced the same decision as the young artist's mother and who chose both responsibilities. Simon's father worked hard, and he raised his child with a determination to do it right.

Simon Fisher, the boy, as hardheaded as his father, saw the great things the life of a self-made man can offer, but as sometimes happens among hardheaded, stubborn men, he would not and could not follow in his father's well-worn footsteps. His was not to be a life of pipe-fitting. He had discovered from a very early age that he felt the beat everywhere he found his feet. As a precocious youth, he had regularly gathered old boxes, pans, and plastic containers from the street and, using two like-sized sticks, he would wail and wail on his little cobbled drum set.

By the age of fifteen he was hanging out at jazz clubs, where he befriended an old-time drummer who gave him a used set—bass drum, snare drum, hi-hat—to practice on. Simon moved the set to the roof of his building and practiced every day. He cracked the face of the snare drum one afternoon in the deep winter, and wearing gloves and a parka he kept going anyway. By nineteen he was getting paid to play live shows with real groups.

When he met the young woman for the first time, he was twenty-five years old, and his hands were some of the most talked-about in the New York jazz scene. They were quick, dependable, and, as was his family's specialty, self-made.

Then there was the portrait. It was after one of Simon's shows, and after being so moved by what he could do, the young woman was overwhelmed with inspiration to show him what she considered her best talent. She couldn't show him at the time, but she spent the next few weeks working on something. She made two—one for him and one for herself—and decided to give him his on their one-month anniversary.

After dinner that night, she gave him the portrait. He took it from her and looked at it for a long time. Then he set it down, put his arms around her, and said, "I always wondered what it would feel like when it happened."

The following show, after she had given him the portrait, it is rumored that there were serious Jazz Men in the club who went to their graves saying that what Simon did that night was one of the great moments in music history. The way he lorded over the club's very real drum set was something that can be compared to a moment in basketball history.

There is a story about an American Olympic basketball

team that was called the "Dream Team." It was called this because at the time it was assembled, there was a perfect storm of Hall-of-Fame talent still playing the game, and they were all united, on the same team, for the first time, under the banner of international competition.

The story goes that after one of their early practices together, they emptied the gym of everyone except those players on the team and a few of their friends, who were spectators. In looking around, the players reasoned that probably never again would this group ever be alone in the same gym together. They were international superstars, and while they would spend the rest of their lives together in some way or another (via appearances and honors and ceremonies and such), they would probably never have another opportunity like this. So they sent everyone out, and two players—two of the greatest guards to ever play the game—picked teams and got started. Under those indifferent lights, far removed from the media world that would have paid any price to cover the game, some of the finest athletes of a massive generation played the game not for money or international glory—they played because greatness responds to the call for greatness.

There are always arguments over what comprises the greatest anything of all time, especially in sports and music. But many times those arguments are centered on moments that were caught by the many media and have been discussed and dissected and talked over many times before. However, never making those lists and discussions are the moments that only a handful of people, if any, ever got to witness. The "greatest painting of all time" may have been the masterpiece of a long-forgotten "no-name" who was so tortured by what he created that he burned it and his studio to the ground. History is judged according to those moments for which we have an account.

The same goes for Simon Fisher's perfect performance the night after the woman he loved painted for him a picture of what she saw when she watched him at work behind his simple set of skins and cymbals. He'd been challenged by greatness and responded with his own.

At the end of the show, the normally reserved jazz crowd rose to its feet and let out a loud peal of appreciation for what they had just experienced.

The young musician and the young artist spent two beautiful years together, but then Simon Fisher was drafted into the Army, and the young woman's lifelong dream came true.

Before he left, on a walk through Central Park, Simon got on his knee and gave the young woman a ring, and they were engaged to be married as soon as he returned from the war.

A man at war needs something to come back to.

Simon was in the heavy jungle, halfway around the world, when an old oil baron and art collector bought one of the young woman's paintings for more money than she had made in the entire previous year. The oil man was also happy to let the charming young artist know that he planned on including the purchased piece in his next public showing.

She wrote Simon a thirty-page letter about it, about what it represented, about her thoughts and feelings, the happiness and sadness over it all—words that needed no expression, because what attracted Simon to the young artist was that very fiery passion which ignited each moment and thought between them.

It is fortunate that they were superfluous words, because the letter reached the front only after a scared-shaking soldier accidentally tripped an improvised jungle trap, which sent about six-hundred metal shards tearing through the man next to him: Pvt. Simon Fisher. According to a soldier who was there, Simon Fisher's last words, before the other soldier tripped the trap, were a very funny description of what he planned on doing in bed with the young woman when the war was over and they were together again.

The news of his death wouldn't reach the young woman for another three days—not until the day of the art exhibition in one of New York's most celebrated spaces. That morning, she was notified by telegram. The most important person in her life was dead, and all she had was a piece of paper in her hand.

When the reality finally hit her, she curled to the ground

and wailed helplessly, with the telegram a crumpled, tear-corroded ball on the floor next to her.

She cried herself to sleep, and she awoke to the sound of a ringing telephone. The young artist had promised to frame the painting for the oil baron, and he was calling to make sure she was on her way to the exhibition.

The young woman arrived as planned, if a little late. What wasn't planned was the painting she brought with her. In a testament to her love of a beloved man now dead in a foreign jungle, she had brought with her not the piece the oil baron had purchased but instead the finest work she ever created.

The piece was met with the heart-rending silence of public indifference.

Nobody commented on the piece; few people looked at it for longer than a cursory glance before moving on to finger an inscrutable statue or hoist another glass of wine. The young artist stood in a dark corner all night, alone. She wanted people to see her painting and weep as she wept, even though she knew that was an impossible hope. But what she found were people who appeared not to even notice her painting. And when they did, their faces did not struggle to disguise a new bliss; they struggled to find a new distraction, bored and unimpressed. Near the end of the night, she saw a curator walking a group through the exhibit, and when they got to the young woman's painting, she heard the curator say, "Here's an oil painting by a new artist. Nice stroke-work and choice of of color, but a bit predictable, no? We've seen oil paintings of people before. If you want transcendence, you simply must see this sculpture over here; it's made of things found in famous New Yorkers' garbage bins."

Uninterested people, with an upturned glance and a shrug, who then moved on to see famous garbage—this is the way the young woman was officially greeted by the art community.

It was the last time anyone in the common public ever saw one of her original works. After that afternoon, Jane Jefferson disappeared.

*****

"You never put anything in another show?" Dalton asked.

"No."

"But it was just one show and a bunch of stupid people who could never know how much that particular piece meant to you. God, on that day, too. I'm so sorry, Jane."

"Would it have been any better if the only reason they liked it was because Simon was my dead lover?"

The question hung in the air.

"No," Dalton admitted.

"They didn't like it, Dalton," she said. "They didn't want it. So tell me why I should have put on another show."

"Because fuck them."

"Now you know why I went into advertising," Jane said with a half-suppressed grin.

After a while, Dalton asked, "What did the rich guy say about it? Did he see it?"

"He saw it. After the show, he pulled me aside. I was crying, but I was trying not to let him see, and he said to me, 'Jane, dear, it has been my experience that you can catch a lot more flies with honey. If you show the world that kind of art, you'll only catch spiders like me. There are very many more flies than spiders out there. You can have either, but you can't have both. It's your decision.'

"I still hear him saying that to me sometimes."

"He was right," Dalton said, upset at the idea but having to accept it. "So you added a cup of sugar and went into advertising."

"Not for a while. I still just wanted to make my art, but nobody wanted it. You're right that he was right—almost got killed at my night job and applied at an agency the next day.

"The first time was the hardest. Always is, probably. Then I just did it. And I actually got quite good, for whatever that's worth."

"I guess he saw that you could have this," Dalton said, indicating the large, beautiful grounds and her personal monument of a house, "and that you should have it. And now you do."

It was a long time before Dalton spoke again.

[83]

"I'm sorry, Jane," he said. "You're such a great person; I wish your life had been easier."

"Thank you, Dalton," Jane said. After a moment, she added, "But I don't."

Dalton looked at her, confused.

"If my life had been easy, I probably never would have turned out like this."

16

THE MAGNIFICENT green lawn in front of the church was, at that time in the early evening, patterned with white-cloth-covered tables, with each table topped by two large hurricane candles. Near the front doors of the church, at the back of the lawn, was a small stage featuring a microphone stand and two large speakers, as well as a large sign reading, "Welcome Brother Nathan!" Strung around the outside of the lawn were white streamers that effectively added a sort of celebratory border to the gathering. It was a perfect evening—the air was still, with a light crispness that served more to sharpen the senses than drive fasciculations through the muscles.

The townspeople, or at least the lion's share of them, were gathered in small social groups around the tables. The city's major players were all there, as well. They were the centerpiece of the largest of the circles, and theirs was also the circle towards which everyone had kept an ear turned—the closest thing one could compare, in this community, to paparazzi. The mayor, the city council members, the police chief, and the Hersheys appeared to be gathered around something and talking animatedly with it and each other. Nearly everyone held red plastic cups, out of which they drank lemon water (and lemon water only, unless they were the more spirited and frowned-upon followers, who made their own gin and smuggled it in). As Jane, Dalton, and Quentin arrived, they observed the social customs of the Luminarians and tried to give off a friendly air.

The three worked their way over to a corner table, one distant from the murmuring social groups, whose discussions grew more animated and agitated when the three well-meaning nonbelievers infiltrated their celebration.

Dalton, Quentin, and Jane had been invited by Head Pastor Phillip Hershey himself, as Jane and Quentin usually had been, which surprised Dalton until Quentin explained the excuses the pastor's "enlightened" views could afford him when discussing moral matters, like he was capable of a level of tolerance and forgiveness so generous that he didn't even request it of his own followers. More pragmatically, their presence also afforded him the corollary benefit of being able to motion to them with an unspoken hostility when making certain points during his occasional speeches.

As the evening sky glowed orange, the three "unwanteds" (as they had overheard someone calling them) were talking. Jane was trying to get Dalton to relax, who squirmed every time he saw the strung banner above the stage and strained against its missing comma. He wanted to run up there and mark one between "Welcome" and "Brother" so much it itched. "I'm being pedantic, aren't I?" Dalton asked, and Quentin laughed and decided to change the subject to how surprisingly nice the lawn looked for the festivities.

All of a sudden Dalton felt a jab at his ribs and saw short strands of fake blonde hair fly by his eyes, and then he was face-to-face with an extraordinarily ordinary-looking doll, whose owner was yelling, "Boo!"

Dalton clutched his chest and faked a heart attack, much to the giggling glee of little Shannon Penrose.

While Dalton played dead on the ground, Jane said, "Hey there, Shannon!"

"Hi, Missus Je-Je-Je-Jefferson," the little imp shyly stuttered, which might have been the most adorable thing any of them ever heard.

"Hello, Miss Penrose," Quentin said in a tone of voice Dalton had never heard out of Mr. Hancock before—almost whimsical. "Where's your father?"

"He's ove' theah," she said, wiping her sniffling nose and pointing to the periphery of the big-time social circle featuring the mayor and the Hersheys.

Shannon began swatting Dalton in the face with her doll, so he laugh-shocked her by springing his eyes open and animatedly hurrying to his seat. The high-pitched rings of laughter must have alerted someone to the goings-on, because once again Shannon was swiftly carted away by her father. This time, though, as she left, she waved and bellowed, "*Byyyeeeee!*"

The three in the corner all waved back happily and called out, "Bye, Shannon!"

Someone hissed at them, but it was forgotten when there was a very deep grunt into the microphone, which squealed momentarily, and then the now-familiar baritone of Augustus Hershey addressed the crowd.

"If I could have everyone's attention, please," the voice boomed over the tables, whose conversations tapered off into attention.

"As you may or may not know, three months ago my sister was on a diplomatic mission to Southern California"—an uncomfortable murmur circled the tables—"when she met a young man. I knew this young man had to be special, because my sister typically doesn't have human emotions"—crowd laughter—"but when she returned, there was something in her face that had changed. We soon learned what that change was: she had met a boy.

"And as you undoubtedly understand, my father didn't take this news very well!"—crowd laughter. "Nevertheless, after some long discussions with the family, we began to warm to the idea of this boy, despite his spiritual handicap"—mild crowd laughter. "And then he arrived here, and we all fell in love with him. We could all see what Victoria saw, but let's not kid ourselves: he still had a long way to go." A few ugly faces turned towards the table in the back corner. Dalton laughed. "But he expressed such a legitimate interest in our Victoria, and through Victoria an interest in our faith, that my father took this young man under his wing and started him on the path—a path that ends tonight with our loving community welcoming our newest fluted instrument in faith: Brother Nathan Cameron!"

The crowd erupted into applause and cheering as a peculiarly attractive young man with a serious face and a flaking sunburn walked onto the stage, waved to the crowd, and timidly tried to walk offstage. Nevertheless, several "Speech!" calls from the audience prompted Augustus to guide the young man over to the microphone, where Nathan Cameron looked over the attendees and simply said, "Thank you."

The crowd again erupted into cheering and applause, and the entire Hershey family joined Nathan onstage, which sent the crowd into a fever pitch. Together, the Hersheys and Nathan joined hands and raised them over the audience. Then Augustus grabbed the microphone and added, "Let's eat!"

Aside from a few home-baked side dishes brought by fellow Luminarians and a few dozen swords of bread baked by Lucy Hait, Dalton knew what was on the meager menu that night because he was there when it was killed.

Before the meal started, when everybody had his or her plate of food at the ready, Pastor Hershey quieted the crowd and said a prayer over their bowed heads, which Quentin scribbled down in a manic shorthand on a piece of paper he'd brought with him, trying not to be noticed.

"We gather this evening in celebration as another of the Lorrah's chosen ones is welcomed to the flock. And we praise the Lorrah with this food, supplied to us by my own son and our fellow friends. Thank you, Lorrah, for the food, the family, the friends, and your infinite goodness."

"Through the Lorrah we are made music," the crowd said back, and everyone dug in. Except Dalton. He kept thinking about how little grace or meaning he could find in the way the little deer just dropped to the ground after the bullet tore through its eye socket and out the back of its little deer head. Just dead and gone like that.

Later, after dinner, as people began picking at pies (Dalton, by this point ravished with hunger, ate half of a cherry pie himself), the loose social circles returned. It was fully dark now, and when Quentin leaned back, stuffed and otherwise content, he saw tiki-torch fire tongues licking at a mesmerizing field of stars above them all.

Below those stars, a baptized Nathan Cameron scanned the crowd as he held a blushing and gushing Victoria's hand under the table. She was so happy it almost appeared as though it were Victoria who had just been baptized into their beloved community.

Dalton found a dark corner of the party, away from the ugly stares in Jane's and Quentin's direction, away from everyone's eyes, and he watched Nathan Cameron. Observed his face and mannerisms. There seemed to be something familiar about him.

But, then, that's what everyone seemed to say about Nathan.

Later, deep into the night, most people had gone home. Quentin was still there, conducting an unofficial interview with the mayor. The entire Hershey family and Nathan Cameron talked while Dalton Hughes, resting his head on his curled arm draped across a white-cloth-covered table, waited for Quentin to finish.

"*There* he is. Hey, Dalton!"

It was Victoria's voice.

Dalton pulled his head off the table and saw the Hersheys and Nathan all looking over at him. Victoria motioned him over.

The Hershey circle opened to a semicircle, and Dalton got to interact with the family all together for the first time. Truly, they had a familial harmony to them. Each looked comfortable with the other. In a way, compared to all the things Dalton had seen so far in the town, it was rather nice. Their faces, with the family's confidence supported by their togetherness, looked warm and welcoming. The boy in the middle, holding Victoria's hand, matched them smile for smile.

"Dalton, I want you to meet Nathan," said Victoria.

"So this is the new guy I heard about," Nathan said with his Augustus-like deep voice, extending his hand.

"I was going to say the same thing," Dalton said, meeting Nathan's hand and looking over at Victoria, who blushed a friendly blush—a blush that didn't go unnoticed by Nathan. "I suppose congratulations are in order."

"Thanks," Nathan said for what must have been too many times that night. He quickly peered, peripherally, up and down the row of Hersheys he stood amongst and, buttressed by their presence, added, "I wish I could explain to you how miraculous it feels."

The Hersheys seemed delighted—though mutedly, diplomatically so—by his statement.

"Speaking of that, you probably know I'm supposed to do a story on all this," Dalton said, gesturing to the tables—the *venison*—the celebration, the baptism.

"I look forward to it," Nathan said.

"Same here," Dalton said.

"Speaking of which," Victoria said. "Dalton, you and my brother here had quite an adventure today."

"It was indeed very exciting," Dalton said. "Your brother is an excellent marksman and a very brave man. I almost owe him my life."

"And perhaps I shall collect," Augustus said with a surprisingly affable tone. His family laughed a bit too hard.

"Well, it looks like I should be getting home," Dalton said. "Good night, Hershey family. Pleasure to meet you, Nathan. And thank you again, Augustus."

The Hersheys all nodded to Dalton—this event being their most straightforward observation of his existence yet—while Nathan offered a small wave, adding, "Be careful out there."

As Dalton walked away, he heard a deep voice say something, and then the family once again erupted into a chorus of laughter.

The following day was his first day off since he arrived, and Dalton slept heavily.

17

DALTON AGAIN awoke to the sound of knocking at his door.

It was just before noon. The weather was warmer than it had been in a while—hot, actually—and Dalton didn't want to pry himself off the bed. The oscillating fan in the corner cooled the heat and chilled the little sweat pools that accumulated in the swirling air's absence, creating a relaxing hot–cool–hot effect that had kept Dalton in quiet rest. But now, it appeared, his rest was over, for he heard the soothing boom of Jane's voice call to him.

"Outta bed, sleepyhead!"

Dalton pulled on some clothes and answered the door.

"Good morning, Dalton," Jane said. "I was wondering if you would like to join me at my house."

Dalton massaged his eye socket with the heel of his hand. "Good morning, Sweet Jane. Of course I'd like to join you."

Jane looked great—much better than when she stopped by the day before, in hysterics. As they walked across the long lawn up toward the back of Jane's house, Dalton noticed a springier step and an altogether more vibrant vitality from her. It made him feel more at ease. He liked it when Jane was happy.

The back of Jane's large house was virtually all windows, except at the base, where a sort of hallway was cut into the rolling hill on top of which the house had been constructed, leading to a double-glass door in what looked like the house's basement. This was the first time Dalton had ever been inside the Jefferson residence.

The air, upon stepping into the dark room, was refreshingly conditioned. The room was dark, and, in stark contrast to the brilliant day behind them, it took several moments for Dalton's eyes to adjust to the dark. But when they did, he noticed he was standing in a surprisingly ordinary basement room. The light streaming in from behind them cast long shadows across the floor and the far wall, shadows shaped like tall silhouettes of their observers. There was one door each on the right and left walls. The right door was painted red, the left blue. They were two very serious doors—full metal jackets, a hundred pounds each.

Jane unlocked and opened the blue door. She reached in and flipped a switch inside the room, and the lights came on.

Dalton entered a private gallery—paintings, sculptures, photographs, and statues all leading into and out of one another. Each was illumined by directed bulbs in the ceiling that made an X of light, in the middle of which the piece of art waited. The light was bright enough for observation but not so bright as to cause any glints from the heavy paints of the paintings or glass frames of the photographs. As Dalton walked among the collected art, he almost immediately noticed that this stuff was different from the few pieces of Jane's he'd seen. The stroke-work and color choices were much more . . . Dalton searched for the word, that was it: reserved. They were masterful, indeed, but they seemed timid. A talent almost ashamed of itself, or abstractly handcuffing itself. Despite detracting from the overall aesthetic of the art, these effects added to the idea at the center.

"This isn't your art, is it?" Dalton asked.

"You got me there, Dalton."

"Whose is it?"

"It's mine."

The voice came from behind him, at the door. It was Victoria Hershey. She was dressed in a painfully simple and beautiful sun dress, her skinny legs sticking out of the bottom by the hem at her knees. Next to her stood Nathan Cameron, whose eyes were coolly taking in the whole scene.

Greetings were exchanged, and each explored Victoria's collection.

Dalton continued looking around. There was a painting of the Crondura River in the spring—the hills of its banks bursting with flowers and color. There was a pencil sketch of Jane that almost brought tears to Dalton's eyes: Jane was seated, palette and brush in hand, looking at the canvas on an easel, but Dalton saw that she was not looking at the canvas at all. Whatever she was seeing broke Dalton's heart, because whatever it was was clearly causing her a thinly disguised, profound internal grief. All the world's pain was in those eyes. Dalton, speechless, his heart in his throat, had to step away from the sketch. He looked at the carpet for a moment, and then he looked up and saw something unusual.

It was himself, sort of. An oil painting resembling a self-portrait, it portrayed what looked like Dalton's face. But it wasn't completely his face. The details were minute and breathtaking, but the image, the object, looked like Dalton and didn't look like Dalton. Compared to the general realistic accuracy of the rest of the paintings, this one stood out because it was realistically inaccurate, and had no setting. It was as if the subject had no object.

"I'm not sure I get this one," Dalton said. "It kind of looks like me."

"I was just about to say that," Nathan said.

"You see it, too?"

"No, I mean, I was about to say it kind of looked like me."

Nathan turned to Victoria and said, "What is this?"

Victoria had several false starts as she tried to explain what the painting was. Eventually, she just told the truth as she knew it.

"I had a dream a few days ago," she said, telling the story primarily to Nathan, but including Dalton and Jane in the telling. "I was in this really posh penthouse of this huge hotel, and there were all these fancy people there, like they were attending a party or something, dressed really nice, and they kept asking me, 'Did you see it?' and 'Did you see it yet?' It's all anyone seemed to want to talk about—who'd *seen it*. Finally, I started asking them where *I* could see it, but they wouldn't tell me. They just wanted to know if I'd seen it yet. Then I saw this strange furry animal step into the room we were in and immediately fall down dead-eyed. I rushed over, and I could see that the room it had just come from was completely dark except for way back in the dark there were these soft yellow-and-red lights that were lighting up something. So while other people were dealing with the passed-out animal

I went into the room and walked toward the light, and it turned out to be a big mirror over a small table. The table held candles that were strangely burning with yellow and red tongues of fire. For some reason, all of this made me really scared, and, when I finally felt like I had enough courage, I looked in the mirror, and . . . this person, this face," she said, indicating the painting, "was my reflection—was looking back at me, making that same expression, and then I passed out and woke up."

There was a long pause. She went on. "Anyway, I could still see that face all morning, and then I realized that my brain had mashed your and Dalton's faces together. See, I had meant to do a painting of each of you, as a gift and because I think you're both interesting-looking, and I ended up with that dream and this one painting. I like it, though."

"I love it," Jane said. "It's one face, but there's so much to see!"

Dalton gave it his best aesthetic appraisal. "It's good," Dalton finally said, turning to Victoria. "It's just different from the other stuff."

"So are you two," Victoria said.

Behind Dalton, Nathan observed the same painting. He said nothing. Finally, Jane said, "It's too bad you and Nathan can't have kids, Dalton. Your child could have been a leading man. People would ask each other if they'd *seen* him."

Dalton laughed.

Nathan chuckled.

Victoria cleared her throat. "Now, you get it, Dalton," she said, "that even though you're a reporter, you're not a reporter right now, right?"

"I think so."

"As a woman Luminarian, I am traditionally forbidden to partake in this sort of thing. Even you being here, on the property of an unmarried woman and with another unmarried woman, is grounds for a very ugly punishment, for all of us. You too, Nathan."

"I don't care," Nathan said, and Victoria squeezed his hand.

"They're beautiful, Victoria," Dalton said. "That's a nice goddam religion you have that would want to stop you from doing this."

He'd gone too far, and he knew it, but he didn't want to apologize.

"Religions are a guide or a path," Victoria said, "but people themselves make all the decisions as they travel that path. Sometimes you have to leave the trail to survive."

"Well that's the first bit of sense I've heard in a while," Jane said, effectively ending the discussion, which was fine with everyone.

"I had a teacher in Long Beach who would have loved this piece," Nathan said, pointing to a photograph of Clem and Hunter snoozing in an open field. "He was an old editor at *Look*. Really cool guy. Would have loved this."

"What would happen to you if this place were discovered by the Luminarians?" Dalton asked.

"They'll never see it," Vee said. "Jane is not a Luminarian, and technically this house is outside of Manta, so her home does not fall under Luminarian domain."

"So what am I doing here?" Dalton couldn't help but ask.

"You're here because I would like us all to be friends," Victoria said. "My father and brother and mother have diplomatic and . . . other . . . reasons for being as fanatical about our religion as they are, and they need to be, but to quote a dead man: 'From childhood's hour I have not been—'"

"'As others were,'" Nathan and Dalton said simultaneously.

"Right," Victoria said, impressed and surprised. "I love Jane very much, and she was kind enough to provide me with this space, where I can create and display my work.

"So you're not a reporter today, Dalton; you're just my friend."

"That could complicate things," Dalton said. "I'm supposed to try to remain objective."

"You can't be an objective reporter and a subjective friend at the same time?" Nathan asked.

"I don't know," Dalton said truthfully. "This is my first

crack at it."

"You'll be fine," Jane said with a particular emphasis that showed she both believed in Dalton's capacity as well as the good things that could result from their united friendship. "There's no such thing as objective journalism, anyway."

They rounded out the morning taking tokes from one of Jane's lucky little sticks, sitting on or journeying across the thick blue carpet and staring at Victoria's prolific work. The blue of the smoke, the carpet, the swirling air, and the occasional bright strikes of Victoria's art . . . to Dalton's dazzled mind, a kind of marvelous indoor thunderhead.

Although Dalton didn't notice it consciously, throughout the rest of that afternoon, in the shifting clouds of the room, Nathan would mimic the physical positions Dalton assumed—two men holding a joint a certain way, two men leaning back on their elbows, two men with their arms crossed, gazing into a painting.

All Dalton knew consciously was that he was warming to this cool, measured young man, and there was something both welcoming and curious about the feeling.

THE CORNER Café wasn't even on the corner. It used to be, but the Luminarian leaders "convinced" the owners to move down the block a bit, and the restaurant now sat between a tailor and an empty storefront. (After the unsolicited move, the owners decided to keep the name the same, as a laugh.)

Like everything else in Manta, The Corner Café was sparsely decorated. It had a weatherworn brick-and-mortar exterior, and a thin red carpet on the sidewalk led into the wood-floored and -paneled room, where, above the white-clothed tables, an interlaced network of exposed, dark-stained rafters crisscrossed a warm flow of sunshine that streamed in through grimy skylight windows.

The food was tasty and unique, and the prices were decent enough, but the main reason this was the most popular restaurant in Manta was because of a little waitress named Marie.

Amidst the smell of fresh ingredients hitting sizzling

pans, boiling spaghetti, and the dulcet punctuation of a small sweets bakery, amidst the sound of cooking and quiet conversation, at seemingly any point in the room at any time was a high-velocity little cutie named Marie, who spun from table to table—filling water glasses, removing plates, and sharing inside jokes with the customers who all beamed back with broad smiles.

She wasn't a Luminarian. ("*A Luminarian doesn't* glow *like that*," Dalton later scribbled in one of his notebooks.) She wasn't even a citizen of the town, but she was the only person who toiled there who was roundly forgiven for being different. The reason for this was something Dalton was learning, because after visiting Victoria's secret gallery, the four gathered therein were munchy-hungry, and the ladies decided to take their boys to everyone's favorite restaurant.

Marie, Marie . . . She was energy and symmetry, and she was almost always very busy, which gave Dalton the opportunity to watch her without being noticed. The way he was feeling—pensive, exhausted, now enamored—it was the only thing he wanted to do: to observe the insuperable perfection of this new living art he had been brought to see.

As for the others at the table, Jane and Victoria had no shortage of opinions and stories, and Nathan filled the conversational gaps with what Dalton noticed was a near-endless parade of one-up floats. "Oh, you have a friend in the military? My cousin's a Green Beret, and he was telling me about . . . ." This tendency wasn't as pronounced or annoying as some one-up people's, but it was something Dalton started to notice about Nathan's company in the mix of these expressive minds. It didn't bother him that much; he just found himself noting the observation. And then Dalton forgot all about it when his head and heart were filled with the affecting sight of sweet Marie.

Finally, she appeared at the table in the corner—four chairs occupied by some of the more famous/infamous citizens of Manta.

"Hi there, girls!" Marie said, pulling out her notebook and pencil. "How are we today?"

"Hello, Marie," Jane said. "I would like you to meet our town's newest customers. This is Dalton, and this is Nathan."

"Oh my, yes, I have heard of you both," Marie said with a mild French accent. "Mr. Nathan, congratulations on your conversion and your happy love with Victoria. She is one of my favorite people here. And you, Mr. Dalton, I read the *Post* story of your bear-hunting adventure with great enjoyment."

Nathan said nothing. He silently shook her hand.

"Thank you," Dalton said, unsure of what else to say—unable to say much else. "Nice to meet you, Marie."

"So, what can I get for you?"

Victoria, Nathan, and Jane gave their orders. Dalton wasn't hungry anymore. "I'm actually just here to enjoy the conversation, though I would like a glass of water, if that's not too much trouble."

"Oh, you are like a green plant," Marie said.

Everyone at the table looked around as if someone else knew what she meant.

"I'm sorry—" Dalton said.

"A green plant. It is a French expression, as we say. A green plant is something that sits in the corner and looks cute, but it does nothing."

Jane had a good laugh about this. "Does nothing but drink water!"

Overwhelmed Dalton didn't know what to make of this, but he got the impression that somewhere within him he liked it. "Thank you, I guess, Marie."

Jane and Victoria talked further about what the green plant thing could have meant, and Marie soon quickly returned to the table and addressed Dalton.

"You still looked confused before, but just to clarify, it was a compliment."

"Well, then, thank you, Marie," Dalton said and felt another wave of anxiety pass over him. His face flushed red. She was even prettier than his short memory had remembered.

"Mr. Hughes," Jane said, "I think she's hitting on you."

"Nonsense," Dalton said. "She's right: I am a green plant. But she's just being nice for the tip."

"You can't think like that, man," Nathan said. He looked at Marie in a way that Victoria did not catch, but which Dalton did, and said, "If it's not you, it'll be someone else, but until you get rejected there's a chance it could be you. And if it is you, dude, your life improves instantaneously, so I say that's always a risk worth taking. You know? You should go for it, man."

Jane could sense that Dalton was too overloaded with phenomena to be a master of the current moment, so she put an end to the discussion by stating, "Well, she's been here for years, Dalton, and as far as I know she'll be here tomorrow. Nathan's got some wisdom there: modest or not, today or not, you make sure she knows you want to get *in there*."

They all burst out laughing and then quieted themselves when they saw how much attention they had attracted.

"I have a question. How come nobody gives Marie a hard time?" Dalton asked the table. The stories he'd heard about Marie involved all sorts of smiles and sunshine. "She's not a Luminarian or a Mantanite; how come people give her a break?"

"Well, maybe consider your reaction," Victoria said. "As you can see, it's just easy to look past that kind of thing with Marie. And anyway, it's not like we're hateful people."

Dalton thought about little Shannon Penrose being toted away by unspeaking interlopers and Quentin Hancock watching piles of his paper burn. He heard Quentin in his head, ". . . and these people have killed before," and thought about Shannon's deceased mother. But instead of saying anything, he turned and gazed at Marie.

Then the food arrived. Marie and the cook were quick, and after she deposited the plates and Dalton's water glass on the table, she was off to the other corner of the room to pick up the sippy-cup that had been tossed to the floor by a cranky child. She lifted the cup off the floor and set it next to the crabby boy and attempted to soothe him by patting him on the head "a few times like a cartoon character" (how Dalton later tried to describe it). Dalton couldn't pull his eyes away from her.

After filling their hunger, the four conversed for a while before they left. Marie was too busy to join them, and the green plant sat in the corner, looked cute, drank water, and did nothing.

But he'd be back.

18

THE CITY of Haverbrook wasn't born with a gunshot, but it was baptized with one.

On the morning of September tenth, 1695, an important summit was called between the native Olwahapa tribe and the European settlers who had claimed the land along the low ridgeline facing the Crondura River as theirs by decree of a long string of politically coercive property manipulations—backed by gunpowder and the invocation of a holy burden. As a show of good faith, the town's mayor and the tribe's chief were to meet with each other and their advisors at the top of the ridgeline above the growing town. They were to discuss their respective futures on the land currently blurred by ambiguous claims.

The morning started off far colder than usual, with a shiny wet dew clinging to everything green and in turn soaking coldly into the wet leather of the Europeans' boots and the natives' soft moccasins. The sun was sluggish, almost hesitant to witness the momentous event. The animals must have been nervous too, because hardly a chirp, bark, or bleat was heard that morning. All was powerfully quiet as the two cultural storm fronts swirled together.

There were, of course, unfortunately aggressive plans on both sides of the meeting, which was requested after a series of recent, violent exchanges. The Europeans had short-term plans of more or less killing off or converting the "noble savage," starting with that morning's ambush, and the natives had short-term plans of more or less killing off the "pale threat," either through direct violence or triple-crossing their treaties between the contending nations. This was the land they loved. They did not own it, and they would not accept it being owned by anyone.

That morning, two unarmed groups, containing some of the finest minds each side had to offer, met at the top of Jacob's Ridge/the Gantroah Overlook—a crest above a fertile stretch of land cleaved by the sparkling blue vein of the Crondura. The air was cold, their feet were wet, the day was young, and then, in that strange quiet, one of the most amazing coincidences in modern military and political history unraveled.

The white men's plan was to ambush all gathered Olwahapa and butcher them, leaving one alive to tell the rest of the tribe that they were now considered illegal inhabitants of properly owned land. The natives' plan was to kill the white leaders in the hopes that a headless flock would eventually plummet off the proverbial cliff. The feeling on both sides was summed up by something the Haverbrook mayor told a concerned housewife on the way to the meeting: "Diplomacy's day is done."

That morning, both sides' sentiments came to a head at the very same moment.

Musketeers hidden in bales of hay, expert marksman warriors who hiked all night to circle around the invaders, and one shot—one terrified young marksman named Dale Goodyear, shaken by the pressure and his nerves, squeezed his trigger when the chief made a wide motion with his hand, as he was pointing and asking the Haverbrook mayor where the proof was that the white man or any man owned any of this land.

Boom.

The back of the Olwahapa chief's head exploded, and his body slumped to the ground.

In the subsequent sixty seconds—this in a time when muskets had very little accuracy and bows had very little benefit when compared to modern weapons—every person from both sides gathered on that ridge was dead.

Twenty seconds of exploding black powder, whizzing arrows, and blood spurting from the necks, chests, arms, and legs of the men gathered there.

Then the muskets fell silent, the arrows stood in their targets, and the proceeding moments were filled with the sound of horrid groaning as all those young and old men bled to death.

Then there was just the wind again, and the women, children, and battle-unworthy men from both sides one by one made their way to the bloody ridgeline to find and cry over their losses. And those sounds never end. Men of great minds and ambition were dead in the name of false peace. The morning fell back to quietness, the dew now mixed with blood, and the sound of the wind was lost to the muffled agony of great sobs shuddering through the souls of people who had lost what they loved. Eventually, the tears gave way to rage.

The Europeans won. The effect of the travesty and subsequent Anglican victory for the town was unexpected. Haverbrook became a town of tolerance and trade, and subsequently it became one of the most successful trading outposts in the then-West and for a very long time was the sort of place that was so ahead of the social curve as to be out of vogue, and therefore it was derided. As America grew up and out and advanced beyond the fur trades, the town's utility and population shrunk to the point where it became a rival with the much less celebrated town of Manta, current home of the religious sect that called themselves Luminarians.

Haverbrook, these days, was, in an odd way, returning to its diverse roots. The fur-trading empire it had once been was long gone, and so was the fifty-fifty split between the Europeans and the natives. The town dwindled and emptied, only to be reborn in later years as the center of an intellectual revolution.

Meyer College, one hour east of Haverbrook, made regular deposits into the town population, and these gathered minds had turned the city into a strange new world. The houses were destroyed, and new ones—fresh designs from the minds of Meyer architects—replaced them.

The town library won a large federal grant after three retired professors petitioned persuasive legislators, turning it into the local rural county's Alexandria (it had books). The economy was stimulated by an illegal, under-the-table marijuana crop, general businesses that were run well, a large industrial engineering firm, and a growing artistic community, the majority of which had been subsidized by a famous filmmaker's estate.

While alive, the filmmaker had established an artistic charity, and shortly before his death, he moved the headquarters to Haverbrook, his hometown. Thus, the new houses faced open stretches of virgin land, pockmarked now and then by barns converted into studios, with their weird, painted faces splashing unusual colors into the day, casting giant glances in the evening, and providing ample cover for the artists who would often lie down to sleep next to their own canvases at night.

MANTA'S CITY history can be much more briefly stated. Its construction was the coordinated effort of a traveling Christian missionary named McDavid Gaines, who claimed to have talked to God. He preached that God instructed him to gather a group of people together to build a truly Christian town, which they named Testament. It went up nearly all at once, though the large church took longer than everything else. They lived there in peace, farming the land to feed themselves, for five years. Then one day, when everyone had gathered in the church for a holy day of obligation, the missionary poisoned the water, and everyone died, including the missionary. For those who know the history, there is an ongoing debate as to why Gaines would go through the trouble of building and living in the town if he only wanted to kill himself and everyone else. Eventually, the town and the bodies were discovered, but nobody wanted to move there, so the buildings were emptied and, besides a small repopulation when the ample logging and bad economy combined to make it necessary, remained predominantly empty . . . until gunshots rang out in the town of Bovary, Ohio.

19

THEY DECIDED to hike through the northern woods, as neither of them had ever been up that way before, and the conversational intimacy of having only the two of them out in the wild would be a good opportunity for Dalton to interview Nathan and find whatever story there was to be found for the *Post*.

Dalton had taken a strong liking to walking around the great woods surrounding the small town. The relative quiet mixed with the copper-mouthed breath of the Natural Wild created in him a primal feeling—like Early Man crossing unknown country in search of betterment from everything behind him and protection from everything to come.

It was obvious to Dalton that Nathan enjoyed hiking, or at least he seemed to enjoy it as much as Dalton did. The two of them made good time (good time going nowhere specific, however) as they leaped streams, climbed over fallen trunks, and shuffled through old dead leaves in the cool afternoon.

Climbing over and through the vegetation within the green-and-brown forest, wet with sweat, they began their inevitable conversation.

"Why do you want to be a reporter?" Nathan asked, turning back briefly before continuing the lead.

"I don't," Dalton replied.

"Oh, okay."

They walked.

"It's not the end for me," Dalton said. "It's the means. It's important work, particularly for my real goals."

"Which are?" Nathan asked.

"Personal," Dalton said. "No offense. It's a long story. Why did you want to become a Luminarian?"

"Are we on the record?" Nathan asked.

"For now, yes."

"Really, it all started with Victoria."

They continued hiking as Nathan talked about Victoria and her family. Unfortunately, it was all stuff Dalton already knew—stuff everyone in town already knew. There was no mention of Luminarianism. It was a fine bit of say-something-while-saying-nothing public relations, and it was useless for Dalton's story. Dalton was beginning to lose his patience when Nathan told him some real truth, off the record.

"Off the record," Nathan continued, "I was working at an art gallery in Long Beach, and she came in to check out some of our stuff, and we started talking. *On the record* (Nathan added his own, spoken italics), we met when I was alone on a lunch break, and she asked me what I was reading. I showed her my book—it was Bob Browne's *The Will to Power* [the book alluded to in Nathan's introductory prologue]—and she asked me if I liked it. We started talking, and she was able to guide the conversation toward religion, and then specifically her religion. Now our religion. It was impressive."

"A stranger talking about a fringe religion didn't make you feel uncomfortable?" Dalton asked.

Nathan stopped. "Dude, she's beautiful. She could have talked about cutting off a dog's head and I would have smiled and nodded and asked if I could sharpen anything for her."

Dalton laughed. "Fair enough."

"So, I asked her how long she was in town," Nathan continued. "She told me she was leaving in a few days. We talked about where she came from, and I admit it sounded interesting, like something I might be interested in, like my kind of place, you know. Plus, I don't know . . . there was something about her. Off the record, I like her. I don't normally like people, especially religious people, but Victoria has this personality, and she's so pretty—"

"Right. So . . ." Dalton trailed off, hoping for Nathan to continue.

"So I was kind of done with Los Angeles and Long Beach anyway. The coast would always be there, but the draw of moving to the almost exact opposite of that area was appealing to me. Don't get me wrong—I really enjoyed L.A., but I grew up in an area kind of like this, and it felt right to come this way in pursuit of possibly the only woman I've ever loved. I'm getting older, man. Time to grow up, maybe, you know?"

Dalton motioned for them to stop and rest a bit. They found a fallen tree and sat on the mighty trunk, in the process disturbing a column of ants marching across its sun-streaked top.

"What happened when you met her family?" Dalton asked.

"At first I only met her father," Nathan said. "He met me outside of the town, and, dude, we had a *very* long talk."

"Anything noteworthy about the talk?"

"You mean besides meeting my girlfriend's father for the first time, who happens to be the leader of a closed-off religious sect?"

Dalton laughed again. "Yeah, besides that."

Nathan leaned back on his hands. "I don't know, we just seemed to understand each other. I liked him, after the initial shock of seeing how big he is. In that sense, he reminds me of my own father. But personality-wise they couldn't be more different. My father is a quiet man. Phillip is also quiet, but his . . . persona . . . is vivid. You could sense his presence before he even walked through the door, you know?"

"Good way of putting it," Dalton said.

"Yeah, and then he told me about the Luminarian rules of courting and dating and marriage and everything else, and we started planning my trip to the desert."

"Why the desert?" Dalton was finally getting where he wanted the interview to go.

"Because that's where my girlfriend's father sent me," Nathan said, effectively suturing the wound before it had a chance to bleed anything interesting.

"Right," Dalton said. "What did you think of the whole pre-baptismal endeavor?"

"It was tough, man. But by the fourth day, I think I started to understand why it was necessary. I started hearing the Voice."

"What did it say?"

Nathan stood up and headed up the hill behind them. Dalton followed.

"No offense, Dalton, but that's the sort of thing you'd have to be a Luminarian—or a *believer*, someone who *believes* in something—to fully understand. The Voice has a language, but there are no words."

"So a week in," Dalton said, "and you consider yourself a full-fledged Luminarian."

"On the record, I don't think that's fair to say. I suppose you're a full-fledged member the moment you really and truly in your heart believe in the Lorrah, but there are so many people in this church who are saintly, just wonderful practitioners, believers, and I think it's unfair to compare myself to them in matters of this religion and these beliefs. But I do take it seriously.

"Off the record, I absolutely do. I've felt this emptiness in my soul for as long as I can remember. I've tried to fill it with women, with sports, with school, with friends . . . and the only thing that's ever felt right for any time longer than a momentary solution to chronic problems is the . . . well, the bell jar of Lorrah's love and protection."

"But isn't that a mixed metaphor?" Dalton asked. "You have an emptiness, and you filled it with a bell jar?"

"Everyone has what I have inside his being, and something will inevitably fill that hole. But it's like nothing suffices. It's like rain soaking into the ground. Luminarians choose instead to cap and protect it and keep anything unsatisfactory from entering the person's instrument. There are more to these barriers than simple xenophobia; the borders we protect shape the music that we are."

THEY KEPT walking for a while, without talking. The autumn air was crisp, and while some of the leaves were still green, most of them were already burnt red, orange, yellow. The brown earth was dark in the shadows and rich in the light. As they walked, they appeared to be the only living beings in the forest, but when they would stop, now and then, to catch their breath or take in the scene, the forest would come to life: butterflies rising and falling as they flapped from tree to tree; dragonflies zipping past and racing up to the multicolored canopy; two squirrels, dashing through the undergrowth, on their own adventure; above them (Dalton, Nathan, the insects, worms, flora, deer, and squirrels), an eagle circled, visible only between the few gaps in the canopy. This is what Dalton and Nathan looked over as they hiked through the woods and waded through creeks that fed the Crondura River.

There was no sign of any bears. Dalton never blinked.

They were quiet for the rest of the hike. Eventually, they reached a clearing, and a wide expanse opened before them. An expanse called the town of Haverbrook.

They took a brief look at the town but had to turn and head back. With the sun setting earlier and earlier every day, time became an issue, because they had forgotten to bring a flashlight.

If they made good time on the hike out, on the hike back they were natural creatures of the forest. They doubled and redoubled their pace as the evening quickly bled into that darkness that always gobbles up every bit of color offered to it.

They came upon the large silhouette of the church just as the sun was puffing its last bit of life into the darkening air, hardly another word spoken between either of them—just the mixed sound of their breath and their steps.

20

DALTON ENDED up writing an informal story about interviewing the newest member of the religion. It was widely praised by the townspeople. The majority of them were at least warming to the idea of tolerating Dalton, as they had warmed to the idea that Quentin could put together a better paper than anyone else in town—they warmed to Dalton because he provided them with a service.

But they still hated him, just as they still hated Quentin, Jane, and Halo Kilgore.

And Clem Lemon.

CLEM LEMON, it should finally be noted, was the most hated man in Manta, more so than anyone else, maybe ever, in the hearts of the townspeople—more than the governor who illegally called for the raid of their former haven, more than the fire-tongued former philosophy and literature professor who haunted the outskirts of their hideaway, more than the government agents who'd killed three Luminarians in the black of night.

For one thing, he was hated because he was the only member of the Luminarian faith who defected and survived. There were murmurs around town, and even some peripheral threats in some of the speeches Dalton read in Quentin's book, that several people throughout the faith's short history had grown dissatisfied with the spiritual guidance offered by the community and had either disappeared or died. Most notable in this group was Shannon Penrose's mother. Her outspoken opinions—loudly protesting the church's baptismal practices—were swiftly silenced by what Head Pastor Hershey referred to as the "decisive hand of the Lorrah" and what Quentin Hancock referred to as "the benefits of modern science handled by poisonous thinkers."

Formerly, the Lemon name was synonymous with the Luminarian faith. Clem's own father was one of the highest-ranking members of the church. Young Clem was the ideal follower in every way throughout his infancy, mild youth, and turbulent teenage years. But it was during those teenage years that his father took to ill health (colon cancer), and, over the course of his four years of medical treatment, the father, sensing the internal growth of his own death, told his son everything about the church and his own faith. And while they say there are no atheists in the trenches, the small trench where Thaddeus Lemon died contained at least one. His last words to his son weren't about Lorrah's grace or the comfort he felt from his faith; they were about how much he loved his son and how much he regretted not taking him out of that town, out of that place. He said he wished he'd shown him just how much of the world there is to see when you allow the soul to fend for itself and wander outside of the veiled bell jar of obsessive spiritual reflection, to listen as the world speaks for itself with its own thaumaturgical voice.

These words and these images—both the literal images of his father reduced to a thin, gray shell, and the mental images of the world's unbridled possibility—were to cause the first foundational crack in the cornerstone of Clem's cathedral of belief.

The entire building collapsed to rubble five years later, when Clem's mother's ribs were broken by a church council that was severely displeased when they learned that Harriet Lemon had slept with Bucky Brooks—the semiretired older gentleman whose wife had died the previous year from a fatal stroke. The two, united by loneliness, found life and comfort in each other's arms. And then Harriet found the hospital, and Bucky found himself being chastised by the men he looked up to most.

A few weeks later, when Harriet had the strength, the three of them packed their things and left the town during a moonless night. Clem wrote the note they taped to the front door, as a sort of goodbye. It said, "May you burn in the Hell you invented for yourselves."

The three moved to another country. Clem went on to become a professor of theology at a small college, while his mother and her new lover tried to make their new lives work. But they couldn't. Manta was the only thing Harriet and Bucky knew. They missed their friends and their old lives. No matter how much they had been wronged, they pined to feel the warm breeze and smell the old dust in the air; they missed the long, hot summer nights, and they missed the music.

Four years after leaving, they returned to the rusty, dusty town of Manta. Clem was well on his way to his theology degrees, and they made their way back to their Luminarian home.

Clem was never able to discover what precisely happened on the night of their return, but his mother and her lover were buried in unmarked graves the next day. Clem didn't know this yet. The only thing he knew was that he talked to his mom the day before she was to get to the town, and then he never heard from her again.

Seeking solace over a fact that he knew but could not admit, he maintained his studies and went on to a long and rewarding teaching career. He retired only a few years before he met Dalton Hughes on a walk outside of town.

There were two reasons he returned to his hometown: the first was that an old friend had asked him to return; the second was that he killed the man who killed his mother.

Two years ago, Clem received an anonymous letter that said the writer knew who had killed Clem's mother and her lover those many years ago. The letter's author referred to himself as a lapsed Luminarian, and the author said he felt terrible because he had taken part in the execution. The letter said the writer was the one who buried the bodies.

Clem had held onto some small hope, for all those years, that his mother and Bucky had been welcomed back to the community and that their punishment was they were never allowed to contact the fallen angel, Clem, again. Clem never made any attempt to reach them, for fear this would rekindle past ugliness and lead to further beatings or excommunications. This silence pained him terribly, because he loved his mother. Nevertheless, he hated her decision, and yet he prayed—in his own way—that she found contentment.

He returned to his hometown and found the bodies where the letter told him they were. They'd been buried in the woods, near a small forest lake, their flesh long gone—two stark-white skeletons in a final embrace. There was no headstone; there were no coffins; there'd been no funeral. He verified his mother's body by remembering where her ribs had been broken and seeing the curative calcium buildup just below her sternum on the right side.

The letter also told him the identity of the man who

petitioned hardest for their execution, who was ultimately guilty of the murder. His name was James Blake—Police Chief Artimus Blake's father. The letter said the church leaders were prepared to welcome Harriet and Bucky back, but James felt it an affront to his personal faith and acknowledged that he could never forgive them for their past indiscretions nor accept their current membership. He argued passionately, and the debate raged for hours. The argument ended with two old people dying at the hands of a man drunk with God and gin.

James Blake's life ended when, after being kidnapped to a then-empty Haverbrook barn and questioned about his actions in the death of a certain fallen angel's mother, he admitted to being the one who argued for their death and even to executing them himself.

Clem hogtied Blake, wrapped him with thick blankets, doused the blankets with gasoline, and set the whole mess on fire. Clem had made an audio recording of the process—the interview, and the execution—and he sent a copy to every household in Manta.

The townspeople went crazy with anger, and many swore if they ever saw Clem Lemon in person, they would kill him then and there.

Which is probably why he was so far outside of town when Dalton ran into him that first day. What he was doing out there had to do with the first reason he returned: his old friend, a man named Halo Kilgore, had written to him asking for his company on a trip he was about to take.

ANOTHER REASON Clem was so despised by the Manta Luminarians—besides the fact that he revenge-murdered one of their most celebrated members—was because during his time teaching theology, he had written a book that had done phenomenally well in academic circles.

Beliefs was, in the relative confines of academia, a best seller, and consequently it became a college-level pedagogical staple. Theology professors around the world chose it to be one of the textbooks required for their introductory classes. The book gave a brief summation of the world's twenty-five largest religions, and while any perfect general religious overview is impossible, it was well-regarded by the leaders of nearly every church who read it. They all felt that he had omitted some details that could have been included without adding an irrational girth to the size of the book, but when multiplied by twenty-five times, those tiny increments would have added up to a book that Clem knew would be so large as to be unwieldy and unapproachable to all but the most eager minds. Other than that, it was noted that he had done a tremendous job at being as objective with regard to fantastically subjective beliefs as a serious man could be.

The book ended up on Halo Kilgore's desk a few years after it was published. He read it with great interest and told his associates to let him know if Dr. Lemon were ever in their area.

He didn't have to wait long, because Clem Lemon was given a visiting professorship at Halo's college the following fall.

On Clem's first day in town, as he looked over the wave of unopened boxes piled in his apartment, he heard a rapping at his door and found the world-renowned provocateur and writer Halo Kilgore—a man with whose work Clem Lemon was well-acquainted—standing there, pointing a shotgun at him.

"Welcome!" Halo shouted and began laughing maniacally. Then Halo was so overcome with his own joke that he had to lower the gun, and Clem realized this was just Halo's odd way and joined in the laughter, though much more nervously.

They sat down on the porch and became acquainted with one another. It was the start of a two-decade friendship.

21

AUGUSTUS HERSHEY was sitting at his desk preparing notes for an upcoming sermon when he heard the unexpected rolling rumble of a car's engine come to a stop outside the house. At once, he felt himself springing from his chair and bounding for the door, which, when he opened it, revealed the long-awaited and welcome sight of Pamela Hait—Augustus Hershey's fiancé—who had returned from her diplomatic mission to the South.

Augustus beamed and held the door open as the tall, beautiful, curly-blonde-haired woman carried two large suitcases up the front steps. The moment she discarded them on the living room floor, the two fell into an incandescent embrace and were not heard from until the following morning.

The following morning was Sunday—the Sabbath. As a result of Pam's return and her and Augustus's . . . "making up for lost time," as he told his father . . . Augustus had forgotten to finish preparing his sermon. But it had been a few weeks since his father had led the mass and tribute, so Augustus would take the week off, for special reasons.

IT WAS also the day Dalton had given himself to returning to The Corner Café to talk to his bewitching waitress.

When he walked in, the first thing he noticed was that his plan was as brilliant as it was obvious: nobody else was there. Everyone in town was at church—everyone but Quentin, who Dalton had left working on next week's crossword puzzle, who was undoubtedly humming to himself alone in his office.

The second thing he noticed was Marie, sitting in a booth, reading a book. Without saying a word, Dalton sat down across from her.

"Oh my, you scared me!" Marie said, putting the book down. "We do not normally have customers at this time. Can I get you something?"

She started standing.

"Please, just relax," Dalton said, gesturing for her to remain seated. "I didn't come here for any food."

"Oh, is there something else I could get you? Are you doing an interview?"

"I just wanted to talk to you."

"For a story?"

Dalton laughed.

"Marie, no. This isn't part of any story. You're just always so busy here—I never get a chance to talk to you. And it's just that every time I see you I feel like we should know each other better. Or like we already do. It's weird. All I know is: I want to know you, but I don't know anything about you other than . . . ." He motioned with his hands to indicate the restaurant.

"Well, that's very . . . interesting. And kind. For a green plant," she said, having studied him and reconfirming her original opinion.

"What were you reading?" Dalton asked.

"It is a book Nathan gave me."

She set it down and pushed it toward Dalton.

"Really? What is it?"

Dalton picked it up.

"It is called *The Will to Power*. It is about—"

Dalton shook his head. "Historical anecdotes and essays concerning people who manipulated their way into gaining power over other people," he said as he looked at the familiar cover.

"Yes, exactly. Have you read it?"

Dalton set the book down on the table, away from them.

"Yes."

"What did you think? I do not think I understand it."

"What don't you understand about it?"

"Well, should I respect these people or feel bad for them?"

"What side are you leaning toward?"

"To be honest, I do not know. They are obviously clever people, but what have they done? They have tricked other people. That is not nice. But they did benefit, and it is true that as far as we know this is the only life that we get, so why not . . . but it just does not seem right."

Marie made him so nervous Dalton found he could barely breathe.

"Exactly," he said. "I thought some of the stories were interesting, but I also found the whole moral of the collection—if there *is* a moral—to be a bit . . . amoral."

"What does 'amoral' mean, Mr. Editor?"

Marie looked at Dalton with a combination of flirtation and inquiry, and in reply to this miracle, Dalton blushed and smiled and became hopelessly lost in reverie.

"I'm sorry," Dalton said, still blushing. "What was your question?"

It must have been a fine moment for Marie, too, because her reaction to Dalton's nervous fluster came in the form of a mellifluous giggle, followed by a concentrated effort to return to the conversation.

"Come back to me, Dalton," she said, grabbing his hand for the greatest moment in Dalton's life. "I am right here. I would like to learn a new word. What is this 'amoral'?"

"Right, sorry," Dalton said, now back in a more vivid reality from Marie's brief, delicate touch, and in no small way also immodestly thrilled by her vocabular curiosity. "If I understand correctly, it's the lack of any sort of morality at all. Like, to be immoral is to have morals and break them, but to be amoral means you don't think anything is right or wrong and that everything is permitted."

He didn't remember thinking or saying any of that. He turned away from her in order to regain his bearings.

"Ah! That is very strange. I think you are right. It is weird that your friend Nathan gave me this book, and weird that you have read it, because I do not think of either of you as lacking morals."

"Sure, but try not to forget that it's not like people who lack morals will look like some bogeyman or something. They look like you and me. But, ultimately, regarding that book and all books, we're more than what we read."

"Though what we read says so much about us."

As she said this, she leaned forward, and as she adjusted her hands on the table, the fingertips of her right hand once again grazed across the back of Dalton's left hand.

Dalton gazed at that beloved spot.

"Yes," Dalton said and cleared his throat. "Consider this, though: the stories in that book should prove to you why it's difficult to identify amoral people if they are clever enough. None of the people in that book gave the outward impression that they were without morals. If anything, it was the opposite—their outward personas were extremely useful and interesting and certainly moral-*looking*—but it's the actions that result from people's underlying philosophy that ultimately matter most."

They sat in silence for a moment, a comfortable quiet between them as they considered the fine things they had found when they walked around in each other's mind this morning.

"I like talking to you, Mr. Dalton. I am glad you came today."

"Me too, Miss Marie," Dalton said, his heart hammering happily in his chest. "I don't know why I didn't just do this earlier."

Behind them, in the kitchen, the cook—another non-Luminarian Dalton had never met—swore loudly as he tried to scrape some gunk off a pan. Dalton and Marie laughed.

"Oh, I meant to tell you, I don't know if you got a chance to read the story I wrote about Nathan—"

"Oh, yes!"

"So you read about how we ended up on the outskirts of your town."

"Yes, I thought that was very interesting, the way you drew the connection between yourself, Mr. Nathan, and my city, how it was only fitting that the two of you should arrive there together. My brother thought that article was very well written."

"You weren't a fan?"

This time it was Marie who blushed, and she gave his hands a playful push.

"Oh, no! I did not mean— No, I do like your stories very much. You are very good."

"I was just teasing. I didn't know you had a brother."

"Oh, yes," Marie said. "He is an engineer at Kellogg Industries." Dalton could sense that she was very proud and fond of him.

Kellogg Industries, Dalton had learned during his *Radical*

Post janitorial cleanup days, was the only major industrial employer in the area. In Haverbrook, you were either an artist on a grant, a drug farmer, or a Kellogg employee. Or something else.

"Wow, it's weird to think of someone being an engineer in Haverbrook. Aren't most of the residents like intellectuals and artists?"

"Yes, they are, and yes he is weird. But I think you would like him. He enjoys reading your stories, and it is easy to like people who like what we do, right?"

"True, especially when they have nothing to gain from it," Dalton said, nodding to Marie's book.

"I agree. Say, would you like to see my town? I am sure my brother would like to meet you, and perhaps you should get to know it better—you know, for your reporting job."

"That actually sounds great, Marie," Dalton said, suppressing his urge to howl, "Yes!"

A jingle at the door and a rush of cool air—the first of the post-sermon Sunday customers had arrived.

"Wonderful," Marie said as they both stood. "I have to get to work now, but let us arrange something very soon."

22

THE CHURCH was candlelit and filled to capacity. The air inside was sweltering despite the freezing winds and rain of late autumn outside. The sound of quiet whispers—pre-sermon offerings borne on beads that clicked together to the rhythm of private prayer—filled the air like the overwhelmed candlelight.

Sunday morning, outside the church, the city was a ghost. Almost all of the townspeople—from a pious-looking Nathan Cameron to little Shannon Penrose in her Sunday best—sat or kneeled in the dark church. Outside the building, the rain hit the surrounding forest, producing a natural pitter-patter rhythm; outside the forest and this thunderhead, the rest of the nation headed to their own religious gatherings, or sat down to watch professional sports, or did whatever the rest of the nation did while Head Pastor Phillip Hershey prepared his remarks in a room behind the altar.

Phillip Hershey had been relieved that his son's fiancé had returned a few days early, because he had planned on trumping his son's sermon today anyway, so when Augustus asked, he was only too happy to oblige. This was to be a homily he'd told many times before, but it was one of his very favorites, and it seemed especially poignant with Nathan and Pam back in town.

"Before our musical offering this morning, my father would like to give today's sermon, which is one of the most important that we have. So I ask that you join me in listening to—and not only listening to, but *hearing*—his wise words for us."

The clicking of the beads stopped, and the whisperers finished whispering their prayers, and the room was again deeply silent and dark.

"The storms come. We know they do, and we know they will come again. Though the rain falls, the Lorrah asks that we rejoice. It might seem unnatural, at first, but it is right that we rejoice. The biggest storms produce the greenest plants, and the healthiest plants feed the hungriest stomachs. When the light of the sun is winked out by dark clouds, we are asked—we are required!—to search out the highest hill and to *embrace* the storm and the fear we feel. The hammer-strike lightning, the roaring thunder, and the relentless rain, a fusillade that freely gives its benefit to everything—to man, to tree, to snake, to soil. It is cold, it is dark, it is loud and frightening, and our Lorrah asks us not to cower in our shelters but to find the highest hill and triumph over our fear and *celebrate* all that is the Lorrah's—to embrace the storm! We embrace it because it is our Lorrah who sends it. We embrace it because it is what scares us. And what scares us is . . . what scares us . . . ."

The crowd trembled with unease; Phillip Hershey was not one to fumble a thought.

"*What scares us is ourselves!* We are the Lorrah's people! We need not fear! We are under her protection, even in *rampaging* storms! Even as the Earth trembles from the force of the thunder, and the air is ripped apart by lightning, and the mightiest branches are shredded and burnt by blue-white surges! We need not fear—we need not *hide*—because we are our Lorrah's people, and ours is the path. The one path. We are the way. We shed our lonely individuality when we walk through those doors. Here, we are the path we seek. Here, we are joined together in a song of peace."

One-two-three. One-two-three.

"Here we are . . . the fluted music of the Lorrah."

One-two-three. One-two-three.

"Here we are, under towering rain clouds, waiting for the storm to abate and the light of Lorrah to shine down again. And it will! And that is why we must find the highest ground, because together we must feel the light of our Lorrah first, for we deserve it. The clouds will part, and the love will pour forward, and her people are her reward, for her reward is her people. And to be the first to feel Lorrah's love is to feel it the longest. And that is why—"

One-two-three. One-two-three.

"That is why we go on. That is why we play our music . . . Even when—"

One-two-three. One-two-three.

"Even when the rain comes."

Phillip Hershey picked up his tenor sax and began his weekly wail. The congregants clapped one-two-three, the piano provided its own peripheral beat, and the music began once again, the wondrous music . . . .

THREE DAYS later, this was the banner story in *The Radical Post*:

TRAGEDY BEFALLS MANTA FAMILY
By Quentin Hancock

MANTA—What began as an autumn storm yesterday afternoon ended in one of the most horrific tragedies in recent Manta history. Shannon Penrose, the daughter of Benjamin Penrose, was found dead on Gray Hill late last night.

"She had been outside playing with her doll when I saw another bad storm coming up the horizon, so I told her to come inside," Mr. Penrose said. "But when the rain started really coming down, I was in my study praying when I felt a cold draft coming from under the door. I yelled for Shannon to shut the window, but she didn't answer. She sometimes liked to nap with the window open when it rained, so I went to find out where the wind was coming from, and I noticed I was alone in the house, and the front door was open."

Mr. Penrose alerted the authorities immediately, and a search was commenced. Police Chief Artimus Blake and deputies Alan Thinne and Lucy Hait searched all the usual spots where kids are often found when they slip past their parents' attention—the playground, the old tractor near the south forest, the church—but they had no luck, and minutes turned into hours as the storm continued.

"We really started to get worried when we didn't find her at the church," Chief Blake said. "Ben told us she liked to go there when the building was empty sometimes, so when she wasn't there, and when Alan and Lucy reported back that they hadn't found her either, we quickly decided to expand the search and enlist some local volunteers."

Friends and neighbors joined the police search (and in the interest of full disclosure, this reporter, as well as *Radical Post* writer/editor Dalton Hughes, also joined the search party), which went deep into the night.

The body was eventually found by reporter Dalton Hughes and Luminarian neophyte Nathan

Cameron.

"I don't know what made me think to look there," Cameron later said. "But I just had a feeling. When we got there, all we could see were some shoes lying under a fallen branch. It looked like it broke in the high winds and fell on her. She was lying face down, and when we finally got the branch off her back it was obvious she had been knocked out, and . . ." Mr. Cameron could not finish his statement.

Hughes was badly shaken by the incident and was the recipient of some frustrated castigations from the outraged and devastated Luminarian community; he was the bearer of bad news to Penrose's father, as Mr. Cameron waited with the body for the authorities to arrive.

"The only consolation I have," Mr. Penrose said, "is that my little girl is with the Lorrah now, and through the Lorrah we are brought to peace."

Shannon Penrose's memorial service and funeral will be held this Wednesday at 10:00 AM at the Luminarian Church.

PART TWO

MUSIC MADE BY BEARS

23

DALTON OPENED his eyes and saw sweet Marie Delphine breathing slowly and deeply with the soothing rhythm of sound sleep. A long band of warm sunlight passed through the slightly opened bedroom shades and cut a long, illuminated scar across the sheets of the bed and over her smooth, warm cheek. In a matter of minutes, the Earth's rotation would cause the light-band to rotate across her closed eyes, and at that point she would awaken and see Dalton readying himself for another long day at work.

This happened around the time Dalton was sleepily wrestling himself into his pants.

"Is it morning already?"

"Kind of."

"But we just went to sleep."

He kissed her. He loved the way she smelled in the morning. Before the lotions and powders and laundered clothes, there was Marie Delphine—a blushing nude who smelled like rich earth. Not sweet like sugar or scentless like empty space, but like fertile ground—his tellurian angel.

They had grown into each other. Throughout Marie's dating life, she had had all options available. She was considered beautiful by most men who saw her, and consequently she'd always had her choice of suitors. In the past, she vacillated between the empty conversations of startlingly attractive men and the vibrant conversations of the, to put it in a euphemism Marie preferred, "unique-looking." When she grew tired of the former, she shifted to the latter, and never was she rightly satisfied—until she met Dalton. In Dalton she discovered the better parts of both. She found him to be an endlessly edifying conversant, and though he too was certainly "unique-looking," it was the right kind of unique for Marie. It was a one-of-a-kind attraction, and it was powerful. Unlike all previous suitors, the more time she spent with Dalton, the more she wanted to be his. He was thoughtful, kind, and though he had flaws—like a tendency to withdraw from people, even her, at times—she found that these mysterious episodes captured her imagination and stoked the fires of her feelings for him. As the French say, at least in the original meaning of the phrase, *Il brille par son absence*—"He shines by his absence."

Throughout Dalton's dating life, he had read books in the school library. He found most of the women he tried to date to be too predictable and impossibly fragile. He was revolted by even the shadow of dependence, and most of these women were monoliths of it. In Marie, he found everything he'd ever wanted in a woman: beauty, independence, kindness, intelligence, and a beaming vitality.

He had never known romantic love, and now he knew it and was filled with it.

They told each other all of this, every day, in the look—the ongoing, longing smile—they exchanged at hello or goodbye.

"Before you go," Marie said, "tell me something."

"What would you like to be told?"

"I do not know," she said. "Tell me something I do not know."

Dalton considered her request while he dressed.

"Okay, well here's something I learned from Quentin yesterday," Dalton said as he pulled on a shoe. "The original title of T. S. Eliot's poem 'The Waste Land' was 'He Do the Police in Different Voices.'"

As Dalton buckled his belt, Marie thought about what he said.

"I like that title!"

"Me, too."

Dalton was dressed. He faced her.

"Okay, that will do for now," Marie said. "You may go."

Dalton took a moment to enjoy the lovely sight of Marie sprawled comfortably in his bed. Then he winked at her and left while the corners of her sleepy mouth started rising to the sky.

He ate an apple on the walk to work. It was summer, three years after the tragic death of Shannon Penrose, and the weather was, as it had been for the last few weeks, relentlessly perfect. The birds and insects were already well into the day's symphony, and the wind was in attendance, coaxing little whispers out of the gently swaying leaves of the trees and grass.

The offices of *The Radical Post* had returned to the disorganized chaos they had been in the years before Dalton arrived. But now, both men knew exactly where everything was—the appearance of clutter simply resulting from the physical laziness of busy minds. A desk had been moved in, replacing some old file cabinets that were now archived in Quentin Hancock's basement, and upon that brought-in desk was a small sign the old man had made.

Dalton Hughes
Associate Editor/Editorialist

Dalton sat down at his desk and began writing.

He and Quentin had moved beyond the realm of hellos and goodbyes each morning and evening. Now they were simply the united, two-organ system that kept *The Radical Post* alive and her readers informed about national news and local goings-on.

Stacks of legal pads had piled up on Dalton's desk, many of them filled with abandoned drafts of editorials or stories saved from the "round file" by one or two gem lines that he would sometimes look back on to provoke new ways of thinking based on his old unused insights. Besides those notepads and the sign Quentin had made, the only personal item on Dalton's desk was a smallish, artistically elaborate frame presenting two photographs. Both photographs were taken in the same place and featured the same people—the screened-in porch of Dalton's cabin, in the middle of a blue-skied weekend afternoon, with Dalton and Marie sitting with each other during a small get-together. In the first picture, Marie was leaning in to whisper something to Dalton, who was looking at the ground in a captured moment of rumination. In the second picture, a moment later, Marie and Dalton were laughing hysterically. Jane had taken the photographs. She made the frame and gave it all to Dalton for his last birthday.

Quentin and Dalton's roles had undergone a certain understandable change in the preceding three years. Quentin had reverted back to what he felt most comfortable doing: the lion's share of actual reporting. He covered almost all of the stories, and Dalton was left to handle the proofreading, layout, and "whatever else you think these monkeys would want to line their cages with."

Despite a growing discomfort over the content of his editorials between the *Post* and the Luminarian church, Dalton opted not to accept the resignation of political cartoonist Wendell Pency, who loved the cartoon and felt the gesture of being willing to resign was enough to satisfy the voices in his head and community that told him that to work under such a heathen would be to subject himself to an unjust punishment. But, it turned out, the unjust punishment was the two weeks Pency didn't create a comic. It was what he loved, and it turned out to be more of a punishment to himself than it was to the uncouth Dalton Hughes—who had simply drawn his own political cartoons. (Dalton's cartoons were not well received, of course.)

The young editorialist was putting the final touches on that week's "laugh-a-palooza" when Wendell Pency stopped by the offices with his cartoon.

Dalton pulled the panel from the envelope and had a look. It was a caricature of the Kellogg Industries headquarters and its CEO Shelton Elliott. Elliott, with money falling out of the pockets of his fancy suit, appeared to be having problems with his skin, as it was flaking and falling off. The caption said: "Progress is money, and money is power, and power corrodes."

"Not very funny this time," Dalton said to Wendell. "But, sure—what the hell."

"You don't like it?" Wendell asked.

"We'll run it, Wendell."

"You don't think money and power are corrosive?"

"Tell me what's funny about that cartoon."

Wendell walked out. Dalton turned back to his writing but stopped almost immediately. Wendell Pency was a much better writer than that. So then the rumors were true: Augustus Hershey was beginning his campaign against the city of Haverbrook.

Jean-Luc Delphine's face lit up when his sister walked into his office. It was the first time he'd seen her in weeks—an absence that was neither's fault entirely. He had recently been promoted to "project coordinator" at Kellogg Industries, and his most recent endeavors were already behind schedule thanks to a litany of bureaucratic nightmares at Haverbrook City Hall.

It was a fast-growing community, and the city of Haverbrook had lately undergone a decidedly progressive political change in direction, reflecting the highly liberal majority of the city population. Because of that, new construction projects had become deluged with a frustrating flood of what Jean-Luc referred to as "nonsense," which he said "hobbled progress to the pace of Dostoyevsky's dead heartbeat."

Jean-Luc had tried to explain that, among many other things, the Environmental Standards Reports the council demanded were already built into the Kellogg Industries business plan and therefore redundant and a waste of time. The reply had been that timeliness and fiscal sacrifice should always take a backseat to the moral imperative of making sure people treat the Earth with as delicate a footstep as possible. To Jean-Luc, it felt like being taught to dance by an elephant.

Marie herself was not exactly guilt-free in their long separation, however. She and her brother were quite close, but with her spending most nights in Manta with Dalton and most of her days working in Manta at the restaurant, the two had drifted an uncomfortable and unusual distance apart. This was something they both lamented, which might be a way of giving a sufficient explanation for the gleeful smile that leapt onto Jean-Luc's face when he saw Marie walk in.

"Marie, what are you doing here? You do not have work?"

He quickly stood, and they both hugged happily, and as

he returned to his seat and gestured for her to sit where she liked, she replied.

"I asked them to cover for me this morning. It is not bad on Mondays, and Dalton and I were thinking about you this weekend and how sad we are with how busy you have become. We are thrilled that you are doing what you love, but we are sad that it means we lose you when you are so happy."

"Dalton has been very busy too, no?"

"Oh my, yes—we are all so busy our heads will fall off!"

"I will tell you what: do not make any plans this weekend, and we will go camping—you, me, and Dalton."

"Well that works out perfectly! Dalton and I already had plans to go camping with Victoria and Nathan."

"Oh, super," Jean-Luc said. "I have been meaning to spend more time with Nathan. He is just a doll, no? So *likeable*."

"Oh, Jean-Luc, stop it. You are being weird like our father sometimes. I like them both, no matter what you say. They are nice."

"You like everyone," Jean-Luc said. "Your opinion should not count."

"Well, that is it!" she said smiling, and she pretended like she was leaping across the desk and slow-motion punching him in the jaw. When the punch landed, she returned to normal and said, "Camping—this weekend." She turned and headed for the door and called over her shoulder, "It will be wonderful and everything else that is good."

Marie Delphine walked out of the office, beaming—happy to have something to look forward to and excited to spend time with her favorite triumvirate: herself, her Dalton, and her brother Jean-Luc.

She rushed back to the restaurant, where the swirling chaos of her labor produced moment-to-moment demands that thankfully drew the workday to a close with merciful haste.

MORE RUMORS began swirling later that day. Big rumors. While Quentin wasn't the first to hear them, he was the first to collect them and try to make sense of them. The long and short of it, however, was that Halo Kilgore and Clem Lemon had returned to the Manta forests.

24

JEAN-LUC AND Marie Delphine were born in France and emigrated with their parents to the United States of America when Jean-Luc was eleven and Marie was nine. Their parents had come for what may be considered a decidedly European reason. Though they loved France, they felt a lust to have America as a mistress. And then it turned out that they loved the mistress, too.

Jean-Luc, much like Dalton, had a scholastic history of being considered, well, a loser. A socially awkward nerd. Despite a charming French accent, which he worked avidly to eliminate (he projected his social shortcomings upon it), he was too smart for his own good in his new country. This was an unfortunate irony considering he'd also been smart in France, and much more popular, which was one of the Delphine parents' arguments in favor of moving—with Jean-Luc's intelligence, he would be well-liked anywhere, but especially in America. They had no worries at all about Marie. Nevertheless, though Jean-Luc's parents had come to America to inject themselves into American culture, their son tried to do the same, but he was rejected by it. His schoolmates were cruel, his teachers were dunces, and every day he went to school he heard cell doors lock behind him.

He never became embittered, though. Instead, he simply studied, figuring he would try to improve all the things that were actually under his control.

Jean-Luc found he was a natural in the natural sciences—so natural in fact, that he was granted an extremely generous scholarship package to one of the country's best engineering schools, a school about an hour east of the city of Haverbrook. Meyer College.

His sister, Marie, never one for studying actual schoolbooks, though smart in a nonacademic way, enrolled in the same college, though for a degree for which the entire department's offices were located in the back of one of the mishmash buildings: Creative Writing. She had grown to love her newly adopted language and was a voracious reader, so it only made sense to her to keep an eye on her older brother while keeping her head in books she probably would have read anyway while at the same time letting the burgeoning quill of her mind take flight on countless white sheets of paper soon tattooed black with poetry and detailed sketches of animals in motion.

Jean-Luc quickly rose to the top of his classes, but unfortunately for the young man, there were only three women in his major. This again perplexed the Delphine parents, who had heard that America was a land of great equals—the birthplace of feminization, individual transcendence, outright rejections of the status quo. But there Jean-Luc found himself: surrounded by foreigners from across the world, all male. Of the three women in the engineering school, two were engaged to fellow foreigners, and the other's face looked like it was on inside-out. This certainly made it much easier for Jean-Luc to concentrate on his studies, and because he'd become used to being a somewhat reclusive social outcast, that's exactly what he remained. While many of his contemporaries were getting drunk and toking dope with some blokes or provoking drunken girlies with a playful grope, Jean-Luc was doing extra-credit mathematics assignments and sometimes letting himself be entertained by his popular younger sister—who was pretty, nice, and self-effacing, so naturally everyone loved her. Marie would sometimes bring a movie or her baseball glove to his off-campus apartment.

They loved baseball, and though they were both terrible at it, they never quite felt so close as when they were playing catch. To them, it felt good to finally be able to put life's turbulence away during the moments they were concentrating on the delivery or the reception of a thrown ball.

We release! and are released in these
loping, concentrating, freethinking
moments, and tranquility calms the
cold waters of the puddle in the field, and,
in these piles of atmosphere, we are revealed the
simple clarity of our moments' purpose,
as a thrown object's reflection
streaks across
the clear water
into our hands.

[excerpt from one of Marie's unnamed poems]

And with Jean-Luc's head flowing with advanced calculations and Marie's head bent with an ear toward life's poetic stream of words and ideas, they both needed the sweet relief of tranquility now and then.

Marie played the part of their barometer. She always arrived just as Jean-Luc's head was about to collapse under its own pressures.

Despite being offered a job in New York, as well as an advanced-degree grant offer from the Massachusetts Institute of Technology, Jean-Luc instead decided to take the job with Kellogg Industries. It having been mentioned that Haverbrook was the emigrant home of many of Meyer College's graduates, the competition at Kellogg was near the top in the country, and Jean-Luc had been offered the very position he'd been aiming for since he first discovered as a child that he felt almost literally forced by something within himself to understand how a suspension bridge near his childhood home could possibly have been constructed and remain standing.

He was hired to be an engineer with no specific specialty. He could be tasked with anything from coming up with a new idea for personal headphones to designing the sewer system for a new community. These latter jobs, of course, typically went to more senior staffers, but Jean-Luc was usually among the first asked anyway due to the unique approach he brought to engineering. For instance, in college one of his favorite assignments involved designing a water park. Jean-Luc's design was that of a water park that could power itself and parts of the surrounding community.

The work itself had turned out to be more bureaucratic than he'd expected. Far more hoops to jump through than during his university studies, where all of the projects existed in a vacuum—free of politics, bosses, and profit expectations. But the new challenges, things for which the only study is the practice itself, had brought out a newer version of Jean-Luc. In having to deal with representatives from a myriad councils, he had, by virtue of necessity, became more confident and charismatic. It was either get swept away and drowned by the city hall, unrealistic client demands, and similar waves of people getting in his projects' way, or jam his feet into the silt and start walking upright, up river.

Jean-Luc Delphine chose the latter.

25

JANE JEFFERSON chose something closer to the former. After the tremendously successful *But Is It Art?* campaign, she was offered a number of different freelance contracts from the world's biggest brands, but she rejected them all. The famous campaign had been another ugly reminder of how much she hated the advertising world—where she kept being told to make her ideas more "approachable," which was a euphemism meant to communicate to Jane that her work should look like everything else out there. It also reminded her of just how hollow and oblivious even wild success at the "advertising racket" (as she called it) made her feel.

Seeing her bank account blossom exponentially felt good, of course, but there was no artist's elation when that new piece was completed. The billboard design would be submitted, the company would approve, sometimes even gleefully and vociferously, and Jane Jefferson would sit in her house and feel a momentary ache. The callus of her life would then cover the ache, and she would go purge her mind on a private canvas.

In the years after the *But Is It Art?* campaign hit its peak, Jane had produced a few personal works, and she had locked the red door behind her.

She continued to be a tutor for Victoria, but whatever artistic inferno had once burned in her was now reduced to a few glowing embers. She felt the same empty ache, but she also felt out of fuel to burn.

Jane found it difficult to feel anything at all about the slow death of the artistic visions that had charmed her suicidal head so many years ago. In a way, that fire died out the night she pulled her painting off the wall at the end of her first and last art showcase. For Jane, it was bittersweet. She was comforted by inner pride that warmed the surface of her heart when she thought about letting all the wretched civilizations die without knowing her work—that her work was something so private and powerful that the largely revolting people of the world didn't deserve to judge it. But she also repressed the private shame that seethed beneath her skin when she thought of all the deserving people who may have found inspiration and beauty in her masterpieces. In the end she figured she would cast them into the world when she died—"when I will have something much more important to worry about than how my art is being received."

Word had gotten around to Augustus Hershey—who in the three years since Shannon Penrose's death had essentially but not officially replaced his semiretired father as the Head Pastor of the Luminarian community—about his sister's near-daily trips to Jane Jefferson's house.

Determined to right one of the wrongs in his heart, Augustus left Manta and went to Jane's house one day, a bold move that was not without risk, for Augustus did not wish to give his beloved community any impression that the Hershey family was falling one by one into alignment with this unusual nonbeliever. But he was faced with a nut he could not seem to crack himself, and he thought maybe Jane had the right hammer.

There was a growing division in the faith regarding the acceptability of nonbelievers. Phillip Hershey had always preached and regarded them as nothing better or worse than a stone or boulder, of no consequence beyond maintaining physical space, and deserving of all the emotional concern as one would grant a rock. Augustus, however, for a number of reasons obvious and unobvious, began to see the utility of others. Maybe they were not merely the nonentities his father saw them as; maybe, rather, they were potentially valuable for the growth of the Luminarian faith, which had for too long remained a quiet song in the shadows of the forest.

Jane Jefferson was just finishing her breakfast when she heard a rare knock at her door. She was surprised, frankly, and mildly disturbed, but certainly not afraid, to see the large frame of Augustus Hershey silhouetted behind the thick, smoky glass. She opened the door.

"Hello, Mr. Hershey. Please, come in out of the heat."

Augustus entered the air-conditioned house. Directly behind Jane was a wall covered with a massive billboard of a basketball player flying through the air during a game—a good two feet higher than any of the defenders against him. Jane had taken the famous photograph of the player's slam dunk in the Eastern Conference Finals and added a combination of paint and digital alteration to lend a surreal quality to the image, thereby giving it a more vivid effect. The result was mesmerizing—so attention-grabbing, in fact, that the billboard had sparked a small national controversy after a number of people got into minor traffic accidents because their eyes were so pulled into the image that they stopped concentrating on the road. This was one of the last billboards of its kind—the work of a real artist looking for a public place to privately wither.

Jane didn't let Augustus very far into her home. After waiting for him to take in her billboard, she leaned against a small table near the wall and asked him what could be so important as to shatter his religion's social boycott of what

Quentin Hancock had jokingly referred to as "us secular pig-shits."

"As you know, Jane, even religions evolve."

"I thought religion was against the theory of evolution."

"Ours is not. We find a sort of harmony in the universal symphony, and we are completely aware that symphonies may change in pitch and tone as they are played."

"Okay. Are you here to ask me if I'd like to perform a duet with you?"

Augustus smirked. "Kind of. I've been told that my sister often comes over here and spends time with you and a few others."

"You'll have to ask her about that," Jane said. "No offense, Mr. Hershey, but I don't owe you any information about your sister."

Augustus returned to grave seriousness. "I would just like to know what she is doing here," he said. "She rarely talks to me anymore. Not in any detail. Not for years."

"And your congregation is getting nervous about it?"

Augustus took a deep, frustrated breath, and let it out as calmly as he could.

"I had just hoped you could help," he said. "She is my sister, and I miss her."

"Well, Mr. Sister Misser, I can't help you. What I do know is: if I don't talk to someone, there's a reason, and usually they know it."

Augustus nodded. "Can you at least tell me this: what can I do? I get the feeling that something is bothering her, but I don't know how to reach her anymore. She won't open up to me."

Jane bit her lip in thought. To admit to knowing anything personal about Victoria would be to admit that whatever Augustus had heard about her coming over and confiding in Jane was true. And Jane didn't even want to give Augustus that satisfaction, despite the fact that she and Victoria were public friends. Nor would she ever betray her friend's trust, and she knew that Victoria was in no great hurry to be closer with her brother.

Finally, she saw that he was offering nothing—less than nothing, actually—while asking Jane for plenty. The feeling brought her back to why she had moved to such an isolated place to begin with, and she began backing Augustus out of her house.

"I really don't know, Mr. Hershey. Women are complicated. You seem like a smart-enough guy; I'd think you would know what your sister's strings look like. And besides, like I said, usually someone knows why someone else won't talk to them. In fact, I bet you know exactly what's going on between you and Victoria, but maybe you're just not willing to face it."

Augustus backed out the door, and Jane finished.

"Leave me out of your problems."

Augustus was surprised by this swift dismissal, and, outside, his face turned to disappointment.

"Thank you for your time, Miss Jefferson. Please tell my sister I miss her."

He told this to a smoky-glass door that was closing in his face.

26

Marie, Dalton, and Jean-Luc loaded their camping gear into Marie's truck.

As before, they would hike out in a different direction from previous trips, humping their gear through the seemingly endless forest, sometimes driving long distances to bask under different tree-shade cathedrals in the rolling woodland hills.

But first they had to make a quick stop.

It had started out as an excuse for Dalton to kill the day-to-day boredom of small-town life, but more than that, to be invigorated by the living forest, while at the same time endeavoring to stumble upon the hermetic home of Dr. Halo

Kilgore.

While the desire to find Kilgore hadn't decreased in the intervening three years, Dalton's burgeoning journalistic responsibilities and the relationship with his sugar-sweet girlfriend meant that for the first time in a long time he had people and things where he was, instead of where he thought he hoped to be.

But then one day Quentin asked him if he would like to edit a book he was writing about the history of Manta. Dalton, honored and thrilled by the offer, took to the project with great interest. He loved Quentin's writing, largely because it required very little effort to read or edit. It *flowed*.

A chapter dedicated to Halo Kilgore and the strange dome he called home reignited the young man's curiosity. Dalton read that chapter over and over again. It included whatever sketchy, sundry, cobbled details Quentin could find—including rumors that the house's architectural design was given to Kilgore by, literally, aliens—of a residence which was somehow almost impossible to find and which included, among other things, a built-in power plant. It also detailed the full history of Kilgore's connection to Clem Lemon (whom Dalton hadn't seen again since first arriving in town) and the arboreal distances Quentin covered as a younger man in search of a building and a man who did not want to be found.

Dalton had not forgotten about the mysterious mind looming somewhere in the forest out there—or not out there, as Jane, as well as frequent rumors, had reported that Clem and Halo took a long trip three years ago. But after the combination of editing Quentin's book and hearing further rumors that Lemon and Kilgore had returned to town, Dalton decided it was time to pick up the torch of trying to meet his literary hero.

Quentin had some helpful advice. Despite his long travels, the old man still had no idea where the house was; Halo had always initiated contact with him. He'd searched as far south and east as fifteen miles, and west to the plains, and he thought he'd searched the forest around the town to the north, but he recommended Dalton start there—"anywhere north, probably by the river."

Dalton gave a copy of his favorite work by Dr. Kilgore—*The Polyglot*—to Marie, who had never heard of the man, though she had heard people saying his name. ("I just thought he was some weird old man in town nobody liked.") She raved about the book. And then, after she had finished it, and they discussed the sweet meat of his writing, as well as its ridiculous characters and brilliantly simple plot (a man who speaks every language in the world finds that he has nothing to say), Dalton told Marie he planned on trying to find the mysterious man's hidden mansion, "somewhere out there in the woods, living in the breathing shadows like the true creep he is."

They laughed, and that's how their camping adventures began.

It really was a win-win for them. First of all, they were able to get out of Manta together and simply coexist for a while. Second of all, even though they had until now never found the house, the excursions were so beautiful and fun that there was no disappointment when they trekked back home without finding any useful clues. In fact, it gave them something to look forward to—their next outdoors adventure.

They stumbled upon Victoria and Nathan one weekend. The two Luminarians were simply camping because they both liked camping. Soon after that, their twosome adventures became a foursome, though only Marie and Dalton had other motives beyond nature's perfect dynamic aesthetics. They decided not to share these motives with their friends because for one, Victoria, though kind, was still a Hershey, and Dalton and Marie worried what would happen if the wrong people discovered Kilgore's location. They didn't tell Nathan because they had no reason to tell him and not Victoria.

Jean-Luc didn't go with them very often, and he had only a cursory understanding of who Dr. Kilgore was, though he too very much enjoyed *The Polyglot* when his sister lent him the copy Dalton gave her, so while he had suspicions that their fawning manhunt was the reason they went camping, he considered himself lucky to just be able to enjoy the feeling of a long hike, a scrounged meal, and the shared intimacy of laughs and stories around a crackling campfire. Not only that, but he was actually curious to see Kilgore's house himself; engineering students at Meyer College talked about its theoretical existence, but nobody could get any confirmation from anyone on staff.

With their gear packed in the back of the truck, Jean-Luc drove with Dalton and Marie in the cab on their way to pick up Victoria and Nathan from the Hershey house adjacent to the church.

They parked behind the church and met Victoria and Nathan in the lot. From there, they shouldered their gear and headed northwest. That was the first direction Dalton and Marie had searched on their initial camping trip, but they had not gone far, as they were both so new to the whole camping experience.

They listened to Jean-Luc describe a particularly heated discussion he had had with Manta Councilman Joe O'Brien about the logistics of reconfiguring the city hall's heating system, which was deplorable in the winter. Jean-Luc had tossed together a design—per his boss's orders—but the city council was dragging its feet. Apparently, O'Brien's brother had a private heating/air-conditioning company, and the brother had also submitted a proposal O'Brien was rushing through the vote by declaring it an emergency. Jean-Luc argued on two logical fronts: one, the brother's proposal was actually somehow functionally worse than the existing system, and two, there was no emergency here. It was still summer, and though to finish the job before the truly bastard weather came would be a rush, the difference between voting now, on a system that would require near-constant tweaking, thereby awarding the councilman's brother a reliable source of income, or holding a vote in two weeks, when quality work had a gasping chance, was all the difference in the world, according to Jean-Luc.

He lost the battle. The city council voted with their colleague, and Joe O'Brien's brother got the contract. However, this was "good" because it meant Jean-Luc could go camping with his sister and friends rather than spend all his time obsessing over every detail of the Manta City Hall heating system and its reconstructive progress.

Victoria's heart went out to Jean-Luc—a young man who bore no grudge against a city that essentially slapped him in the face because of a combination of nepotism and his (lack of their) beliefs—but there was very little she could do to help him. Her mother was of course the city controller, but the heating vote exceeded her purview, and either way, Victoria had little sway with her family. Never had. None of the Hershey women ever did. Sometimes it really bothered Victoria, and understandably so. She felt resentful, and then she resented that feeling, which she felt was unfair to her family and community.

Dalton was already compiling notes for a possible editorial, though the prospect of this editorial scared him because whenever he got this charged up about something the tongue of his pen would fork, and the mix of his vitriol and vocabulary had a way of both offending and alienating the source of his ire, and in this case the source of his ire was in many ways his and Quentin's entire readership.

Nathan contributed a few humorous insights about various characters who popped up in Jean-Luc's story.

Marie was so proud of her brother she could just float and explode—no matter that he and his plan had been rejected. Her pride stemmed from the facts. She knew his design was better, and he had gone up against an almost-hopeless situation and returned from the loss not embittered but merely happy to be able to spend some time on other things he enjoyed in life.

They hiked over snarled roots and the soft scrape of fuzzy leaves and discussed these and many things. They felt the sun run down their arms as they walked under openings in the canopy, their salty sweat holding their clothes to their skin. Shouldering their backpacks, heavy with sections of tent, sleeping bags, water, and food, they rested infrequently, preferring to muscle through the exhaustion in order to rest hard when they stopped.

After nearly two hours of hiking and talking, they found a

beautiful flat opening about fifty yards from the river and decided to set up their tents. Within a half-hour, three tents were erected, and the groundwork for a campfire in the middle of the tent-triangle was laid out. The couples (Dalton/Marie, Victoria/Nathan) set out to gather firewood while Jean-Luc made sense of the food and water rations.

Bearing armloads of branches and handfuls of tinder, Dalton and Marie came back quickly, hoping to spend as much time as they could with Jean-Luc, who was happy to see them return. The three sat down and let the light breeze tickle and cool their sweat-soaked skin.

A half-hour passed and Nathan/Victoria had not returned, but this didn't surprise anyone, because the two of them often ventured out for long periods. Dalton and the Delphines talked about how unusually quiet Nathan was. Marie said she had noticed that Nathan was always quiet in mixed company.

"It is weird. He is one of those people who I like very much when it is him and me or him and me and Dalton," Marie said. "But when there is a mix of people, he is unknown."

"I noticed that too," Dalton said. "Exactly. I love the guy when he and I are just hiking around or smoking a joint on my porch, but, and I guess maybe this is just a Luminarian thing, though I doubt it, but whenever he's around a mix of us and them, it's like he's neither. Normally I'd find that unsettling, but with him it's different. But you know what, either way, I think we should talk about something else. Let's not worry about Nathan."

"I agree," Marie said and turned to her brother. "Jean-Luc, it has been so long since I could talk to you; do you have any love prospects?"

"My love will always be Madame Engineering," Jean-Luc said with a poetic grin, which unfolded into a smile and then returned to seriousness. "Actually, I have gone on a few dates lately, but I have to tell you, Marie: women are dumb."

"Hear, hear," Dalton said and sarcastically toasted water bottles with Jean-Luc.

"You do not have to tell me twice," Marie said. "Or maybe

you do, with how dumb I am."

Jean-Luc chuckled. "It is obviously not all women, but so many of them are so . . . scared, and dependent, and they choose to be ignorant, as if that were ever good. It is very frustrating."

"Before I found you, Marie," Dalton said, "I'd been in a grand total of two relationships, both of which didn't last longer than a few months."

"I had a feeling about that," Marie said. "You seemed like a really big loser. I had never dated one of those before." She looked at him with an impish grin.

"I prefer to look at it like I don't play the same game as most people," Dalton said.

"Yes, that is how losers comfort themselves," she said, and the two men laughed.

"*Anyway*," Dalton said, playfully moving past Marie's dig, "I would meet these girls in my hometown, and it was like they were these fragile, frightened children. I mean, I understand how women like to feel protected, but Marie, I would give my life for you, right? But don't you feel even more protected because you also know how to protect yourself? Why would anyone forego having the option of independence?"

"You are lucky you met a French girl," Jean-Luc said. "They are tremendously proud of themselves. Most French people are, but the men usually do not have a good reason."

"The women always do," Marie said.

"Hear, hear," Dalton said and toasted water bottles with Marie.

Jean-Luc relaxed back on his elbows and looked up into the forest sky. As he reclined, the length of his body rested along the soft underbelly of the leafy forest floor, and he took in a large breath and exhaled all that cluttered his mind.

The sun, tiptoeing to the far western horizon, began its daily smolder from yellow to orange. There was about an hour of sunlight left, so the three at camp readied the fire and walked down to the Crondura River, where they washed their hands and let the gurgling chatter of the running water lay a relaxing soundtrack to their by-now sparse insights. It was too relaxing to enjoy with a fully charged brain. They let their concerns drift down the moving water tinted sparkling gold between the long shadows of the evening.

Just before sundown, with Jean-Luc having already returned to camp, Dalton and Marie were sitting on a tree stump near the river when they heard the expert padding of a young deer scuffling through the undergrowth and settling its hoofs into the river's muddy sediment. The two watched the young doe wordlessly as it drank with caution—its movements poetic from perfect coordination, from a life of living on the move, on the run, on the go, into and out of shrubs and shadows, slashing through sun puddles. Finally, behind them, Jean-Luc's heavy boot snapped a branch, and the deer shot off toward the sunset with a fluid, animal grace.

"Victoria and Nathan are back," he said.

"Okay, brother, we will be there soon," Marie said.

She and Dalton sat for a while, leaning together, fingers interlaced, gazing at the water and the sky.

"Dalton," Marie said.

"Marie," Dalton said.

"I did not think you were a big loser."

Dalton laughed softly.

"I know," he said.

"Actually," she said, "I thought you were mysterious and quite sexy."

She could feel him smile.

"What did you think of me?" she asked.

It took a while before Dalton responded, and he dropped Marie's hand and stood before her.

"I've always . . ." he said. "I've never, I should say—"

"Are you all right?" Marie asked.

Dalton reached in his pocket and pulled out a folded-up piece of paper. It was not the article about "The Odd Light in the Forest" that had brought him to Manta, because three years ago Dalton had replaced that page, which he had always carried with him, like a torch in the existential night, with something he himself had written—about Marie.

He unfolded it.

"I was so overwhelmed, when I met you, by how much you already meant to me, that I ended up writing a poem about meeting you. I had to. It leapt out of me."

"You wrote a poem about me? That is it in your hand?! I must see it—now."

She held out her hand, but he withheld the poem.

"You're the poet, you know?" Dalton said. "I'm embarrassed. I've always worried that if I showed it to you and you didn't like it, you wouldn't respect me anymore."

"Give me the poem, Dalton, or I am going to get violent."

Dalton laughed.

"Okay."

He handed her the poem.

To Be Struck by the Lightning Bolt
For Marie

Can these new thoughts reach beyond the
closed window of my self,
where, in this overcrowded house, they press their wet eyes against
the glass and long to find a home within another?
Can I say what it is to be me
and to meet and be observed by her?

It is to begin as a flat little blue balloon, dropped and forgotten in the
bottom of a child's toy chest,
and then, years later, covered with dust,
folded upon itself in a helpless shrug,
to be retrieved and at last to feel the first rush of
expansion and fulfillment—
to be inflated and float!
That!

To stretch my growing boundaries and rise into the warm air and be
what I was made to be,
and to register no sound but the soft thud as my
head bumps against the ceiling, safe and swaying,
rejoicing in these heights, buoyed here by thoughts of her being.

To be a massive lifeless rock surging through vast space, the

distances and solitude giving
impatient length to my cold journey,
and to suddenly slam into a brilliant world blindly and find
enlightenment and warmth
in the beautiful force of our colliding energies—
That!

The force of her is a force I had never believed to be.
(I thought I knew and could rely upon the knowledge of all forces,
but of hers I know nothing yet thirst for all knowing of it,
like green plants made alive by the glory of sunlight.)

To be bewitched whichever way I turn,
to have my life raft snag
on dazzling coral in the middle of a flat ocean,
to walk along a lake from my childhood, and, on the far shores,
amongst the reeds waving in a breeze muted by the surrounding
forest of trees,
to see the peripheral golden glint of some memory or forgotten
dream,
as it slowly disappears in the gloaming,
as the insects begin their summer symphony,
which I requested,
which I dedicate to her.

Do my words have any power?
Yes, they have their own self-propelled power,
and they shoot into history like beams of light into space,
where, unseen for ages, they might one day
produce a flicker of illumination in a secluded patch of darkness—
the children of a deep future gazing upon it and giving it a name.
It will be her name.

Marie finished reading the poem, and Dalton watched her chin fall to her chest.

"Oh, no—you don't love me anymore," Dalton said, worried.

She looked up, and her eyes were red and wet with tears, and her mouth was turned to a crying curl.

She stood, clutching the poem in her hand, ran over, and threw her arms and legs around him.

They held each other and felt the warmth of the love between themselves. She set her feet down, and, with her head against his chest, she told Dalton a story.

"When I was a little girl, I had a beautiful dream about falling in love. But in the dream, I could not see the person I had fallen in love with. It was just this . . . presence . . . but I knew I was in love, and I was so comforted by the feeling. It was the most wonderful feeling of my life, and when I woke up, I was so sad. It was only a dream. And for a long time I worried that maybe I could not feel love like that in my real life, because it had only ever happened in that one dream."

He felt Marie pull her head off his chest, and they looked at each other.

"What I am saying is: I am awake, Dalton, and here you are, and it is love!"

Her eyes were still red, and she had long streaks down her cheeks from the tears that cleaned away the debris of the day's trek. The surge of emotion within Dalton produced a hard-looking shell, a strong face, but within himself, every blood cell was a popping skyrocket.

They held each other, on the banks of the glowing river, and felt the sweet sweep of a cool breeze brush across their skin.

They kissed.

Eventually, they returned to camp, where the fire was roasting hot dogs affixed to sticks Jean-Luc had driven into the ground while everyone else set up makeshift chairs. The sky was all but dark—a mellow purple blush on the horizon, not visible to the five in the forest—and the air under the canopy was cooling.

"I got a letter today from my friend in Long Beach," Nathan said.

"Excellent," Dalton said. "Big news, or just catching up?"

"A little of both," Nathan said. "He just got a promotion at work, and he's thinking about coming out for a visit. Said he needs to get out of town for a while, and when I told him about this place, he said it sounded like exactly what he needed."

"How do you know him?" Marie asked.

"Friend of a friend, who became my friend."

"I imagine a person like you," Jean-Luc said, "must have many friends—unlike Dalton here."

Dalton laughed at the truth of Jean-Luc's observation.

"I mean, you are handsome, literate, an obvious armchair student of psychology, so you must have had interactions with many people," Jean-Luc continued. "So, please, tell us about this friend."

"If that is sarcasm I hear, brother, you are being rude," Marie said.

"What? I did not mean to be rude, and it was not sarcasm," Jean-Luc quickly replied, backpedaling. "Nathan, I just know so little about you considering all the time we have spent together, camping and otherwise. I would like to hear about your life before Manta."

It was a long moment before Nathan responded. "Billy is from my hometown. We both moved out to California together. He's one of the best friends I've ever had."

"Why? What makes him such a good friend?"

Nathan considered his answer to that question.

"This is boring," Victoria said, breaking her long and seemingly half-interested silence. She stepped in front of the bullet to save her boyfriend from Jean-Luc's sudden interrogatory fusillade. "And besides," she continued, "the food's ready."

The conversation came to a brief, if awkward, conclusion. The famished campers ravaged the fire-cooked food.

The insects in the orchestra of the woods went into full swing, and the white noise of their layered calls produced a merciful soundtrack to check against the campers' silence. They chewed their food and ruminated. Dalton, with his shoulder pressed against Marie's shoulder, could do nothing but smile (inwardly) at Jean-Luc for mixing things up a little bit. The outward smile on his face, however, came from the pressure of Marie's body leaning against his own—how that little bit of contact represented almost everything he loved in the world.

Nathan and Victoria said little else that night and retired to their tent far earlier than usual. Before they fell asleep, Nathan told Victoria he preferred not to hang out with Jean-Luc anymore, and Victoria understood.

Victoria once told Jane that it felt like Nathan could help her understand anything.

It had been a long day, so Dalton and the Delphines also decided to retire to their tents.

Before they fell asleep, Dalton and Marie gazed together at a patch of the night sky visible through the mesh of their tent and an opening in the canopy. The patch was packed with stars that shined distantly and twinkled to the rhythm of the world's turning symphony.

THEY SET out early in the morning—the three of them: Marie, Dalton, and Jean-Luc—while Nathan and Victoria were still asleep. They headed farther north and west, looking for something, ignorant of what exactly they were looking for other than an unusual home owned by an unusual man, possibly near the river.

The cold morning air always made Dalton shiver in a particularly uncomfortable way, but as the march of his legs spurred the muscle and heat of his heart, the rapid flow of his blood began to warm him up, and not long into their hike he started to feel as awake as he was going to feel at that awful hour. They say it's always darkest before sunrise, and, at least to Dalton, it's always coldest then, too. When the situations of his life forced him into action at those hours, it was not without his miserable face sitting grumpily twisted, almost like his countenance refused to untangle the folds of sleep—its only way of protesting.

Despite having learned to appreciate the morning with Jane, who introduced him to the cabin's river-mumbling, pastel dawns on the porch, which they still shared frequently, often with Marie there, to wrap themselves in the morning splendor, the cold pre-sunrise hours were no less unpleasant for any of them. Fortunately, they finally set out on their search just around ten minutes before the sun would appear on the unseen horizon. The air was already filling with color.

Marie and Jean-Luc hiked while quietly playing a vocabulary game. They were both working on mastering their use of the English language, and their parents taught them a game when they were younger in which they challenged each other to define and properly use words they learned recently. Dalton, when not learning new words himself, played the role of referee. As they hiked and talked, the sun rose over the green leaves at the roof of the forest.

Coincidentally, they were discussing the definition and use of the word "peculiar" when they came across a peculiar sight: a metal tube, three inches in diameter, sticking five inches out of the forest floor.

As they looked around, they saw other little aberrations in the landscape. A lump in a hill that seemed to jut out a bit farther than would be naturally expected. Another metal tube about twenty-five feet from the first one. To glance around carelessly, it would appear to be any other section of the hilly forest. But the metal tubes belied the natural landscape, and almost immediately Dalton felt himself fill with a nervous excitement.

This had to be it.

But this was a house?

Jean-Luc bounded up and over the hill overlooking the river and excitedly called for them to join him.

He was at the edge of the river, looking straight at the hill Dalton and Marie were quickly hustling down. When they were at his side they saw what he saw: dirt, bushes, and long windows set into the hill. To travel down the river without paying attention, the casual observer would never notice the well-hidden windows, but Jean-Luc was hardly a casual observer, and he had a lead thanks to the quest initiated by Dalton.

They walked up and down the "property" and couldn't seem to find an entrance, only long dark windows set deep in the hill, covered with shrubs and bushes. They settled on rapping loudly on one of the windows until they got a response. But a response would be a long time coming, because nobody was home. Apparently the rumors swirling around town about the return of the infamous Halo Kilgore and Clem Lemon were false. Or perhaps the friends had simply gone somewhere else for a while. Dalton couldn't help but feel a tremendous disappointment.

But then they heard a dog bark, and before he knew what was happening Dalton felt a familiar lick at his hand and turned to the smiling black Labrador he knew to be Clem Lemon's best friend, Hunter.

Dalton excitedly gave Hunter the petting of a lifetime until the curious dog went ahead and gave Marie and Jean-Luc a nice little sniff-and-hand-lick themselves. Soon all four were the best of friends, and Dalton, unable to resist the temptation, asked Hunter where Clem could be found. Before Jean-Luc could joke about the extraordinarily limited range of a dog's vocabulary, let alone its knowledge of verb tenses, the dog shot over the hill, and the three followed with haste.

They didn't have to follow far, because at the top of the hill they were greeted by two old men pointing shotguns at them.

"Welcome!" Clem Lemon said with a wide smile. "Now get the hell out of here!"

Jean-Luc's face went pale. Marie grasped Dalton's hand and half-hid behind his arm.

"Clem?" Dalton said. "It's me—Dalton Hughes!"

"Who's that now?" the other man said. "Should I kill him?"

"Not yet," Clem said and gave Dalton a curious up-and-down look.

"I really want to kill him, Clem," the other man said. "Real quick? C'mon."

"Easy now, Huck," Clem said to the man. "This is the boy I was telling you about. Welcome to Hell, Dalton."

"Glad to be here!"

They shook hands. Clem was still deceptively strong.

"I admit I'm a bit surprised to see you're still here," Clem said.

"Dalton, I think I know that man," Marie said.

"What'd she say?" Clem asked.

"This is Marie. She said she thinks she knows you," Dalton said and turned to Marie. "From where?"

"He eats at the restaurant sometimes," she said. "A very generous tipper." She turned to Clem. "Hello, sir!"

"Well, hey—if it isn't Lambchop," Clem said with another big smile. "What's shakin', bacon?"

"Keeping it cool," she said. (This seems to have been a little friendly dialogue they'd developed.)

Clem turned to the other man. "And this is that lovely waitress I told you about."

"I like her," the man said. He pointed to Dalton, "Him, I don't like." He pointed to Jean-Luc, "And why do I recognize you?"

"You were a guest lecturer in my philosophy class in school!" Jean-Luc said, scraping his jaw off the ground. "But I take it your name is not really Yancy Morningbone, is it?"

"I think I'm going to be sick," Dalton said as he realized whom and what he was looking at.

"Perhaps we should all go inside for a bit and get our shit together," Clem advised, and they all happily if confusedly agreed.

27

THERE WAS no traditional "front door," but there was a way in.

A large hinged metal door in the ground, with fake plants, dirt, and debris stuck to it, glided open from Clem's expert touch. They all looked down into a short stairwell leading to an open elevator, and Clem advised the young ones to go ahead, so he and Huck could shut the forest floor behind them.

They walked down a few steps into the small elevator, which hummed softly as they felt themselves being lowered farther underground. When the elevator stopped, the door in front of them opened, and they entered a massive room unlike anything any of them had seen before. At the far wall were the windows they'd seen from the river's edge, which somehow let a surprising amount of light into the room despite being shielded by shrubs. The ceiling had to be about fifteen to twenty feet high in most places, and what they noticed almost immediately was that despite it being an unusually hot late-summer morning, the room was perfectly cool. From the looks of it, the residence was one massive room sectioned off according to utility. No walls save for the ceiling, which curved down to the ground at each end of the room—certainly a structure to pique the interest of an architect or an engineer.

The look on Jean-Luc's face as he observed the residence reminded Dalton of a funny story Marie had told him.

When he came to America, in an attempt to integrate himself with his new peers, Jean-Luc tried, and failed, to play American football. Luckily for Jean-Luc, he went to a public school, and there were no cuts. If you tried out for the team, you made it. Jean-Luc tried out, and he received a uniform and the unspoken knowledge that it would be a silly day in Hell when he would ever see the field in a game.

That silly day came during the second-to-last game of his sophomore year, when his junior-varsity team was up by twenty-eight points late in the fourth quarter. The contest was all but over, and the coach, after much prompting from the kids on the team—everyone had gotten to play in that game but Jean-Luc—put the "little French loser" (as the coach referred to him behind closed doors) into the game to field a punt.

Marie, who was in the stands that game, lost her voice because she was cheering so loudly and animatedly when her brother stepped onto the field. As Marie described it: "Jean-Luc stood back where you are supposed to stand to catch the punt, and the ball was hiked, and the punt went into the air, and, if you can believe it, he caught it! But then I guess he got so excited that he caught the ball that, well, it looked like he was trying to run in every direction at the same time!

"Brother was, of course, soon tackled for a big loss of yards."

The story had always made Dalton laugh, and he was reminded of it as he watched Jean-Luc enter Halo Kilgore's house. It looked like his brain was trying to run in every direction at the same time. His eyes shot from the tall ceiling to the long arches down to the ground, up to the wide windows, over to the ventilation system, the fireplace . . . the little engineer in his head calculating and contemplating a whole host of unusual and innovative designs.

"I bet you have no need for any air conditioning and only minimal heating in this place," Jean-Luc said excitedly. "Built right into the earth. Amazing."

Dalton's eyes were a nervous mess. He found himself concentrating on Jean-Luc's appreciation for the design because he had hardly the intestinal fortitude necessary to gather the nerve to look over at the grinning aspect of Halo Kilgore—the man who, whether he liked it or not, taught Dalton more than anyone else in the world about the things he loved.

Marie's eyes danced from her brother to Dalton to the weird and wonderful home in which she found herself that morning. Whether she knew it or not, her hand clutched Dalton's with an excited strength. She felt as though she were the checkered flag being held out the window of a racing champion's car as it sped around on its victory lap.

"Well then, what do you say we all have a seat?" Clem said, gesturing to a large, wooden cube underneath one of the wide windows.

They all walked over to the cube, but the campers didn't exactly know what to make of it. Laughing, Halo Kilgore ran his finger along the top edge of the table until he caught what he was groping for—a small, nearly indiscernible ledge, which he pulled at—and the cube released a chair. Clem did the same, and the others discovered that the sides of the cube were composed of chairs designed so that when they were all pushed in, they made the table into a seamless block.

"Perfect," Jean-Luc said, sitting down. "Just beautiful."

"So the rumors are true—that you have returned," Marie said to Clem.

"Yeah, I couldn't keep Huck from this place."

"I can see why," Jean-Luc said, looking around and then over to Halo "Huck" Kilgore. At which point he stood and walked over to the man. "I apologize for not doing this sooner: I am Jean-Luc Delphine, and it is an honor to be received into your beautiful house, Dr. Kilgore."

"My pleasure, Jean-Luc," Huck said and turned to Clem. "What a *nice young man*."

"And I am Jean-Luc's younger sister, Marie Delphine." She too rose and shook his hand, and Dalton was both happy and surprised to find the old man blush a bit.

"This guy, if I'm right," Clem started, motioning to Dalton, "has probably got a cinderblock tongue right now."

Clem, Marie, and Jean-Luc laughed.

Dalton walked over to Huck.

"My name is Dalton Hughes." The two met each other's eyes and recognized something that went down to the very root of their natures, and both felt that warm recognition of a new friendship. Sometimes, it's that easy. He continued: "A Miss Jane Jefferson told me that if I ever found you to send her best regards."

"Nice to be found, Dalton," Huck said. "Jane is a wonderful woman. I'm sure I'll see her soon enough."

"So, Mr. Keep It Cool," Marie said, addressing Clem, "where have you both been for so long?"

Clem and Halo looked at each other briefly and shrugged.

THREE YEARS ago, Clem Lemon and Halo Kilgore were called to visit a mutual friend in Salt Lake City. The friend, another retired professor, had been diagnosed with the same fatal disease that had killed Lou "The Iron Horse" Gehrig—Amyotrophic Lateral Sclerosis.

During his many hours poring over the variety of periodicals available to him as a night janitor in the school library, Dalton had discovered a book concerning fatal diseases and had read much of it, sometimes finding himself literally crying as he read—crying while he read the sterile, objective voice of a medical description. For instance, this particular disease—"A.L.S."—has no known cure or vaccination, yet, and what happens if you develop it is that every muscle in your entire body atrophies until, if left untreated, you starve to death from no longer being able to swallow, or you suffocate from no longer having the strength to inhale. With treatment, they put you on a respirator and feed you through your stomach, while you lie there and slowly fade to death. The thought of perfectly normal, nice people going through that wretchedness had made Dalton cry. But at some point between then and now, that response area in his brain had changed, because now the thought of that injustice made him smolder with quiet, unsure-of-where-to-be-directed anger.

The man in Salt Lake City whom Clem and Huck went to visit had, fortunately for him, lived an exciting and fulfilling life, so although he was of course devastated to have been stricken with such a terrible, maddening, and fatal disease, he was better-prepared for his demise than most of the damned.

But he had no family. He had a lifelong partner who had died the previous winter, and both his parents were long since dead. He had a global network of former students who would have lit themselves on fire and jumped into a pool of kerosene for him, but what he really missed was the company of the two best friends he ever had—two friends he made while teaching at a prestigious university many years ago—so he called them, and because they were both retired and restless and concerned for their friend, his two friends met in Manta and drove out to Salt Lake City to be with him as long as was necessary.

At first it was his leg. It was weak and only getting weaker. And then they noticed he began slurring a few words. This was "remarkable" because he was one of the great orators either Clem or Huck had ever heard. The weakness spread to his other leg, then his arms.

At first, when he began to choke while trying to swallow food, he refused intensive care. He said he wanted to just die and be done with it. But he soon caved and was put on a respirator. Though he couldn't talk with his friends anymore, he could sit and be with them, and that was preferable to the great mystery awaiting him, coming after him.

He was diagnosed three years ago, and he died two weeks ago on a gray day in a hospital outside Salt Lake City. Through the hospital room window, they could barely see the outline of mountains through the fog and mist. Nurses and orderlies indifferently walked past the open door sometimes, which seemed like an indignity to Clem and Huck. Their friend deserved a pyramid.

One night, in a contemplative quiet, they heard the shrill, unbroken note of a stopped heart on the monitor.

The staff elevated the indignity—they could do nothing to help him. The doctors signed the paperwork, and the nurses left, and the friends shed their tears together. When they buried him, a few days later, they shared stories with his former students. And then the two friends came back to the only place either of them cared about.

And then they found three kids standing outside Huck's house, and they let them inside.

Marie, Jean-Luc, and Dalton wiped tears from their faces. The men's story had added an element of subjective affection to Dalton's injustice-rage, which had turned it back into a deep, painful sadness. Meanwhile, Clem and Huck were through with crying over their friend. They preferred to look back on the good times, because to do otherwise is a form of torture, and nobody should torture the elderly. (Except maybe God.)

"That is a very sad story," Marie said. "I am almost sorry I asked."

"Don't be," Huck said. "The sad part is over. He's dead now. His pain and fear are gone."

"Thank Fuck," said Clem. (It was one of his caustic sayings, something he'd started saying after one of his colleagues had written a best-selling, scandalous philosophy book about the idea that "Intercourse Is God.")

"Oh, my goodness—Victoria and Nathan!" Marie said, suddenly remembering they weren't alone on this expedition.

"There were others with you?" Clem asked, almost nervously.

"Yes! We left them at the campsite hours ago. We should get back!"

"That's probably best," Clem said. "Now I don't need to tell you three to keep this place to yourselves, do I?"

"Of course not," Dalton said. "But we'll be back soon. There is too much for us to talk about."

"Indeed," Huck said, and they shook hands again.

As they left, a starving-for-attention Hunter the Smiling Dog blocked their way until Dalton and Marie gave him another good petting and a few rib-slaps for good measure. And then they rode the elevator up to the surface, where they opened the overhead metal doors and were immersed in the late-morning light and heat.

They double-timed it back to camp and told Victoria and Nathan they had tried—and failed at—survivalist fishing.

28

ANTAEUS "ACE" Dugan grew up in Haverbrook, graduated from Meyer College, and made a fortune as a producer in the movie business. When he died, the main benefactor of Haverbrook's artistic community left behind a two-hundred-million-dollar bequeathment and a plan for its use.

Half of the money would be donated to a variety of programs doing advanced medical and technological research at Meyer College. He had never allowed himself to spend any time thinking about the grim institution of the death process, and finally when it was time to be put through the mortal thresher himself, he found it to be as awful as he knew it would be.

He had already written the checks to Meyer College when he wrote his last will and testament. The memo on the checks read, "Re: Immortality."

The other half of the inheritance was to be used on the expansion and enhancement of the city of Haverbrook itself, the city where Dugan grew up and which he loved so much.

A few months before his death, the benefactor visited Haverbrook and noted with displeasure how long and difficult a drive it was from the nearest major airport to the town. In response to Mr. Dugan's complaint, the city council proposed a location for a bridge that would link the nearest major roadway—the same road that led into Manta—to a road leading into Haverbrook. The project had been shelved due to shortage of funding, but it came back to life when the city council received its hundred-million-dollar apportionment.

A wave of hurrahs and huzzahs ripped through the town. The city council praised the name of the benefactor, renamed the city's main road after him, and immediately petitioned Kellogg Industries to get started on a design.

The morning of the big announcement, Jean-Luc was called into his boss's office. When Jean-Luc arrived, he could barely squeeze into the room—seemingly the entire engineering department was in attendance. The boss told them that they were to form teams and submit design ideas for a potential bridge that would span the Crondura River.

The city of Haverbrook, it seemed, was about to get a profound facelift.

The town of Manta was apoplectic. The townspeople, in their enlightened fury, could be accurately described as having the antithesis of the Haverbrook reaction. The Luminarians did not choose this isolated island in the forest in order to witness the rebirth of Manhattan across the shore from their sought seclusion.

"Ban the Bridge!" signs were erected, and "Burn the Bridge!" speeches were made. Wendell Pency, the councilman and town editorial cartoonist, concentrated nearly all of his efforts on this and related Haverbrook projects (with one of them captioned: "We don't want out, and we don't want *you* in!").

If the Mantanites' irate reactions were any indicator, the forthcoming "Haverbrook Revolution" threatened to utterly destroy every fundamental concept of the Luminarian faith.

Quentin and Dalton, understanding their readership, had their own thoughts on the matter, but they bit their editorial lip and gave their readers a wide variety of perspectives concerning the project—a wide variety of voices all calling for the destruction of Haverbrook.

Marie Delphine looked forward to the day the bridge would be in working order, not only because her brother would be associated with a major civil project, but also because it would save her a lot of driving time on her commute. She wrote a letter to the editor about just that, but Dalton wouldn't print it.

"There's no need for you and the restaurant to suffer from the pernicious reactions that seem to deluge anyone and anything involved with the project," he told her.

That her brother was taking part in the bridge's design was bad enough.

ALL OF which should help in describing the level of stress Augustus Hershey found himself under when his father's failing health and the Clergy of Twelve left Augustus as the full-fledged leader—the Head Pastor—of the Luminarian community. The stress changed the man. Alienated by a sister almost entirely devoted to a boy who Augustus would often complain "never seems to do anything!" and a mother who was looking after his ailing father, Augustus's temperament had gone from reticent, pious student of Luminarianism to a sort of high-energy spiritual cosmonaut, constantly tinkering with the satellite he piloted over the planet.

Shelly White, Marcia's young daughter, three years old and walking but still not talking much, returned from her baptismal weekend with Augustus and cried every time Marcia mentioned their going to church or a church function or anywhere he and the other church leaders would be. It got to the point that she couldn't even bring her daughter to mass on Sundays, because she had to spend nearly the entire service in the church foyer as her too-old-to-be-crying-like-this daughter wailed insufferably. Marcia began formulating weekly excuses for why Shelly wasn't there—sickness, visiting family, et cetera. Excuses that ran thin quickly. Excuses that led to a particularly stressed-out Augustus Hershey knocking on her door one dark Saturday night.

Upon the sound of the knocking, little Shelly immediately fell into hysterics. Marcia carried the gasping child to her room and tried to comfort and coo her to rest, because she knew exactly who was at the door, and it would be best for everyone if she could somehow get Shelly to relax and avoid making the scene any worse than it had to be.

Marcia answered the door and found Augustus Hershey standing there in a long, black duster. The evening was wet with drizzle, and Marcia invited the large man inside.

"Where's Shelly?" Augustus asked as he sat down at the table. "Not visiting family again, is she?"

Marcia could feel her throat tightening further from the moment she answered the door. Her breaths were more shallow than normal, and this lack of oxygen made her body feel cold. She hugged herself and shivered.

"She'sss," Marcia said stuttering, "sss-sleeping."

"Ah," Augustus added cogitatively. "Are you okay? You seem . . . nervous."

"I'mfine," she said, trying her best to maintain a level voice, but her anxiety drove the words into each other.

"You're anything but fine," Augustus said. "You're shivering, and your voice is quaking. Are you feeling guilty about something? You don't look like you are filled and fluted with the love of the Lorrah, Marcia."

Augustus went to the window.

"Shelly's just been such a h-h-handful," Marcia said. "She's always cryinnng."

"Perhaps she misses the glorious music of our weekly church sermons," he said. "Or perhaps you don't know how to care for her?"

Marcia's blood boiled, but she couldn't answer back, so she watched as Augustus opened and closed her window blinds a few times, seemingly playing with them like he was playing with her.

"Many of us in the church and city council are worried about you, Marcia—you and Shelly. Some of us think you've lost your faith."

"I have n-n-not," she said.

"No?"

"N-no."

"Well, like I said, we're all worried about you, Marcia. I find myself constantly defending your spiritual constitution against many people who disagree with me. Let me ask you something: do you, Ms. White, think you could convince me of the quality of that constitution, if it were demanded of you?"

The man's big hand grasped a silver-gray Luminarian necklace hanging around Marcia's neck—featuring a plain, open circle—and he gazed into it as he held it, and then he laid it gently back against her throat.

He stood.

"And with that damned bridge . . . We need solidarity, Marcia. We need to show the world that we are united in our faith and worship. We cannot *waver* in the face of what is coming!"

"I was born into this community, Augustus." Marcia said in her defense. "It's my whole life."

"Is it?"

Outside, she heard voices and the scuffling of boots on her wooden porch, and then her heart was in her ears, and she was bent doubled-over from the internal cold. She could hardly breathe.

"You do know why I'm here . . ." Augustus said and let the statement hang in the air.

She thought she did. She'd heard stories like this before, but she'd prayed that they were just that—stories. Augustus especially didn't seem like his father. The young man couldn't be the kind of person who would maintain the old practices of the church's sometimes revolting past.

But then she heard the door open, and she began to black

out, unable to breathe, terrified out of her wits—a waking nightmare she gagged upon as she found herself fading to unconsciousness.

Augustus softly slapped her awake. She opened her eyes and saw several of the church leaders, including Councilman Joe O'Brien and Police Chief Artimus Blake, standing over her. She heard Shelly crying again. She tried to back away from the table and hurry over to her daughter, but the councilman's hand caught her arm and forced her back into her seat.

Then they were on top of her.

In the middle of it, at the height of her terror, at the bottom of her soul, she could hear something.

One-two-three. One-two-three.

She heard music.

One-two-three. One-two-three.

She fought and cried.

One-two-three. One-two-three.

Inside herself, closed off from the horrors of the outside, almost as in prayer, she wailed, and it was turned to music that burned intensely in the depths of her dark universe. Every musician and piece of music joined her in the ongoing, layered soundtrack of all worlds, between, through, and with the beat that is found within everything, from the beads of a rosary to the heartsong in little Shelly's chest—it is the song of all existence.

One-two-three.

One-two-three.

She fought and cried.

She listened and survived.

29

Pamela Hait sat in the middle of the bed she shared with

Augustus Hershey, surrounded by photographs, and frowned. They were photographs of her, Augustus, smiling Luminarians, and the town itself. There were pictures from Manta's four seasons: the poetic *memento mori* of autumn leaves piled on the forest floor; landscapes of wintry fields, unbroken, diamond-white; the surreal colors exploding out of a rolling hill of wild flowers in the spring; and summer just outside the woods, under the long shadows of early evening or in the yawning mists of morning.

She didn't know exactly why, but Pam felt vulnerable and alone as she sat there in the midst of those powerful memories and moments.

She'd noticed a gradual change in Augustus over the past few years. He was no longer the boyish man-child she fell in love with; he was now the man she always knew and was afraid he would become. She felt divided, which was perhaps the cause of her vulnerability. She loved him, but she was not proud of him, and she wanted to be proud of him—oh, yes, of course—but she was not.

She had put this time aside—time when Augustus would be at the church preparing notes for the coming sermon and musical offering—to surround herself with thoughts of where her life stood.

She loved Augustus the man—the man he was when it was just the two of them. She was uneasy about Augustus the spiritual leader—the man he was when he became overtaken by the importance of his beliefs, when he made her feel almost like a decoration, like the flowers a bride carries. (She remembered thinking that the flowers a bride carries are beautiful, but they are also dead.)

Looking over the pictures spread across the bed, she saw what a fine life she had. The pictures, most of them taken by Victoria, revealed glimpses into a truly charmed life, and she felt lucky for those long, beautiful moments that, unfortunately, like everything else, eventually had to end. She suffered alone that emotionally destabilizing dichotomy, which seemed to turn up everywhere she found herself.

She turned and looked toward the door when she heard a

few quiet steps in the hall and saw Nathan Cameron lean his head into the room.

"Sorry, I thought I heard something," Nathan said. He looked at the pictures and then at the look on her face and asked, "Everything hunky-dory?"

She looked over and shrugged slowly. "I guess so," she said. "Just thinking."

"I try not to do that," Nathan joked. "Thinking always gets me in trouble."

"I never get in trouble," Pam said, staring at a picture next to her. Which was true. With her sister being a town police officer and her father a powerful disciplinarian, Pam hadn't had many occasions in life where she had done something anyone could consider *wrong*. Even her relationship with Augustus was based on what she viewed as a macroscopic, objective right-thing.

"Everyone gets in trouble," Nathan said.

"Not me," Pam said. "I always do the stupid right thing."

Nathan stepped into the room, and Pam made some space for him, moving a low-angle shot of Augustus standing on the stage the night Nathan was introduced to the Luminarian community. Augustus looked even more massive than usual in the photograph, and he was being set aside so Nathan could sit down.

"You've never wanted to do the wrong thing?" Nathan asked.

Pam didn't answer. She'd never really had the ability to be bad. She enjoyed the structure of rules because she knew, deep down, she was in complete disarray—a chaotic, insufferable mess. But if she did what others whose respect she wanted thought was right, she believed she would then become a good person. Or at least pass as one. And it was working. Wasn't it?

There was something she liked about Nathan being there. He was no authority—he was quite the opposite, actually. Her fiancé alternately loved and hated this boy. He saw inspiration in him, and need. He loved him for the inspiration, and for the need. They got along like brothers, most of the time.

Every now and then, though, he found that he hated Nathan. He would complain to Pam, "Sometimes I feel like there is nothing *real* there! He's a snake-man!" This feeling bothered Augustus, partly because he wanted to feel like he had at least one honest friendship and partly because Augustus sometimes felt like he himself was an insincere, unreal snake-man, too, and it was his way of facing it. In short, they got along, very much, like brothers.

But Nathan was real and doing something now. He was helping Pamela Hait get through a vulnerable, lonely moment by holding her hand.

"What do you think would happen if you did something that you weren't supposed to?" Nathan asked.

Blushing, Pam replied by not replying, by not pulling away.

"If I'm being honest, it doesn't look like doing the right thing has made you very happy," Nathan said, getting closer. "Maybe you'd feel better if you tried something new."

And then they kissed while Victoria napped in the next room.

30

JANE JEFFERSON checked her mailbox and saw two checks. One was from Prask Impressions Advertising, LLC—the last *But Is It Art?* payment. She had officially retired. The success of the campaign led to dozens of similar offers from similarly large companies, but she told them all she had enough money to give to three generations of a family she didn't have, and she couldn't find the point in continuing to do something that made her feel empty.

She'd found herself in the surprising position of being inspired by the people in the Luminarian community. They were in such a state of agitation that eventually, as she saw the legitimate swirls of fear and hate one morning in a young townswoman's eyes, she asked herself when was the last time she was that agitated about anything, and she was surprised to find that that time was right now.

More than a few of the representatives she told this to laughed and agreed with her—that they too weren't exactly in love with what they did. But, Jane, my dear, they implied, they had mouths to feed, boats to fuel, and much more sophist work to do. Can't stop now, now can we?

Jane's bank account held a staggering number of commas for a girl who grew up thinking about different ways she might kill herself. Though her mother and father made a living in the entertainment industry, being a celebrated jazz singer is akin to being a celebrated poet. At any given time, a troublingly small portion of the world's population likes jazz or poetry so much they pay money for it. So while her family was able to get by (at least until her mother killed herself), she had very little knowledge of opulence—besides the man who showcased her portrait of Simon Fisher, the rich man who told her what her choices were—until she found herself seated on a leather couch looking at a bank statement that took her breath away.

The second check was from a small publishing company. They were paying her for designing the cover of Quentin Hancock's forthcoming book about Manta.

A happy smile broke over Dalton's face when Jane told him that her career in advertising was over.

Together with Marie and Victoria and Nathan, they all celebrated with great enthusiasm, because everyone could plainly see that a heavy shroud had been lifted from Jane's shoulders, and her smiles seemed to beam inwardly as much as outwardly for once. They drank and smoked and played loud music, and at the end of the night, as the others had fallen away in pairs or simply passed out, Dalton and Jane sat with their backs against the front door, looking up at the massive billboard that had so confounded Augustus during his brief visit.

"It really is a wonderful piece of art," Dalton said.

"I know," Jane said, gazing into a glass of wine. "For an advertisement."

Dalton chuckled exhaustedly.

"How did you think of making something like this?" he asked.

Jane, though she had the answer, let the balloons of question and speculation rise before she popped them with the response Dalton should have expected.

"I just thought about Simon . . . and what I would want him to see."

31

THE CITY hall's main room was packed from front to back. Dozens of sweaty citizens fanned themselves in the sweltering, stuffy air, which swirled lazily with the flick of the attendees' handheld, opened fans. The heat and sweat raised a heavy stink, which only added to the displeasure of the gathered citizens.

Everyone wanted—demanded—to know what the city of Manta could and would do about the encroaching Haverbrook menace. This bridge. This audacious attempt to subvert the quiet privacy of a small church community and cut open its belly to the delight and spectacle of the unwanted masses.

Dalton and Quentin both had to cover the meeting, as there was more than one story going on. Additionally, Quentin was called in to testify before the city council about the relatively quiet editorial pen he and his associate editor had held regarding the coming change. Though his voice had always been a semi-contrarian jolt, Dalton's lack of exposition on his thoughts regarding the Haverbrook expansion was itself unacceptable to the townspeople—like the young heathen was hiding something.

But first there was the addressing of old business, which

itself churned the stomachs of the community: the heating and cooling system for the city hall remained incomplete and behind schedule.

"Unacceptable!"

"What is wrong with this place?"

Loud scoffing and derision for "trying to do better than what the Lorrah provided."

Mayor Tony Capps—a small man, bespectacled, red-faced, white-whiskered across his upper lip and about his under-chin—rocked his gavel against the podium in an attempt to hush the agitated crowd.

"*People!* I have been reassured by Councilman O'Brien and his brother that the most difficult portions of the renovation are past us, and the project should be completed soon."

"Horseshit!" someone called out, and Dalton took down this note with a laugh.

The stink seemed to flex. An unmistakable look of concern found its way to Charlotte Hershey's face throughout the meeting. The wondrous music of the Lorrah sounded much like angry pontifications, frustrated squeals calling for the neck of whatever foe was most convenient.

Perhaps Quentin Hancock would suffice, as he was the first person called to the stand on new business.

The pushy voices, combined with the general instability of the hot, muddled, city-hall meeting, created the sort of environment where you'd expect to hear from anyone but Quentin Hancock, who was a man of few words, and softly spoken those. Nevertheless, he trumped the irate madness by remaining more quiet and patient than usual, giving his contrasting persona a certain weight that the other braying donkeys lacked.

"The townspeople—your readership, I need not remind you—are gravely concerned about your young editor's lack of response to the Haverbrook bridge plans," Councilman Joe O'Brien offered. "Many of us believe his and your reticence is a sign that you agree with the proposal. Perhaps, given the boy's *numerous* connections to Haverbrook—"

The members of the audience who hadn't heard this yet

or just now realized it were triggered into an even greater outrage at the thought of it, and they shouted their disapproval. The ones who had heard about this or already realized it simply made vocal agreements in the forms of grunts as they fanned themselves angrily. In short, the unfinished statement was met with a unanimous binge of Luminarian support.

Quentin waited until they all stopped grunting and shouting.

"Mr. Hughes and I share the same opinion on this editorial subject: we feel it is best to give voice to the people most notably affected by this currently hypothetical bridge. As journalists and non-Luminarian citizens, our opinion is far afield from that of our readership, and, if you've noticed, Dalton, without my asking him to, has given twice as much editorial space to the letters we receive from the aforementioned affected citizens, many of whom are with us here today."

"So you're in favor of a proposal that would forever damage Luminarian tradition," Joe O'Brien said, both question and statement.

"'We are as indifferent to it as a mountain is to the ocean,'" Quentin replied, which was a line from Halo Kilgore. "However, if it would please the townspeople for Dalton to further stoke their ire by explicating his indifference in a five-hundred-word column, we would be willing to do that.

"We would look like idiots, but we wouldn't be the only ones."

At that, without being prompted or dismissed by the council, Quentin walked back to his seat and took up his pen and notebook.

Tony Capps once again was forced to gavel the meeting to order.

"My *word*, people! We've all heard your protestations by now, and we agree with them," he said. "Just please know that we are looking into every legal recourse available to us. Town lawyers are working around the clock, and we promise we will provide you with our findings the moment we decide on the best course of action."

"Would the lawyers benefit from the help of our townspeople?" a man in the back asked. "We're all willing to do whatever it takes to help in the fight for what's right."

"We'll get back to you on that," Capps replied to the grumbling crowd.

Dalton decided to ask a question.

"Would the town lawyers be further ahead in their research if they didn't have to spend three nights a week and every Sunday afternoon attending church services?"

The reader can well imagine how that went over.

32

JEAN-LUC DELPHINE walked into his boss's office with a large folder tucked under his right arm. Normally, Jean-Luc would have been knee-shakingly nervous to do what he was about to do, but he had an extraordinary faith in what he had done, and he entered the office with a calmness and certainty that felt exhilarating. It was not that he thought that he himself was so great; it was that the design in his hands was an opus, and he loved it so much he felt like he should be wearing gloves while he held it.

"What is it, J.L.?" his boss asked.

Jean-Luc placed the folder on the large, polished, mahogany desk and stepped back.

"It is my bridge design."

"Oh," his boss said. "I've been meaning to talk to you about that."

It was one of those sentences where the way it is said instigates an internal, "Abandon hope . . . ."

Jean-Luc felt sick.

"We're facing some goddam political pressure from the goddam people of Manta, and while our lawyers say we're in the right, the goddam Manta freaks plan to battle us through every appeals court available. This project might not get off the ground for years. I'm sorry I didn't tell you earlier, J.L. I've been fighting the creepy bastards on my end of things all week."

"I understand," Jean-Luc lied. "There is my plan anyway. Perhaps you could file it away for whenever it will be needed."

Jean-Luc turned to go.

"Jean-Luc," his boss called out.

"Sir?"

"I told you to break up into teams. What happened to your team?"

As he walked to the door, Jean-Luc said to his boss, "I am sorry, sir." And when he got to the door, he turned back and said, "They could not keep up."

INSIDE THE office, his boss left the bridge design in its folder for the rest of a busy day spent screaming into a phone at a loop of bureaucratic ambiguity. He was just as upset about the city of Manta blocking the project as he could tell Jean-Luc was, and it tore up his insides to see how quickly the young man had gone from nervous excitement to the drudgery of expected disappointment. It hurt him to see that.

But then, at day's end, with the night air pressing black against his office window, the boss put his feet up on his desk and pulled open the folder.

The plan fell to his lap, and he picked it up and took a look.

33

IT WAS early on a cool Saturday morning when Dalton and Marie knocked on the riverfront windows of Halo Kilgore's unusual home. Then they headed up the hill, pulled open the camouflaged steel doors, closed them, and descended in the elevator, which then opened, and they entered the dark subterranean house hand-in-hand.

The light was low, reflecting the early morning's shade, and the music that seemingly manifested itself straight from the air they breathed was melodic, tranquil, and congruently brooding.

The previous Thursday, Dalton found a note taped to his front door.

My place. Saturday morning.
—H.

He had only shown it to Marie.

Inside, they found Huck Kilgore draped across his couch, a cigarette in his hand, the smoke floating up softly, swirling in the window light and sliding up a ventilation chamber. Dalton unslung the heavy backpack he carried and set it on the counter. The two walked softly over to the relaxed old man and sat down in a black leather loveseat.

"Good morning, Dr. Kilgore!" Marie playfully shouted, and an appreciative grin leaked onto the side of Huck's mouth. He opened his eyes.

"Good morning, Little Miss Marie."

He turned to Dalton. "Jesus, Dalton . . . what a wonder it must be to wake up with her," he said.

"Every day is the greatest day of my life," Dalton said.

"Yeah, it is," Huck said. "Either of you eaten yet?"

"Funny you should mention that—" Dalton said.

"I thought I would make you boys some breakfast," Marie said. "We brought some food, and it would be an honor to cook you something, Mr. Huck."

Halo softly laughed. "Anything cooked by a woman as beautiful as you, Marie, and, well, I'm afraid I wouldn't know whether to eat it or take it to bed."

They all laughed.

"Thank you for your perverse compliment," Marie said, standing. "Now I will get to work."

"Please do," Halo said. "Feel free to ask if you need help finding anything."

And with that he turned his full attention to Dalton.

"You do good work, boy," he said. "I've been reading Quentin's paper, and it's better now. That's part of the reason I invited you here this morning."

"Thank you, Dr. Kilgore," Dalton said. "I think you know how much that means to me. It's all thanks to you, too, because your books were instrumental in helping shape my voice, in getting me here, you know?"

Shrugging the awkward compliment aside, Huck waved his hand. "I know, I know . . . Christ."

Dalton—inured to Huck's aversion to praise—dropped the subject and adjusted his position on the loveseat.

"So, what's up?" Dalton asked.

Dalton turned in his seat so he could watch sweet Marie preparing the meal as Halo considered the question.

"To put it frankly, Dalton, I'm not long for this world."

"Of course," Dalton said. "You're a sour old man."

"Thanks," Halo said. "And I know I look all right, but trust me, Dalton, I'm dying."

For a while, Dalton didn't say anything.

"So, what? You need pallbearers or something? Because neither of us has many friends here, and Jean-Luc—"

"Shut up, Dalton." Halo said with a sly smile. Sadly, he turned serious again. "I had you come here because there are a few things I think we need to discuss before I can move on."

Dalton sat back.

"You're going to kill yourself," Dalton deduced, more a statement than a question.

"Yes," Halo said. "I goddam am."

Dalton's throat closed. The way the man said it—like he'd seen everything he cared to see, and the only thing left for him was to snip the tattered cordage of his life and slip peacefully into a deeply desired ocean of nothingness—sent a horrified shiver down Dalton's spine. If this man, this mental beast, this colossus . . . if Halo Kilgore could resign himself to the hopelessness of self-destruction after a lifetime of original and world-challenging thoughts and mental creations, what hope was there for someone like Dalton? He would never approach Huck's tremendous perspicacity.

"Why?"

"That's what you're here to discuss," Huck said.

Marie, blissfully ignorant of their topic, continued her energetic preparations. The lovely soft humming and singing coming from the kitchen took on a peculiar and incongruous tone amidst the heavy morbid clouds of their conversation.

"Do you believe in God, Dalton?"

"Well, to be honest, I can't really say either way. I have no proof, for or against."

"So you're agnostic."

"I guess that's it."

"Isn't that kind of pussyfooting around the issue?"

"Maybe. But like I said, the arguments for and against are both wanting, as neither is definitely provable, so if I ever pray it's for help with the things I can't control."

For a moment, Dalton thought back on some of those times. He hated to think of them—couldn't stand the way they made him feel about himself. He hated the feeling of needing to ask for help even though there was literally nothing else he could do to try to change the situation. He was reminded of something Quentin said to him once: "Hell is helplessness."

"Have you ever wondered why that was?" Halo asked.

"Why what?"

"Why a man without an organized faith would pray for help."

Dalton always assumed it was a remnant of the fundamentalist religion he'd been forced to follow as a child. He looked at Huck and shook his head thoughtfully.

"Do you believe in God?" Dalton asked.

"No."

"How do you know for sure?"

"I watched my friend's muscles break down to the point that he suffocated from not being strong enough to draw a breath. I felt the life leave my wife's hand as I tried to pull her from the cracked ice of a frozen lake. I've seen children die of terrible diseases, and I have friends whose children and loved ones died from errant bullets and falling debris. I've seen the world taken over by throngs of idiots, all of whom chugged faulty philosophy in order to fill a hole in their being left there by what I can only deduce is a godless universe. I mean, if there really were a God, there would be no need for these faulty philosophies because that emptiness within them would be filled by *true religion*."

"What about 'The Lord Works In Mysterious Ways'?"

"A philosophical catchall that presupposes the 'Lord' even exists."

"Right . . . so why did you ask me if I believed in God?"

"I was getting at something," Halo said. "I wanted to make a point about prayer."

"Prayer? You pray?" Dalton asked skeptically.

"Sometimes."

Dalton sat forward, intrigued.

"There are those who say we were created in God's image, but it might be true the other way, that God was invented in our image. Think about it: isn't God just the ideal person? Man seeks knowledge, and God is called omniscient. Man desires ability, and God is called omnipotent. Man endeavors to do good, and God is called omnibenevolent."

"Sure," Dalton said. "Makes sense so far."

"So what about prayer? It seems to make sense to me that even if there is no God—if God is merely a mental creation to help us try to understand this generally inexplicable existence—then there still might be a psychological benefit to prayer, because if the idea of God is the idea of the ultimate person, then when we pray we are aligning our most important and passionate thoughts and concerns with the concept of the very best person we could want to become."

Dalton wished Marie had heard that. He made a mental note to tell her about it later.

"Huck, I can't deny that there is something to consider there," Dalton said. "So when do you actually pray?"

"Not often—kind of like you, only when there's nothing else I can do about something that's important to me." After a moment, he added, "And that's more and more lately."

Dalton sat back again.

"What does Clem think about that?"

"Clem's a theologian-academic; my argument would be destroyed before he even got done dismissing all of my premises as inaccurate," Halo said with a wry grin, which Dalton, knowing Clem, shared.

"But, basically, it's the only thing stopping me," Halo said.

"From killing yourself?"

"I've got nothing left, boy," Halo said reservedly. "I'm falling apart. My brain ain't what it was, my joints ache, my family are all dead, it hurts when I piss, and I piss all the time, and I just want to die. The beautiful world . . . it just makes me angry now. I can't enjoy it like I could before. Probably never can again. Never will. But every time I try to do it . . . to . . . kill myself . . . I think you're right. I don't want to believe in a god that could let so many awful things happen, yet I can't help but think that all of this was created for a reason, for the gods we could become, and I should just try to enjoy my debilitating slide down the sordid tube of time."

"You're not enjoying it anymore," Dalton said—both statement and question.

"Not like I used to, and I've just run out of the energy to make it better. I used to be able to make it better; now I just crawl around and mewl and try not to be noticed."

Dalton had no reply for that, and they both sat there in deep rumination.

The music whispering into the air from Huck's ubiquitous yet seemingly invisible speakers came to a quiet end, and a new song began.

One-two-three.

One-two-three.

Ch-ch-ch.

Ch-ch-ch.

"What is this?"

"The song?"

A man on the track began to speak:

Peace is a united effort for coordinated control.

Peace is the will of the people and the will of the land.
With peace we can move ahead—together.
We want you to join us this evening in this universal prayer.
This universal prayer for peace,
For every man.
All you've got to do is clap your hands.
One-two-three.
One-two-three.
One-two-three.

"I know this song!"

"You know Pharoah Sanders and Leon Thomas? I underestimated today's youth, boy."

"Pharoah Sanders? This is a Luminarian church song."

Halo laughed.

"Dalton, trust me: it's Pharoah Sanders."

"Huck, you don't understand. The first day I was here, they were performing this song in the church. I snuck in, and this was the song they were playing! I loved it. Hell, I almost converted. It's so beautiful."

"It *is* beautiful," Huck admitted. "It's called 'Hum-Allah-Hum-Allah-Hum-Allah.'"

Dalton laughed.

"They were singing 'Hum-Lorrah-Hum-Lorrah-Hum-Lorrah.'"

Halo's eyes sadly pored the floor.

"Religions take the accomplishments or beliefs of men and retool them to fit a spiritual worldview they created and say was sent to them by their god. That or they destroy any art not directly celebrating their spiritual constructs."

"This is unacceptable!" Dalton said, standing, hearing more of the song unfold.

Huck raised an eyebrow in Dalton's direction.

"Me killing myself you take with grace; Phillip Hershey stealing an old jazz song, and it's unacceptable," Huck said. "You're a crazy son of a bitch."

Marie had only heard the last part.

"Yes, he is," she said with a smile and a wink as she laid

out a platter of fruit. "You're both crazy sons of bitches. Eat some fruit." She went back to the kitchen area and manned the sizzling griddle.

"I'm going to do something about this plagiarism," Dalton said. "The singing music of the Lorrah is nothing but the stolen music of Pharoah Sanders."

"Nothing but—? You do see how they could argue back to you, right? Yes, the music may have been first presented by Mr. Sanders, but he was merely being guided through the Lorrah—who works in mysterious ways."

"Yeah, but—"

"There's no beating them, Mr. Hughes," Halo said. "Any argument you put before them will be riddled with the unstoppable counterarguments based entirely in faith, and how do you argue with someone who's mentally certain without physical evidence? How do you burn down a house that's not made of anything tangible?"

Dalton had nothing. He sat back with a grape and chewed it thoughtfully, listening to the painful wail of Pharoah Sanders' sax. The real song was so beautiful that it felt like something sacred within himself had been violated.

"Winter's coming . . ." Halo said, gazing out the window at the colorful leaves. They danced somberly in a cool, quiet breeze.

"Winter's always coming, Huck," Dalton said. "If that's what you want."

"*Heeeeeere* is breakfast!" Marie happily announced, carrying two steaming plates of food.

Halo changed the conversation, not because Marie was out of her depth discussing such matters but because her presence gave him a sweet relief from his miseries, and instead he found he could just enjoy her as a person and a work of art.

IN TOWN, the citizens of Manta gathered for a special church service honoring the fallen Shannon Penrose, on the three-year anniversary of her death.

They wore dark clothing and spoke in whispers, their fingers working prayer beads, their hearts longing to embrace the pain of the moment, so to be better-able to express the spiritual ache through the voice of their fluted selves.

One-two-three. One-two-three.

Across the dark church, Pam Hait met eyes with Nathan Cameron, and each held the other's gaze until it was broken by the first wailing note from Augustus's saxophone. Inside Nathan's hand, Victoria's hand sweated lightly in the warm air, and she squeezed tighter for a moment as the song ascended.

Nathan turned his head and saw Lacey O'Brien—Councilman Joe O'Brien's twenty-year-old daughter—and she too held his gaze and then quickly looked away. They had met a few months before, and they met in secret a few days later. And every few days after that.

The citizen-orchestra redoubled their efforts as the layers of the song worked into each other, and only they could bring their music to the level of the Lorrah, or, as Dalton would say, to a level somewhere far below that of Pharoah Sanders and Leon Thomas and all the other greats who actually wrote the music the Hersheys claimed to have been singing through them and their church by the fiery soul of their loving Lorrah.

As the music roared, a video montage of pictures of little Shannon taken by Victoria Hershey and others played across the far wall of the church, with the tear-streaked, red faces of Luminarian worshippers bellowing a musical expression of their grief.

And then there was a speech.

"WHAT DO you think, Marie?"

They had finished eating, and they returned to their previous discussion.

"I think I will miss our good doctor very much," Marie said with a small tear in her eye as she looked at old Huck. "But if he is no longer happy, then asking him to stay alive would be cruel, would it not?"

After a pause she added, "And what could be worse than that?"

With a twinge of discomfort, Dalton realized that he wasn't arguing for Huck Kilgore to live, but for himself. Neither man had a family, both had traveled vast philosophical distances, lumbering up cold mountains of thought and through the raging tempest of experience, and what Huck found (and what Dalton was afraid he too would find) was that there were certain limits that men's brains could never move beyond—that a true and full spectrum of knowledge of life and the universe was in fact denied to serious thinking men, that because he and his brain were constructed by the same matter and physical laws that created everything else in the known universe, he was a part of that system, and he would never be able to fully understand its entirety.

Those who know almost nothing at least have the bliss of ignorance. The smarter a person became, it seemed, the more likely he or she was to find that existence is a bittersweet proposition—far more bitter than sweet. And sometimes far more sweet than bitter. Every moment Dalton spent with Marie was as beautiful as anything he could imagine, but then he thought about how eventually they would each die separately, and his soul swelled with pain. They would melt into nothingness, and the uncaring gearwork of the universe would grind on in its grand indifference.

"MY FRIENDS, my brothers, my sisters . . . today we ruminate upon a dark moment in the history of our church. Three years ago, we lost one of our beloved sisters, a child brimming with the hope and love of the Lorrah, and while we can celebrate her memory with our music and love, we must also—because we are men—we must ask ourselves what there is to be learned from this horrible tragedy. So, what have we learned?

"We have learned once again that sometimes the Lorrah's actions are not easily interpreted. We don't know our Lorrah's final plan for man, nor why an innocent can be taken before an infidel or one of our pious and prepared elderly. Perhaps it is because the Lorrah, in order to make our instruments as pure as they are capable of being, afforded us a natural will to act through a combination of our own impulses and the larger, philosophical impulses of the world. But man being man, and the world doing what it does, those personal impulses can be maladjusted and corrupted, as was the case with our Shannon, who had been corrupted by the darkness."

"So then what do you want me here for?" Dalton asked Huck. Dalton was still knocked sideways by Kilgore's morbid thoughts.

"You, Dalton," Huck started, "are the other main reason I haven't killed myself yet. I've done almost everything I could ever hope or want to do, but there is still so much that I see in you.

"Last night, as I was shaving, I felt so tired. I could barely look at myself in the mirror. The tattered and aged face of the man I've become. This goddam grotesque face. And I wanted to do it right then. I had a razor and a warm bath running. It was raining; I was cold; I felt at peace with it all . . . except for you and Marie. You two remind me so much of myself and Ariel that I just ended up quietly finishing my shaving and taking my bath. Goddam I miss that woman."

Huck fell into silence.

"I'm still alive because I feel like there's unfinished business here," he said. "There has to be. I'm not one to dawdle like this."

"Perhaps we should not force it, then," Marie said, beginning to clear the dishes.

"Let me help you with those," Dalton said, needing to stand and clear his mind a bit, and needing to be near Marie.

"Yes, the darkness, the cloak of evil, the black veil that surrounds and abounds, my brothers and sisters! The darkness works through the infidels and philistines and through those unacquainted with the righteous love of the Lorrah. The darkness sits and stirs in the hearts of men like Quentin Hancock and Dalton Hughes. The darkness embeds itself and sleeps in their brains, and it seeps into their heart's beat, casting forth a towering shadow over the bright lights of the Lorrah's universe. Yes, life is an endless dance and battle between the forces of light and the forces of darkness. Does not our newspaper cast a shadow? Do not the maniacal comic books that other religions call 'holy texts' cast shadows? We sit here in our darkness to remind ourselves of evil's omnipresence. We sit here in the dark because only then can we, the true believers, fully understand and reflect the light of the Lorrah.

"Shadows, the darkness of evil, are cast everywhere. There is darkness in you, in me, in the walls we use to keep others out or ourselves in. But the music of the Lorrah is without shadow. It is what is good. Our bodies may cast a shadow, but our actions do not. Through the musical wonder of the Lorrah's bounty we see a synchronized world that could be. A world that is light!

"And what should we do with that light? We should—we must!—do everything in our power to chase the shadows from our world. We must cast them out! It is our duty and our purpose!"

DALTON AND Marie cleaned dishes while Halo Kilgore picked himself up off the couch and made his way over to the fireplace, where he warmed his hands. Another multilayered Pharoah Sanders song—Dalton's favorite, a masterful jazz composition called "Thembi"—crawled along the walls and bounced around the room.

When the young lovers were finished cleaning the kitchen mess, they joined Huck by the fireplace, settling into a warm loveseat. Huck sat directly on the ground in a position that appeared to be second nature in this house.

"Things aren't going to get any easier for you, Dalton," Halo said. "I thought they would when I was your age. The years leading up to my twenty-fourth birthday had been difficult. A blooming teenaged brain is not nearly as graceful and beautiful as that of the blooming flower. The pulsing of thought mixed with uncertain hormonal changes and imbalances took the pendulum of my consciousness and both shattered it and inverted the pieces, resulting in what could be described, if I were to twist my metaphor a bit, as the delusional insanity of thinking that the most difficult part of my journey would end when my brain fully bloomed and finally welcomed the sun's warm rays into its growing. I was wrong. The bloom of my brain resulted in my turning into a sort of dream catcher, soaking up the influences and aspirations of the world around me. Even meeting Ariel—meeting the woman I would love forever—was difficult. She was a medical student where I was a grad student. We met after a bicycling accident sheared a long chunk of skin off my leg, and the first time she touched me was also the first time the wound was being treated with antiseptic, and the pain—"

Halo laughed quietly at the memory.

"The pain was outrageous, but I wanted to look tough for her, so I gritted my teeth so hard that I succeeded in masking my pain, but the deception was quickly uncovered when the force of my inward grunt resulted in my letting out a ripping fart."

Dalton and Marie laughed.

"I was so embarrassed," Halo recalled with a smile. "But Ariel just laughed and literally belched the words, 'Don't worry about it.' Then we both fell in love."

"What was it like to finally be published?" Marie asked. Unbeknownst to Dalton and even to her brother, Marie had been tinkering with the idea of putting together a collection of her poems. She could not decide, however, whether to send them out for publication or ritualistically burn the manuscript. She found the same beauty in an immortal collection as she did in the sweeping of an intricate sand mandala.

"Marie, at the beginning, nobody had any reason to care about me and my weird writings. I sent them to magazines and publishing houses, and not only did I never get published, but all I ever got in reply were any artist's two great spirit-killers: silence, and indifference."

"So when did that change?"

"It didn't," Halo said. "Eventually Ariel convinced me to publish the books myself, citing the fact that *Leaves of Grass*, the collection that inspired me to be a writer when I was ten years old, was unabashedly self-published by Mr. Whitman.

"And after the succcess of *The Polyglot*, I sold the company for a mint and dedicated myself to academia. I had made my money, and I had proven the professional publishers and magazines they were visionless, stuffy humps.

"After that, I just did whatever the hell I wanted."

"Let us close our eyes and pray that our bodies and message might be made clear for use by the Lorrah. In this anniversary of a tragic loss, let us put our hearts onto the altar and pray for the light of the Lorrah to guide our path toward divinity. Let it start in our hearts, and let us sing it into the world. Let it end with the voice we give to the Lorrah, and let those who stand against us meet their end with a rope around their neck or at the bottom of the ocean."

And with that, the music picked up again—the opening notes of Pharoah Sanders' magnum opus, "The Creator Has a Master Plan."

Which also began playing in Halo Kilgore's dark underground house. The music sprang from the walls around them and settled into their ears, and the three let their discussion dissolve, watching instead as the day, the leaves, and the dancing tips of the river glinted through the long windows in the hill.

"I had an idea once for a movie I wanted to shoot using this song as the soundtrack," Halo said. "I was wondering if you would like to help me with it, Dalton. It will be the last piece of art I ever create."

34

Quentin couldn't help but grin giddily as he set his notes down and leaned back in his chair and took a deep breath. The lean back and the deep breath were a prewriting ritual for him, but the elation, however, was new. It was the surface-breaking tip of a tremendous iceberg of emotion. He held the breath for a moment, letting his thoughts and memories from the day become organized in his mind, and when he was ready to write, he found that the story began with a blinking red light.

THE FIRST thing Quentin noticed when he walked in the door on that bright blue Saturday morning was the indicative light of the office's message machine.

He put his things on the desk and dialed up the message and listened to the familiar voice of a friendly editor from *The Haverbrook Sun*. They had met years ago while covering the same local event (a small defense contract had been awarded to Kellogg Industries), and Quentin had liked the young reporter, so he sometimes lent an objective ear and the benefit of his local experiences when the kid asked for his help. Over the years, that young reporter had risen to associate editor, and that morning the associate editor had an important lead for Mr. Hancock.

As Quentin listened to the message, his mind shifted quickly from recognition to urgency. The message ended, he slammed the phone down, grabbed his things, and rocketed out the door. He left with such speed that he seemed to be in his car and driving down the street by the time his footsteps made their first thumping sound on the wooden walkway in front of the building.

Within forty minutes, Quentin was pulling up to the Dugan Arts and Innovation building. Without realizing it or legally needing to, he applied the brakes when he saw it. It had been years since he'd last traveled, even to Haverbrook, and the sameness of the Manta architecture had produced a hard callus that covered the aesthetic sensitivity in his brain. As he looked at the sweeping grace of the building, with its delicate band of windows and the skeletal strength of its exposed steel beams, he was taken aback, if only momentarily.

He parked and went inside and followed the editor's instructions to a meeting room in the back of the building. Sitting just outside the door was a city reporter for *The Haver-*

brook Sun—his friend's employee.

"It's really happening?" Quentin asked.

Before the other reporter could answer, he was interrupted by the sound of two doors being thrown open, numerous hard-bottomed shoes clacking across the marble floor, and multilayered voices resonating from the other end of the hallway. Three well-dressed people—two men and a woman—having an animated discussion, which was impossible to understand because of the echoes, clattered busily in Quentin's direction and, ignoring the two reporters, right through the doorway outside of which the reporters sat. The muffled conversation continued and then died down quickly, and then a voice from within the room asked the reporters to come in.

"I'll take that as a yes," Quentin said.

Two groups of people were seated at a large conference table. On the far end were Kellogg Industries CEO Shelton Elliott, Haverbrook Mayor Joe Valaitis, Ace Dugan estate lawyer Graham Hanley, and next to him his two paralegals, a male and female whose names Quentin never got. On the closer end of the table, with several chairs separating them from the other party on both sides, sat the other group: Luminarian Head Pastor Augustus Hershey, who eyed both reporters icily when they entered, and Manta Mayor Tony Capps, who looked aloofly detached from the whole affair.

Graham Hanley was the first to speak.

"Gentlemen," he said addressing the Manta half of the table, "I'm going to keep this brief. In the hopes of having a swift decision rendered, and in response to the town of Manta's numerous protests and complaints about our ongoing development plans, the Dugan Institute, Kellogg Industries, and the city of Haverbrook took our case to State Controller Danielle McHale.

"After looking at the arguments from both sides of the case, her office delivered this ruling last night."

He handed out copies of the document to everyone in the room.

"In short, this document says that Mrs. McHale and the

rest of the lawyers and legislators in the statehouse can find no compelling reason to further entertain the protests coming from the town of Manta. Their ruling is that ours is a perfectly legal project on properly owned land, and they find that the arguments from the Luminarian and Manta communities are lacking in any truly measurable pernicious effect that would warrant a further deliberation on these matters. The bridge is approved, as are all other Haverbrook reconstruction plans."

In the moments that followed, the room would have been completely silent if it weren't for the furious scratching of pencils on paper between the two reporters.

The Haverbrook leaders had already heard this news and had celebrated amongst themselves, but they wanted to appear austere in the face of the total defeat of the other side; the Manta leaders were struck silent by the final legality of the ruling.

While the other reporter asked some Haverbrook-centered questions to Graham Hanley and Mayor Valaitis, Quentin took notes and watched the faces of Augustus Hershey and Tony Capps. Never in his life had he seen Mayor Capps without one of those big beefy smiles on his face. That indulgent, boozy grin was replaced by what looked like an umbrella, mid-collapse. All the corners were pointed down, and the folded fabric of his lips said everything his voice could not. And Augustus . . . .

It's possible that this was only the second time in his life Augustus didn't get what he wanted. The effect it had on him was a bit more curious than what happened with Mayor Capps. Instead of looking unhappy, he stared at the table steadily; he was not sure what to do.

Augustus was not one for deliberation, so this previously untapped mode of being left Quentin feeling frightened. Although Augustus was obviously in thought, it looked as though he couldn't understand the writing on the document in front of him. His eyes scanned and re-scanned it, but it never produced any visible, cognitive effect.

"Pastor Hershey," Quentin said, holding up his tape recorder, "what do you—"

Augustus Hershey slowly turned and looked at Quentin.

Quentin looked up from his notes and saw that there was more than a touch of madness in Augustus's eyes, and Quentin was so shaken by the man-child's grim aspect that he didn't finish his question.

The meeting was adjourned, and Quentin and the other reporter were the last to leave—still scribbling down notes. Then, with a reaffirming glance at each other, they parted ways.

On the drive back to Manta, Quentin made a short detour, to the south side of town, where the bridge was to be constructed. There were a few groups of people already there, and they were probably doing the same thing Quentin was doing: trying to picture the spectacle.

Eventually, Quentin's eyes fell across the small canyon, to the forest beyond. The leaves turned their faces in the breeze, and Quentin stood there for a long time. He thought about the country outside of this area and about how little any of this could mean to them, and then he thought about the citizens on the other side of that canyon, in a small town hidden in the endless forest.

He looked down the canyon at the river below. It ran forward like all rivers do, and he followed the powerful gash with his eyes all the way to where it turned and disappeared in the army of dark trees.

Then he got in his car and drove back to the office and sat down to write.

QUENTIN EXHALED and began typing the first story in decades that made him feel good, good, good.

35

MARIE RETURNED to Haverbrook after she received an urgent

message from her brother. She was trying not to cry after the long discussion about life and mortality between herself, Huck, and Dalton.

As she drove, she ruminated upon a part of that conversation.

"I think there's an interesting juxtaposition between time and gravity," Dalton had said, "like the way time heals all wounds and like the way gravity pulls all things together. But while time heals wounds, nobody ever talks about how time is also a part of their cause; and while gravity keeps us on the planet, it is also that persistent pull that builds enough friction between hydrogen atoms to cause stars to spark to life and create a twelve-billion-year blast of heat and light."

"So you're saying our wounds—the pains in our life—are like stars?" Halo replied.

"I'm saying—I don't know what I'm saying," Dalton said. "I just see something there."

She found that the time it took to drive to Haverbrook had pulled her back together after the deep sadness of the morning's conversation, but the strain in her brother's voice made her worried what he could need so urgently, and her worries began to collide and cause friction in her mind.

DALTON RETURNED to his place by the river in a somber mood. The cabin was dark except for a light left on in the kitchen. He had lately heard something or someone walking around the cabin at night—people or animals, he wasn't sure. Either way, he left the light on. Now, at night, after the existential conversation with Halo and Marie, Dalton stood outside the cabin in reverie, recognizing how much he loved how beautiful it looked in the inky darkness like this, near the soughing run of the river—like a lone campfire flaring on the desolate face of an abandoned continent.

Exhausted, he trudged up the steps and let himself in, barely making it to the couch before he was asleep.

He was shocked awake by the terrible sound of breaking glass and a loud thud against the wall near his kitchen. He heard voices and footsteps, but before he could wash the grog off himself the noises were gone, replaced by a light breeze whistling in through the shattered window on his front door.

He rushed to the window, but he could only make out the silhouettes of four figures sprinting across Jane's backyard. He briefly sighed, and for the first time in three years he was glad Marie was not with him.

Across the lawn, he saw a few lights come on in Jane's house, and he knew she was already hurrying to see if he was all right. He put on some shoes and started sweeping up the broken glass. He looked around but couldn't find the object that had gone through the window and thudded against the wall.

The door flew open and a huffing-and-puffing Jane burst into the cabin with her eyes wide, scanning for bodies or smoke, waving a fire stoker.

"I'm all right," Dalton said. "It's okay."

"Those bastards!" Jane said. "This ain't even your cabin!"

"Just some kids causing trouble," Dalton said. "I'll talk to Augustus tomorrow and see if we can get this straightened out."

"I'm just glad you're okay," Jane said, dropping to the couch. "Ow!"

As she sat, her foot jammed up against a red brick with a note attached to it.

"There it is," Dalton said.

Jane picked it up.

"Yours?" she asked.

"It is now," he said, taking it from her. "Let's see what it says—something really deep, no doubt."

Dalton unwrapped the note and held it to the light. *"The darkness is coming for you."*

"Is that all?" Jane asked.

"Looks like it," Dalton said.

"Do you have any idea what it means?"

Dalton pulled out Quentin's notebook and turned to a well-worn section on the matters of good and evil, highlighting a particular favorite speech of the pastor's.

"Yes, I think I do," he said and took a seat next to Jane, his heart in tenth gear as his body flooded with adrenaline in the aftershock.

36

MARIE PARKED at the Kellogg Industries engineering campus and was directed to her brother's office, which was empty.

Everyone in the building seemed to be in high spirits, but she wasn't going to stop feeling funny until she saw that her brother was fine.

In an instant, the door flew open, and her smiling brother erupted into the room.

"Ah, you are here!"

He danced over to his sister, picked her up off the chair, and twirled her. "It is happening, and they are using my design!"

"Whoa, whoa, whoa—slow down, brother!" Marie said, relieved that everything was okay but still not comprehending what was said.

Jean-Luc swung her down to one of the seats in front of his desk, and he sat on the arm of the other one.

"Mr. Dugan's lawyers steamrolled the city of Manta, and now Haverbrook and Kellogg are moving forward with the big bridge!"

"Wow!" Marie said. "Wait a minute, so that means—"

"Took you long enough! Yes! They chose my design!"

"Oh my goodness, Jean-Luc, I am so happy!" She stood and they hugged. "We must celebrate! You and me!"

They set out immediately, and because it was the only place Jean-Luc ever went (he had a secret crush on a bartender who worked there), they headed to the bar across the street. It was crowded with other Kellogg Industries employees, all celebrating the bounteous event.

Marie and Jean-Luc had two places specially set aside for

them by Jean-Luc's coworkers. Everyone bought drinks for everyone as the jukebox helped trumpet their glee into the vibrating air. All night, glasses were raised and glad toasts were given. At one point, someone shouted out, "If anyone goes to bed alone tonight, they're fired!" and all voices cried out in exuberant celebration.

The news of Jean-Luc's triumph had already spread among the Kellogg crowd, and he couldn't go anywhere without being paddled forward by hard, jovial slaps on the back—"Attaboy, Jean-Luc!"

Also there that night, by chance, in a dark corner, mixed congruously in the general celebration, was Nathan Cameron, a hat pulled low over his eyes as he talked to a flirting, intoxicated woman.

Marie noticed, and her brother, returning with two handfuls of free drinks he'd been given, noticed her notice.

"Should we tell Victoria?" Marie asked, their secrets protected by the loud clamor of the crowd.

"No," Jean-Luc said, setting down the drinks. "I like Victoria, too, but there is nothing good that comes from our meddling in that mess, sister."

Marie thought about it. She shrugged.

"I guess you are right," she said. Turning the corner, but staying in the same neighborhood, she asked. "Do you know who the woman is?"

"Leslie Boyd," Jean-Luc said. "She works for me."

"She is older than you," Marie noticed.

"She hates me."

"She is jealous, brother."

"Why should she be jealous?" Jean-Luc asked. "She has Nathan."

They both laughed.

AUGUSTUS HERSHEY could hardly breathe. The late news from the city of Haverbrook was, of course, devastating. He had lost his first public battle with the resurgent forces of anti-Luminarianism, and his congregation (his now that his father was in the last throes of a terminal disease) was nothing short of petulant. Visitors poured into and out of his home and his church office continually. They offered help or they vented about the world's profound injustices and their personal miseries. Whether the visits were positive or negative in nature, they summed in fraying Augustus's nerves to an exposed, open rawness.

He sat in his office, quietly and mournfully playing a soft melody his father had plagiarized from Donald Byrd, when he heard an uncharacteristic knock at his door, and at once he knew who it was.

"Come in, Mr. Hughes."

Dalton entered quietly, holding something in his hand. He set it down on the desk with a heavy thud.

"I am here to issue a request that you pay Jane Jefferson for the window some of your followers broke last night," Dalton said.

"What are you talking about?"

"This town is too small for me to believe you don't know about the incident to which I am referring, so I would ask that you not treat me like one of your parishioners. Please send Jane a check, and I'm willing to forget about the whole thing. I won't even ask for an apology."

Augustus, who was sitting forward over his instrument, set the trumpet on its stand next to his two saxophones (alto and tenor) and leaned back in his chair and studied Dalton.

"So you're claiming a group of Luminarians broke a window at your cabin with that?" he said, motioning to the brick.

"Yes, sir."

"I'm sorry, Dalton, but with only your word against nobody else's, there's really not much of a charge here, and the Luminarian community just doesn't have the funds to go around repairing other people's broken windows."

"You're probably right," Dalton said. "Your followers are uneducated and have virtually no use except as accompanying thieves in your weekly rip-off sessions, forced to sign over their rights and children to you so you can bask in your own controlling perversion, so I can't see how they'd be able to offer much money. But either way, you're going to pay Miss

Jefferson back."

"Mr. Hughes, I'm a very busy man . . ." Augustus said, rising to dismiss his guest.

"I understand, Augustus," Dalton said. "And you're going to become much busier, what with the whole world about to drive through your front door. But, before I go, I have to ask one last time: you won't be repaying Miss Jefferson?"

"Get out of here."

"Okay."

Dalton stood and turned. He took a step and then turned back. He grabbed the brick off the desk with one hand and fished in his pocket with the other. He threw a piece of paper down on the desk.

"See you soon," Dalton said as he walked out.

Augustus picked up the piece of paper and read it. "*The darkness is coming for you*," was crossed out.

"*Let there be light*," was written above it.

Augustus frowned and again leaned back in his chair. Then he heard the sound of shattering glass.

37

CLEM LEMON arrived late in the afternoon with the items Halo requested. He knew what Huck was planning, but it did not make him happy, even if he could understand the point his now-frail friend was endeavoring to make. They were old now—time-withered husks of the great men they once were. But despite Clem being able to understand Halo's intentions, he was reminded of a cogent thought he'd once overheard between two students back in his teaching days. One student had said to the other, "There's a big difference between being okay with something and not being able to do anything about it."

It was exactly how he felt now.

All the discomforts of being old and thinking about the end of their lives made him wonder if living this long had been worth it—if living at all were worth it at all.

Sure it was, Clem thought. He figured that was all the immortal knowledge he would achieve in this life. Despite his many degrees and titles, he still grappled with the enigma of seeking enlightenment by trying to free himself from desire—goals that seemed at odds to him. So this little self-assurance, this approving nod to the life he had lived and was living, seemed to be sufficient.

It was not enough for Halo Kilgore.

Clem could see that old age had sent Huck down a morbid path, but instead of following his friend down it, Clem traversed over to a well-worn-though-long-neglected path of his own: a return to his love of hunting.

He found he enjoyed the sport of it, rather than the murder, so he replaced his old rifle with a paintball gun. He figured that hunting with a modern, scoped rifle is like stepping into a boxing ring wielding a sword—it's just cheating. A game plan, patience, the pressure of combining coordination with silence . . . it made him almost feel young again. The point wasn't the kill; it was the skill. Even better than that, it was the feeling of being completely immersed in the moment.

In an essay he wrote about it, which he shared with Dalton and Halo, who had both mildly mocked his paintball-hunting excursions, he wrote, "We are all hunting, always, in a great many ways. For most people, their hunt ends at the most convenient edible plants, and there they are sated. But we would still be eating ticks off of each other on the floor of the forest if there weren't those of us who preferred something far more challenging and rewarding. But, in the modern world, why should I kill these animals when it is unnecessary? Instead, I simply shoot them in their ribcage, near their heart, with a pellet of paint that, when it hits, sits on their chest as the only full stop I should ever wish to impart to them."

Meanwhile, Huck couldn't stop feeling old. Whereas he'd once been a sprightly, intelligent dynamo with a wit as quick and powerful as a lightning strike, he could now see that his barbs were more blunted, his memory spotty, and his pen, while still formidable, losing its luster. He'd been to the top of the highest mountains his mind could climb, and now he was finding that the sturdy legs and Himalayan heart that once braved the thin air of those isolated peaks had decayed, and the feeling was made so much worse because of what he once had been. It was a long, devastating fall from those heights.

Whether or not he would ever see his wife again—in some sort of post-mortem hyper-reality—he just wanted to be able to sleep and rest. It had been so long. His sleep came in fits, and his rest was never restful. He awoke more tired than before he slept, with the constant ache of his mortality keeping his mind terribly occupied on the misery of his physical and mental dégringolade.

But the two men, despite their deepening age, and perhaps even because of it, maintained their friendship. They missed youth. They missed who they were and what they could do. They were quietly envious of the ignorant, who can die so seamlessly. They sat together and talked and watched long afternoons fade into darkness, and they thought about what that meant, those evenings slowly peeling the night sky.

Clem set the camera equipment on the cube and walked over to the fireplace, which was more or less where Huck spent most of his time now, warming his cold hands, thinking, reflecting, and preparing himself. The two reclined, tired, and let the day crawl past the long windows above their heads as they contemplatively drank old wine and listened to the perfect notes of pained jazz combine with the concordant notes of their own existential atrophy.

38

"The window repairs should be finished by midweek. I apologize for the ghastly look of our church foyer, and I humbly ask that our community refrain from taking any retribution; I will deal with the guilty party personally. Let us move on, now, to the keynote of today's sermon.

"I'm afraid I must compound our despair with still further bad news. We lost, my brothers and sisters. Our bid to keep our harmonious community unspoiled by the rot of nonbelievers was overruled earlier this week by the city council of Haverbrook and the state government, and construction on the Dugan Bridge will begin soon. We stand now in the quiet before the tempest. In many ways, such is our life. We live in the still before the storm, and the things that happen to us are mere glimpses into the power of what comes after we die.

"Because when we die, true believers in the universal music of the Lorrah are reconnected totally to the wondrous form of the Infinite Choir. We set off on an endless adventure within the all-encompassing body of the fluted universe. Shannon Penrose is there, her adventure unfolding as we sit and pray and toil on this earthly soil. She is with the Lorrah now, and the Lorrah is all that is good, and even we are distant memories to Shannon, for where she is now is so complete and so glorious that it's impossible for her to think of anything about her shortened life on Earth.

"But for the nonbelievers, death is an unending deployment to The Void. A man who's never felt the music of the Lorrah flow through his soul dies and comes upon a limitless emptiness, where forever he floats, disembodied, unable to tear himself apart, howling with madness and loneliness. This loneliness envelops him like a death shroud, but it has not the mercy of death. Whether his eyes are open or closed, it does not matter; nothingness finds him. He is ground into irreducibility, and all memories of his life are at the tip of his consciousness, but the only thing he can think about and wonder is where he could have gone wrong to end up in such a lonely and impossibly empty place.

"The nothingness will suffocate him, but he will not die. He will howl, but nothing will sound.

"Let us rise and fill the air with the music of the Lorrah, for such is our purpose, and such is our duty."

The music began.

NATHAN CAMERON stopped by *The Radical Post* at the end of Dalton's workday, and he walked with Dalton back to the cabin by the river, where they took a seat across from each other on the porch and shared a joint.

Nathan had something to tell Dalton, and he lit the joint and handed it over.

Dalton pinched the slim joint between his thumb and index finger and, before he took a drag, asked, "So what's up, Nathan? You're making me nervous."

He took a hit and passed it to Nathan, who also pinched the joint between thumb and index finger in the "OK" sign.

"I was able to talk to Augustus about that window thing," he said, looking over to the pane of cardboard Dalton was using to cover the gap of the door's broken window. "I was able to convince him of the point you were making. Nobody saw who broke your window, and nobody saw you break the window at the church. We all just have our words now." He took a drag and handed it back.

He continued. "But that's just for now, and that's just Augustus. Pretty much everyone else has kind of turned you into the scapegoat for this whole mess. I really think you should get out of town for a while. I feel like some bad things are coming."

"Like what?"

"Like I said, it's just a feeling. I don't even know how to explain it, but I definitely feel something strange in the air out there."

"That's a huge surprise," Dalton said sarcastically. "But why me? What about you? Or Quentin? Or Jane?"

"Well, they talk a lot about you, Quentin, *and* Jane, but

those two have a deep history with this town. The church existed for many years with their . . . let's call it . . . 'unwanted' . . . presence, but then you arrived, and things started getting slippery for them. First Shannon died, and Phillip got sick, and then Ace Dugan died and kick-started this whole bridge mess, and . . . you know."

"And you? You arrived a little before I did."

"Yeah, but I'm a believer."

"Are you?"

"What's that mean? Of course I am."

Dalton looked at Nathan skeptically. He probed.

"Nathan, people like you don't actually join anything."

It took a few moments before Nathan replied.

"I don't know what you're talking about, man."

"You don't know what I'm talking about . . ." Dalton said. The orange wink of the joint grew brighter as he inhaled. "I guess that makes sense." Dalton thought to himself, *When you do something long enough, it becomes a part of who you are, and to have someone point it out would probably seem confusing.*

"Hey, man, I don't need this," Nathan said, turning to leave. "I just wanted to catch up and warn you because I think you're a good dude and some of these people are nuts. That's all."

"Thank you, Nathan," Dalton said and handed the joint back to him as a kind of peace offering. "I apologize for the psychological profile. My mouth gets ahead of me sometimes."

"Yeah," Nathan said.

"The thing is, though," Dalton said, "I don't see what they can do to me. This cabin is Jane's, and the rest of my life has been a ginger walk across thin ice, summoning only enough will and resolve to make it across, for fear that too much of anything would sink me. Intentionally, I don't have much to take."

"Do you suppose that whatever you do have means that much more to you than it would to most people?" Nathan asked.

"Maybe," Dalton said, weighing it in his mind. "Or that much less."

The joust paused for a moment. Dalton gazed at the dark-stained planks of wood on the creaking porch floor.

"And anyway," Dalton said, "what's the problem with having a new bridge outside of town? Even Augustus said the Luminarian Church recognizes that the universal symphony changes pitch and tune and tempo. Isn't that what's happening here?"

Nathan took a hit and stubbed out the joint. "There is a revulsion to the idea of the bridge that runs through our church's core, Dalton. And have you ever known anything that could change its core without being destroyed?"

Dalton looked at Nathan, and the look was his reply.

In Haverbrook, Mayor Valaitis held an impromptu press conference/civic rally. All day, people had been gathering near the canyon, and some even climbed down to the river itself and sat on its banks and watched it run its course. There was excitement in the air. The attendees were a mix of Haverbrook and Manta citizens.

A person could easily tell one from the other. A Haverbrook man or woman was dressed simply but comfortably—old country boots; a well-worn pair of jeans; a loose, casual T-shirt. A Manta man or woman was dressed in the coarse blandness of the pious—black boots; a black, stiff pair of pants; a starched, white, collared shirt beneath a black jacket; and an unusual hat. The men's hats were black, about eight inches tall, square in shape but rounded slightly at the corners, with a thin brim all the way around. Around the "mid-barrel" of the hat were three holes of about a half-inch diameter on each side. For women, the design was the same, but it was white, and the front of the hat was cut out, and the hat was pulled down over the ears like a bonnet. Otherwise, the women wore loose-fitting, neck-to-ankle length, black dresses.

A Haverbrook face showed curiosity and a general excitement about the proceedings; a Manta face showed the down-turned corners of the bitter-mouthed, and the expression otherwise seemed to suggest a sort of condescending hatred. Each face, from both sides, was now turned to Mayor Valaitis, who addressed them all.

"Today is a new beginning for the city of Haverbrook! Today, we break ground on the biggest civil plan in our town's great history. Today, the lifelong dream of our friend and benefactor—the great Antaeus Chapman Dugan—takes a first step toward becoming an amazing reality!"

The gathered crowd erupted into loud noise divided along the factional lines—cheers and jeers.

Large construction machines sat idle, waiting to be put to use on the project that would span the river's heavy rush near the southern tip of Haverbrook. A large, watercolor drawing of the completed project stood next to the Haverbrook mayor as he gave his speech. Many in the crowd remarked at the bridge's unusual design, and opinions were split as to its aesthetic value. Some considered it overly ambitious, and some just gazed in awe at the sight of what was there now and what would be there soon—reveling in the inspiration of what a man could do with the right motivations.

39

CLEM LEMON taught theology courses at some of the world's most prestigious universities, and only once in his career did he let his own personal theology be known—during the last class he would ever teach.

Sitting in the back of the room on that day was an already-retired Halo Kilgore, who'd grown a gruff beard and donned unusually normal clothes (Huck typically had a flair for the sartorially absurd) so as not to attract attention to himself and away from his dear friend during what was to be a particularly difficult class. Clem loved teaching, but he was done—like a ballplayer who wakes up one morning and realizes that the best and brightest moments of his playing days are in the past, and the only thing, the most painful thing, left to do is to put an end to his daily attempts to rekindle the dying embers of his ability, to stop fanning his own ashes.

"It has long been debated around silly academic circles what my own personal thoughts on theology might be, and I never wanted to disclose the information because I was afraid it would slant my students' understanding of my lessons and give greater weight to those ideas, ideals, and idols I personally held than those I merely taught, out of a respect for the wide breadth of religious traditions the world over. However, now that I am retiring forever from this job I've loved for as long as I've done it, I am going to let my personal religion be known, to silence some of the preposterous things I've heard referenced in my name."

At that point one of the brighter students in the class raised her hand. "Professor Clem, won't this disclosure proactively slant the future students of your book in the way that you worried it would? Just because you won't be around to teach anymore doesn't mean your book will vanish and other teachers will stop assigning it."

"Good question," Clem replied. "I have two answers: one, I don't care." The class had a small laugh at that. "And two, my religion isn't in my book.

"It's a one-man gospel."

He began pacing the room.

"There is no name for my religion. It is mine, and to name it would do it a disservice, as anything given a name can be so easily pigeonholed, manacled, and mocked. In the words of the immortal *Tao Te Ching*, 'The whole world says that my way is vast and resembles nothing. It is because it is vast that it resembles nothing. If it resembled anything, it would, long before now, have become small.' So I'm not going to name it, but I will tell you—just so you can possibly get an approximate picture of the sunny coast of my beliefs—that the closest established religion to it is the Theravada sect of Buddhism. But I would add that my little raft has a number of odd-looking outriggers and pontoons.

"I've never been able to fully embrace the idea that life has any sort of intracollective meaning. Each of us is born alone, and each of us will die alone. Even in the company of our friends and family, it is an uncompromisingly individual passage, which to me means that the struggle to understand the nature of the universe and the bodies we inhabit is essentially a personal and individual battle.

"I believe in quiet meditation, whether it be on paradoxes and koans or merely an attempt to let the rushing buzz of my brain settle. I like to think of it as giving the mud of my mind an opportunity to be dried, and to separate the water from the dirt. The human brain is the most impressive organ in the universe, and it is capable of so many profound things. But it is also capable of turning against itself—of becoming so full of fluff and useless toil that it effectively overheats, and the many machinations it's capable of become a tangled mess, and what results is what I call busy nothing.

"Whether we are reincarnated after we die or whether we merely turn to dust in a state not unlike the feeling of sleep—meaning the feeling of no feeling—is not something for which I have an answer. Nor do I even try anymore. What I do try is to keep my mind from being overrun with busy nothing, and I try to find little universal insights during my trek through this inexplicable existence.

"I believe in impermanence, which isn't even a matter of faith. Look around at your life, at the way the mountains are shaped, the way that rivers run the course of least resistance, the way that animal species die out while others are discovered. Whether that impermanence is guided by the spiritual forces of some all-knowing godhead or whether it is governed by the physical laws born from of a universe that spun itself into existence is again something for which I do not and cannot have the answer: the only answer that matters is impermanence. I am getting older, and I will die. And not only will I die, but my body will turn to dust. The layers of my life will peel away until all that I am is the skeletal form of what I was, and even that will decay, and I will be gone completely. So will you. So will your children and heroes. We all die, and we are all replaced. Nothing is permanent but the impermanence.

"But that isn't to say that impermanence is what is beautiful. The lifespan of a flower is certainly a wonderful thing, but is not its fullest and finest bloom a rare bit of pure universal poetry? There are moments in this kaleidoscopic universe that are so beautiful as to be beyond my ability to assemble descriptive words—grunts—that would do them any of the justice they deserve, and it is those moments that we must recognize and cherish, for they are the flashbulbs in the universal swirl, and they are what fill our lives with experiences of value and meaning.

"Life is bitter and sweet. It is a finite look at an infinite universe. It is an impermanent mix of the glorious and the horrible. We love and we hate. We lust and we feel shame. We see an animal kingdom that appears to be in perfect harmony, and then we zoom in and we see a pride of lions biting chunks of flesh out of a living zebra.

"We are the universe's eyes, brain, and heart. This universe, which for so long existed as an impossibly vast landscape dotted intermittently with bright stars and devoted planets, eventually produced mankind, a truly rare species—a metaphysical manifestation of life, sight, thought, and feeling. We are the universe observing itself and changing itself.

"That constant universal change. You can see it everywhere if you just pull back far enough and look. That is just the beginning of what I believe, and it is also the end.

"It's all I need."

Clem and Huck Kilgore recalled that speech with fine affection during a gray Sunday morning in late autumn. It was Halo who'd brought it up, because he had something important he wanted to discuss with his friend.

"Do you still believe all that?" Halo asked.

"I still believe in the basic ideas of what I said that day, yes," Clem said. "But as I mentioned so many times, life is impermanence. Some ideas have changed."

"Do you remember those pictures you showed me, of that final meditation outside that village?"

"Yes," Clem said, already knowing where his friend was going with this.

"Will you . . . do it?"

Clem could feel the muscles in his throat tighten while at the same time a tear welled at the corner of his eye.

"When?"

"Soon enough."

Outside, the season's first snow began to fall. It silently accumulated.

40

DALTON HUGHES sat forward and ran his fingers through his hair while he let out a long breath of stale air. He'd been poring over the contents of six different letters to the editor in which he himself was referred to in a wide array of unprintable epithets. He had to choose which three of the six would be best for the publication, but the prospect had grown taxing. They were all so poorly written and so rife with frustration that he almost felt bad for the citizens, for being so unreasonably scared of what was happening. But mostly he was feeling the same fury that always resulted when he was involved in any kind of incompetence, particularly when it involved something he revered so deeply, like writing, that it caused him physical pain.

There was a brief knock at the office front door, and the timid figure of a terrified-looking Marcia White stepped inside. The first thing Dalton noticed after the sadness and fear in her face was the large bruise on the inside of her forearm as she wrestled with her winter jacket.

Dalton sat up immediately and turned all his attention to her.

"Marcia," Dalton said. "Are you all right?"

"I wrote a letter," Marcia said, but though she held the

sturdy folder in front of her, she did not hand it to the young man.

"Oh, good," Dalton said. "I was just going over some letters. Perfect timing."

Marcia didn't move.

"May I see it?" Dalton asked.

"This was a bad idea," Marcia said, and she turned to go.

Dalton followed her outside.

"I don't have to print the letter," Dalton said. "If you've got something to get off your chest, it might be wise to . . . whether it's in this letter or if you just want to step back inside and talk to someone."

Dalton was fond of Marcia, the first Luminarian he ever saw. These days he knew her—held her in high regard, even—because of the quality of her writing. He had published several of her letters to the editor.

"I mean, this can be just between you and me, if the newspaper thing worries you."

Marcia stopped walking and turned around. As she was about to address Dalton, Councilman Joe O'Brien emerged from a nearby general store and saw the two of them talking. His face became serious. He didn't want anyone in the community talking to a non-Luminarian, and certainly not Dalton Hughes—not now.

"I know we have our differences, Ms. White," Dalton said, eyeing Councilman O'Brien, "but I don't appreciate you saying those sorts of things about Mr. Hancock, especially when he's not here to defend himself. Frankly, it's rude."

At that, Dalton caught Marcia's eye for a moment and turned back inside. Marcia played her part perfectly. She followed him inside as she said, "I can talk about that old rat any way I want!"

Councilman O'Brien looked pleased and walked on.

After the two watched the councilman's squat figure disappear into an office across the street, Marcia turned back to Dalton and threw herself into him—hugging him, crying.

She cried horribly and quickly. When she was finished, when the sobs and shudders ceased, she wiped her eyes clean and said, "It's all in the letter."

She walked to the door, turned, and said, "Please . . . I need help." And then she walked out.

Dalton sat in the morose silence for a moment, letting pure emotion and intrigue rush over him, and he let it all recede. Then he turned his attention to the folder and the letter inside.

> *Dear Editor,*
>
> *I have been a Luminarian all my life. Every branch in my family tree is watered by the Luminarian baptismal fountain. I am just like many of the people in our town. This community is all I know, all I've ever known, and I too have been affected by the goings-on in Haverbrook. But not in the same way as most people.*
>
> *Augustus and Phillip Hershey taught us that the true path to the Lorrah is the light, and that all shadow is created when there are obstructions between the Lorrah and our souls. And if light can be related to truth, as our leaders imply, then it is time for our community to see the light and know it and not be hidden from it.*
>
> *The truth is that I was physically and sexually assaulted by six members of the church community in punishment for trying to keep my child away from the very Luminarian leaders who attacked me.*
>
> *When they returned my Shelly from her genesis weekend, she cried for three days. I found blood. I don't know what they did to her, but she hasn't been the same ever since. She recoils from me—her mother! my child!—and she recoils from all human contact. My greatest fear is that she and I have in common the horrible reality that we were both sexually assaulted by the very men who claim to protect us and keep us in the Lorrah's so-called good grace.*
>
> *That is the dark light which you all worship! Those are the vicious actions of our best church*

members!

I cheer in my heart when I hear the loud protests against the construction of the Dugan Bridge, not because I side with the protestors but because I celebrate their pathetic frustration. Let the light of knowledge infiltrate this backwards town! Let the light of the Lorrah truly shine upon the dark hearts of her leaders! I salute the work of Kellogg Industries and worship at the feet of young Jean-Luc Delphine. That is a man of noble virtue—a man who creates with his mind a world of opportunities for everyone! Ten-thousand Augustus Hersheys and Nathan Camerons could never make up for one Jean-Luc Delphine.

A person's spirit is his own, and it cannot be tended to by foolish leaders high on their own self-proclaimed importance. A person's spirit is his own, and yet at least two individual spirits in this community were not sublimated but coldly extinguished by these horrible, "important" spiritual leaders. My heart and my daughter's heart are forever hardened by the cruel actions of these men, and to quote another great man, "May you burn in the Hell you invented for yourselves."

Sincerely,
Marcia White

THE FOLLOWING night, a familiar old man in a familiar truck, who'd given Dalton his phone number before they departed each other's company three years ago, picked up Marcia and Shelly White and drove them to a women's shelter in the city of Dover. It was a long drive that took them through the night, and they arrived as the orange sun was halfway up the horizon-line. Before they left, they said goodbye to Dalton and Jane—the only two people in town who knew they were leaving.

Jane had packed them a basket of food and provisions for the road. She had also signed a traveler's check over to Marcia for half-a-million dollars. Marcia found the check later that day, as she and her daughter ate lunch out of the basket at a picnic table. She burst into tears, her body shuddering from the storm of conflicting emotions—the horror of what had happened before, and the blessing of what was finally happening now.

Little Shelly confusedly watched her mom. They had been eating lunch, and then her mother picked up a piece of paper and started crying, and the table shook from her mother's shudders. Scared, little Shelly started crying, too.

Marcia picked up her head, and then she picked up her daughter and set her on her lap.

"What is that, Mama?" Shelly asked, pointing to the piece of paper through her still-falling tears.

The piece of paper was a note from Jane.

Don't ever worry about paying me back. You deserve more than hope, and I still have more money than I'll ever need. Please, be smart and safe. Be wise and well. Be good.
  —Jane

41

DALTON READ the contents of Marcia's letter to a haggard-looking Huck Kilgore, who listened quietly. During the more unpleasant passages, Dalton could see a wince of pain in the man's face, which he had tried and failed to mask.

"You're going to publish it?"

"Mr. Hancock's thinking about it, but there are some legal ramifications to consider," Dalton said.

"You should publish it."

"I agree, but it's *The Radical Post*, not *The Bulletproof Vest*."

Halo chuckled.

"Dalton, what will you do when I'm gone?"

Dalton took a moment to consider a truthful reply.

"I guess I'll do whatever comes naturally, Huck," Dalton said.

"Why did you come here? I know you think you followed me here, but that's not all of it."

Huck leaned up on his elbow, turning his eyes away from the dancing reflection of the fireplace's flames glowing on the curved metal wall. He watched the living flesh of the young man's thoughtful face.

Dalton's eyes scanned back and forth rapidly as his brain tried to cobble it all together. Then, Huck saw the end of that cogitative process: the boy's face indicated he had put together a sufficient answer. Dalton took a breath.

"Something happened to me when I matured. I had a happy childhood, and a wonderful family, and I was safe. And then I grew into my teenage years, and I got very sad. There are many reasons for why this could be, and I've thought over them many times, but nothing permanently satisfies, and, because of that, I don't know how to correct whatever it is that went wrong—especially if it's, as I sometimes suspect, purely physiological, bad wiring. What I do know is that as I developed and changed from boy to man, there began a long succession of these morbid images that would flash through my mind—images of me putting a gun to my head and blasting my brains in a wide spray, relieving all that *pressure* inside of myself. Images of taking a large knife and pulling it roughly up the veins of my forearms. Images of leaping from lethal heights, and boom. Sweet nothing. Something went wrong, and in the subsequent years I felt myself drifting further and further from the world and the people around me. Like a ship with broken navigation that loses sight of the shore and can never find it again . . . Or . . . .

"Another idea that flashed through my mind was that human interaction is based on a sort of shared gravitational wavelength, like the planets that circle the sun. Some people are highly attuned to this wavelength—people like Nathan Cameron, who can somehow get along perfectly with everyone from outsiders like me to insiders like Augustus Hershey. They are highly attuned to the shared social gravity of humanity. And then there are people who are pathetically out of tune with this wavelength, and at times I felt this way, like I was a false planet on a slow and ever-widening trajectory away from the pull of that gravity—that so-important gravity that is the catalyst for all human civilization and life.

"I felt like a mistake—a lonely mistake with the superior privilege of being capable of destroying itself.

"But I didn't do it.

"Though I was a lonely planet falling away from everything that was supposed to matter, I still found bits of powerful beauty in my life and the universe into which I quietly flew. I was able to look out over the field of stars I was entering and feel the amazing potential of the goodness in everything, and that kept me going. And I found this beauty in all sorts of things. Things like . . . like I remember arcing a basketball through the air and knowing, with this metaphysical *certainty*, that it was going in, and then the still-surprising satisfaction when it did, with the ball slipping soundlessly through the rim and snapping the net—the sound of a moment's perfection. Or out in nature, on daily walks, watching the green leaves of summer torched by the cool air of autumn—wandering pensively through the valleys of that colorful inferno. Or when I was a janitor. The older janitors would have these conversations—during work breaks we'd all go to Carl's office—and these guys were so *dumb*. They were so dumb it, like, flipped the scales and became brilliant, the way they talked. It broke my heart, you know, and filled me with like this intoxicating combination of pity and humility. Or as a kid taking my bike to the top of this giant hill in my hometown, having to walk it up there because it was too steep to ride, and at the flat top, pedaling my hardest to build up a real world-blurring velocity, and then rocketing down the hill, whipping past cars, feeling the shaking hum in my handlebars vibrating up from the black blur of my tires on the pavement, with wind-tears flying from my eyes all the way down the twisting hill and then slinging along the flat land at the base, until my momentum ran out, and that crackling feeling as my heart tried to decelerate itself, my hands not to jitter. Or like that first day in the spring when the sharp angles of winter winds are widened, you know, and *rounded*, and change from an assault to an embrace—my old friend called it The Day—and the way people walk freely that day, and smile at each other hopefully, relieved by winter's sweet decay.

"Things like that.

"It was enough to keep me going.

"I read a lot. It was one of the things I legitimately enjoyed, or at least when I was reading good writing. In all of the passages I read, Dr. Kilgore, you were the only other person I found who I thought could relate to the things I carried within myself. The way you wrote, I could feel how you had taken that estranged loneliness and turned it into a brilliant life.

"So I thought I would follow in the wake of your own existential drift, having nothing better to do.

"I saw a beacon in the oblivion and followed it here.

"And then I met Marie, and that's when I knew I did the right thing. The force of her being was able to pull me back toward the life that I was missing. And meeting you was only natural after that."

Huck shifted his position to get a better look at the young man staring into the fire. For a moment, they sat quietly, thinking about what Dalton had just said.

"Nice try," Huck said.

"Thanks."

"It was a nice rant, but it didn't exactly answer my question. What are you doing here now? What's next? *'What's it going to be then, eh?'*"

Dalton stared at the fire and smirked.

"Why, Huck—immortality, of course."

Huck smiled faintly. Sadly, he then grew serious.

"I can't stand the thought of it," he said.

"Of being gone?"

"Yeah," Huck said. "Had we met at any earlier point in my life, we could have been great friends. I wrote those books for myself, Dalton. They were my way of entertaining myself during my drift into my own oblivion, but that they helped you through your tumult is a deeply rewarding bit of causation. To think that I played any part in aiding in the impressive young man you are today makes me as contented as I've felt in years.

"But I can't be the friend I was, Dalton. I'm not the man I was. I'm barely myself anymore. And it's all only going away."

"You're here now, Huck," Dalton said. "In whatever form you are, you are loved now, by great people. And if that's not enough, then piss off."

Dalton looked at Huck for a reaction, and happily he got the smirk he was hoping for.

"Anyway, what about your estate? What about what's next for you? What will become of the finances from your books and lectures and your property?"

"I don't know. I just can't bring myself to care about any of that."

"So you don't have a will?"

"I don't have a family. I don't have anyone to give anything to."

"What about giving it away?"

"To whom? You?"

Dalton laughed.

"No," he said. "Medical research or something, like Ace Dugan. The money is going to go somewhere; you might as well give it to organizations you believe in, if there are any."

Huck mused on that as they sat in the yellow light of the fireplace.

"Okay. Clem knows a lawyer. Have him draft up a will, giving all my money to Marie," he said. "Tell her what you just told me."

Halo Kilgore started coughing. Long and loud. He'd been doing it more and more lately, but it being the height of flu season, Dalton wasn't overly concerned—until he saw blood in the expectoration.

"Shit, Huck," Dalton said, grabbing a tissue and handing it to his friend. "How long has that been happening?"

"Couple weeks," Huck said.

Dalton sat back down and watched as Huck dribbled mucus and blood clumsily into the tissue.

"I can feel it growing inside me," Huck said, and Dalton could see him searching within himself to fully feel the feeling, to investigate it. When he returned, he said, "It's death."

"Why don't you get Clem or Quentin to take you to a doctor?"

"I don't plan on living much longer, Dalton. I want to go home."

Dalton leaned back and looked around the spacious room.

"No," Huck said. "My real home—not my exile."

Halo was looking at something that wasn't in the room, something that was the opposite of the place he went to investigate what was within himself. In his mind, he was in Ariel's arms, and she was in his, and he was looking at his own death.

42

Marcia White's letter ran in the next day's paper. The Luminarian reaction was predictably vitriolic. The home Marcia and Shelly lived in was burned to the ground despite the fact that they didn't own it. (It was owned by the church.) The four-man Manta Fire Department was never called to the scene—the townspeople let the house burn to its foundation.

It snowed that night, and most of the snow in the sky fell to the ground and piled into a bright white erasure. The snow above the burning house melted into a whisper of rain that landed on the upturned faces of the angry citizens.

The flames licked at the sides of the houses surrounding it, and that caused an uproar amongst the neighbors, but the church leaders explained it was an apt metaphor for what happens when the church is deserted and "lies" are allowed to spread like volatile fuel.

That night, Dalton and Quentin returned to their respective homes and found them to be surrounded by Luminarians. There were no injuries, but the message was clear.

Dalton wrote an editorial about the town's reaction to the letter, but by then the entire town was boycotting the paper.

BECAUSE OF her connection to Dalton, Marie was also feeling the reactionary response to the letter. Attendance at the restaurant was down, and she began to feel an undeniable coldness coming from the Manta townspeople.

She received another strange call from her brother while she was at work—strange because he rarely ever called anyone—and he asked her to please stop by his apartment before she went home that night, and to bring Dalton. Thinking there was some snag with the bridge construction, which was coming along at a much faster pace than anyone expected (in addition to the construction firm officially hired for the project, nearly the entire School of Engineering from Meyer College had volunteered to help), she put the thought out of her mind until after work, when she could fully look forward to the prospect of unwinding with her brother and her boyfriend.

She worked late, trying to make up for the smaller number of customers all day. Dalton met her at the restaurant.

They drove to Jean-Luc's apartment, and, as they parked on the street, they both noticed that the light was on in the bedroom upstairs, and the window was open. It was odd because Jean-Luc never kept any windows open at all during the winter, as he had always been prone to feeling chilly. He was a slight boy who grew into a slight man. The sight of the open window gave them both an unexpected wave of anxiety.

Then Marie noticed that the window wasn't open, but rather it was broken, and at that moment poor Marie's mighty heart almost ripped in half.

She ran to the building.

Dalton called out, "Marie, what's—"

But then he noticed the jagged edges, too, and ran with

her.

Marie was already crying by the time she reached the door.

She yelled and searched and yelled, but nobody answered. The place was an unusual mess. The lights were still on, and the front door was unlocked.

Her brother was gone.

THE HAVERBROOK Police Department was on the case immediately. The hatred the Mantanites felt for Clem Lemon was the exact opposite of the way the city of Haverbrook had embraced Jean-Luc Delphine—their brilliant engineering wunderkind.

One week later, Jean-Luc Delphine was still missing, and this article ran as the banner story in *The Radical Post*.

COMMUNITY MOURNS DEATH OF CHURCH LEADER
By Quentin Hancock

MANTA—The Luminarian community has been dealt another painful blow.

Yesterday evening the beloved former Head Pastor of the Luminarian Church—Phillip Augustus Hershey—passed away.

Hershey, 64, had developed a severe case of pneumonia over the last three months, and yesterday, around 6:00 PM, surrounded by friends and family, he succumbed to the disease in his own home.

His reign as church leader marked an eventful time in the history of the community. He oversaw the church grow by 11 percent, the highest growth rate under any Luminarian leader on record besides church founder Aaron Wells. He presided over an adoring community in faith who each week sought and were rewarded by the profound creations of his well-regarded tongue and powerful tenor saxophone.

A man of larger-than-life proportions, Hershey's passing comes at an inopportune time for the church. No members of the Luminarian community allowed themselves to be interviewed for this story, but last night's highly attended makeshift vigil was glowing proof that Hershey is already missed. Dozens of Luminarians braved the cold of winter to let their mourning begin outside the Hershey home.

    The father of two is survived by his children and wife. Daughter Victoria Kathleen, 26, is a highly respected citizen of Manta. Son Augustus Alexander, 31, is the church's newly appointed and youngest ever Head Pastor and was recently engaged to fiancée Pamela Hait, 30. Hershey's wife of 21 years, Charlotte Hershey (née Swallows), has recently fallen ill herself and is being cared for by daughter Victoria and family friend Nathan Cameron. Her medical condition is at present unknown, but it was relayed to the *Post* that on top of her illness she is suffering tremendous grief at the loss of her late husband.

    Funeral services will be Thursday, from noon to 3:00 PM, at the Luminarian Church.

43

THE HAVERBROOK Police Department's widespread efforts to locate Jean-Luc Delphine had been frustrated by the scornful town of Manta, whose city council, in an emergency session, had legally rejected Haverbrook's pleas to extend their search into Manta. Compounding that frustration was the vastness of the surrounding forest, wherein a great—yet, compared to the size of the forest, unsubstantial—number of search parties had also tried to help.

If Jean-Luc was being held captive within the town of Manta, it would be up to Marie and Dalton to find him.

With her brother missing for longer than a week now, Marie hadn't eaten in days and was losing hope rapidly. She looked pale and sickly.

Her parents had been notified, and they were flying in from France, where they had been visiting family on an extended vacation.

Dalton and Marie searched day and night, every opportunity they could. They tromped through the snow-white woods surrounding the city, calling his name, and they listened desperately as they walked past the old houses in town, listening for anything, clutching together for warmth, looking for any clue they could find.

Despite all that, the searches had yielded no progress or leads.

Marie spent every night in Dalton's cabin, staying up late by the fireplace, crying in profound worry about her brother and "what those crazies might be doing to him!"

Meanwhile, construction on the bridge continued in earnest and with haste, despite the winter weather. Jean-Luc's disappearance drove the city of Haverbrook and the students of Meyer College to work even harder, in tribute to the missing young man.

Those who were not participating in any of the searches could be found at the bridge.

44

Two weeks later, a hunter from the distant city of Wellington, in the forest ten miles south of Manta, came across the ghastly sight of dark red blood soaked into the otherwise ubiquitously white snow. The blood led to a dead body, pale and affected by exposure, tied to the trunk of a tree, the frozen eyes being pecked at by crows.

The Haverbrook police were immediately notified, and the body was returned to town, where a crowd of citizens and students gathered outside the funeral home to pay homage to a young engineer from France who was kidnapped from his home, bound, starved, stabbed, and strangled. So many deaths for one young man.

The wake was a closed-casket affair, as weeks of open exposure in the wilderness had left Jean-Luc's body bloated and grotesque—an unjust last image of a peaceful man who lived privately and well.

Marie, Dalton, and the Delphine parents fell into deep mourning.

The day after the funeral, Dalton had to publish two letters to the editor in which his friend's death was celebrated by the Manta townspeople and church leaders. Dalton's brain was too far gone into its own shadows to craft a meaningful counterpoint. All the words in the world were nothing—were pointless grunts at the sun—compared to the mournful look on Marie's tear-streaked face, compared to the helpless fury he felt. The sight of those letters made him irate; the sight of Jean-Luc's small urn of ashes made him cry; the sight of his girlfriend's endless tears broke his heart.

He and Marie both left their jobs indefinitely, with the understanding of their bosses.

Before Dalton left, Quentin said to him, "Go mourn with Marie; I can handle the paper. You suck at it, anyway." It was the only thing he could think of to distract Dalton from the loss of his friend. It worked. Dalton broke his frown, and the corner of his lips lifted for a moment. Then they shook hands, and Dalton walked out.

The Delphine parents arrived, and they, with Dalton and Marie, drove to a distant state park—Jean-Luc's favorite place in the world—where they climbed a hill overlooking a mountain lake, and they scattered his ashes into the blustery wind.

They stayed for several weeks, in that secluded spot, not saying much to each other—comforted by each other's presence, trying to let time heal a wound that can never be fully healed.

Eventually, they returned to town, upon receiving word from Quentin that a date had been set for when the newly completed Dugan Bridge was scheduled to be opened to the traveling public.

The Delphine parents wouldn't think of staying in the city where their son was killed; they went to the state capital, with the Luminarian Church on their lips.

Marie and Dalton returned to Manta.

They returned in the rain.

45

IT WAS early spring.

As the air warmed more each day, the snowpack began to recede. Additionally, it had rained for the previous three days, which greatly sped up the thaw.

Because of this combination of rain and melting snow, the Crondura River flowed mightily, heavily, powerfully, roaring as it went. Some of the mystics in the more freethinking circles of Haverbrook considered it nature's tribute to the dead engineer.

Manta and Haverbrook citizens alike had never seen the swollen river rush with such force and speed. The rain kept coming; the snow kept melting; and the river sprinted down its serpentine path and ran south heavily and took everything with it.

And then, finally, an hour before the sun would rise, as the eastern sky yielded its stormy black mourning to a misty blue-gray pre-dawn yawn, the skies cleared, and the day turned its face to the sun.

The Manta rhetoric, which had been building in Dalton's absence, reached a fever pitch as the weather warmed.

Outsiders were warned by church officials not to use the bridge, for fear of violent reprisal by the Luminarians. Because of this, police officers were brought in from surrounding towns and counties in an attempt to keep all concerned parties safely separated. An officer from Wellington recalled, "It was just this odd-looking bridge in the middle of nowhere, and these folks was going apeshit."

The sight at the bridge that that officer looked over was unadulterated back-country pandemonium: angry Haverbrook citizens shouting pointed obscenities at the Luminarians; intoxicated Haverbrook artists just looking for a scene; celebratory Haverbrook officials turning nervous at the contentious spectacle; serious-looking Manta citizens in prayer circles, humming and chanting prayers into the all-accepting air; virulent Manta citizens waving threatening protest pickets.

Blame. Rage. Fear. Animated and in action—masses of people idealistically divided. Acids and bases in a blender, producing noxious fumes.

The mayor of Haverbrook tried to improve the situation with a brief speech, barely audible over the hollering and ruckus of the agitated crowds.

"Today we pay tribute to two great Haverbrook friends: Antaeus 'Ace' Dugan, one of the world's great creative fountainheads and philanthropists, and Jean-Luc Delphine, a phenomenally talented young man who was taken from us far too early. With this bridge, designed by our friend Jean-Luc and financed by our friend Antaeus, we open the two sides of this great countryside to be traveled and enjoyed by any and all who wish to come and visit. The world shrinks every day and brings us closer together. This is human progress. As we open lines of travel, communication, and commerce, we are strengthened by the ease with which we can come and go and by what we can learn when regions that were formerly foreign are opened to be explored by the knowledge-hungry best of who and what we are. And so today it is with great honor that I declare this perfect tribute to the best of humanity open for travel!"

The mayor performed a ceremonial ribbon-cutting, and the Haverbrook citizens erupted into massive applause and cheer.

The Luminarians shouted down the mayor with personified contempt.

The bridge stood stationary, hanging in the air untouched, bright in the sunshine.

The warnings coming from Manta included threats of physical injury for anyone who chose to cross the bridge.

Nobody had taken the threats very seriously until now. Now, after seeing what the scene had become, nobody moved.

Marie Delphine, who could not pull her eyes from Jean-Luc's bridge, clung tight to Dalton's hand. Dalton's gaze swung from the bridge to Marie's tear-swollen eyes and down to her little frown.

Eventually, the cheers on one side and the jeers on the other side faded into silence. And still nobody moved. A vast quiet descended over the area.

Marie looked around. She saw her friends from Haverbrook. She saw her friends from Manta. She saw the Hersheys, standing together across the bridge, looking vulnerable and afraid. She saw Jane Jefferson and Quentin Hancock. They were still looking at the bridge, sadly and proudly.

She stepped off the raised platform and worked her way through the crowd with a curious look on her face, confused and determined to take action. She walked past protesters, politicians, and police officers, each making way for the dead boy's pretty sister. She walked through these crowds until she reached the foot of the bridge, and then she stopped.

Dalton followed close behind and stood next to her reassuringly as they both observed the graceful lines of Jean-Luc's beautiful creation.

"Why did they kill him, Dalton?" Marie asked, her voice quivering with every consonant. "Why would they do that to him?"

Through his welling tears, Dalton looked across the bridge, at the townspeople of Manta, and turned his face back to Marie's. "There's something I want to show you—something I wrote. It's in Jane's cabin." His voice was shaky, too. He couldn't continue.

With the slightest movement of her overwhelmed head, Marie nodded.

Then they both kissed and hugged and held each other in shared mourning. Within that moment, there was nothing else in the world but the two young lovers and the bridge they were about to cross.

With her head pressed to Dalton's chest, Marie finally

said, "Let's go."

Dalton wiped a tear from her eye, and they both began walking across the bridge.

The Haverbrook citizens exploded in loud elation, and the Luminarians made no sound at all. They watched with loathing.

Marie's eyes welled again, and Dalton's throat was so tight his breaths came in labored gulps. They both mournfully thought about Jean-Luc—the beloved, the fallen, the creator of this wonderful work of functional art beneath their feet, how honest and smart and earnest he was.

Had been.

As he walked, Dalton found himself thinking of the way Jean-Luc had always blushed whenever he ordered a drink from his favorite bartender. As Marie walked, she remembered watching her ten-year-old brother from her secret perch in the tree in their front yard, where she sometimes read, as he bounced a ball off their garage door, for hours, occasionally laughing to himself as he tossed and received the ball, thinking about something, entertaining himself, seeing how he, like she, was alone but not lonely. *We are both alone, but we are both here, so we are not alone*, she remembered thinking.

She cried.

He wasn't here anymore.

As Dalton and Marie walked across the bridge, the weight of their many emotions forced both to lean against the other, buttressed by each other's strength.

The water rushed with white tips thirty-five feet below them. The steady rocking rush of that water down there contrasted with the thin band of concrete upon which they walked, two hands joined, fingers interlaced.

The bridge beneath their feet felt firm. Stronger and bouncier than earth. Like now that it was completed, it could never give way.

Until it did.

The charge was set, and the first sticks of dynamite exploded fifteen feet ahead of them, where the bridge's primary arc was centered. When it happened, the only thing that Dalton registered was that he could feel a tremble of fear rip through Marie as she clenched his hand even harder. Behind them, the townspeople of Haverbrook stood in shock, and their gasps could be heard even over the cracking concrete, which was further drowned out by the citizens of Manta letting out a barbaric yawp of celebration at the other end of the bridge.

The dynamite was perfectly placed, and with only two alternately timed rocking jolts, the major buttresses of the bridge were exploded out, and the bridge disintegrated into falling chunks.

The concrete beneath their feet buckled and then gave way, and Dalton and Marie were falling. It happened so suddenly they were not a moment past their initial shock when they began to plummet. As they fell, as large slabs of concrete fell beside them, as they felt the sudden emptiness from the void created by unchecked gravity, Dalton and Marie pulled close to each other.

Clung together.

And plunged heavily into the rushing river.

Beneath the surface, the icy combination of thawed snow and cold spring rain engulfed the lovers in a paralyzing universe of pain, and the force of the water swept them rapidly downstream, smashing them into large rocks at the river's bottom, where they were then dragged along the jagged silt. Two intertwining spirits of blood joined the river's run, and large chunks of the bridge fell from above and churned the red ribbons into an ambiguous pink froth.

The two young lovers held each other as the powerful world around them gurgled into a suffocating chaos. Even as they both struggled to help each other reach the surface and survive, even as they let out their final breaths and met their individual deaths, they held each other.

AN HOUR later, two grotesquely battered corpses in a dead embrace were discovered on a sandy bank of the Crondura River a few miles downstream by a whimpering black Labrador named Hunter. A grief-stricken Clem Lemon made an anonymous call to the Haverbrook Police Department, and the bodies were collected.

46

EARLY ON a May morning of that year—three days after the deaths of Marie Delphine and Dalton Hughes, a day after Marie's cremation and Dalton's burial—Clem Lemon, who was now tending to his dying friend Halo Kilgore, set up a video camera in the middle of Kilgore's underground home. The two busted out all of the windows and threw open every door and every available portal to the outside forest. The old hinges of the curved roof were oiled and engaged, and with the sound of a small motor, the floor of the forest opened, and its cool, civilized, jazz-filled belly was exposed to the wild.

Most of the sunlight above was caught by the green canopy of the forest, but there were several showers of light between the leaves, and they left little puddles of sunlight on the living-room floor where Huck and Clem hugged and cried a tearful last goodbye.

Halo Kilgore sat down mid-frame in front of the video camera and before a large white canvas and put on some of his favorite music while Clem Lemon pressed the record button and then kneeled on a worn prayer mat.

"There is so much of this life that I have loved, and so much that has broken my heart. Now, I rest. I understand no more now than I ever have about this life of ours, and I don't have the will for the riddle any longer. I'm a tired, old man, and this is my goddam right."

Then Halo Kilgore fitted the wide barrel of his shotgun in his mouth.

His eyes settled on the quivering edge of one of those puddles of light on the ground, and his muscles went rigid with unease. There were a few moments of deliberation, and then his whole body seemed to relax as a small smirk curled onto the corner of his barrel-filled mouth.

The buckshot ripped through the contents of his skull and scattered them onto the canvas—a starburst mix of red, gray, white, and yellow. The body slumped lifelessly to the ground, and instantly the weight of the physical and intellectual world was lifted from Halo Kilgore, and he joined his wife and young friends in ugly death.

Before he died, because he did not have Marie to give them to, he burned all his money and private possessions.

Clem Lemon, who had learned about a special Buddhist practice during his teaching years at the university, settled into a meditation, and with the camera angled over his shoulder, he and Halo made a movie.

The camera was repeatedly loaded with enough film for a time-elapsed sequence, and for as long as it took, Clem Lemon meditated while Halo Kilgore's body decayed and was consumed.

Open to all the greedy forces of the awakening forest, Halo Kilgore's flesh flaked away, eaten by parasites, bugs, worms, and rats, and because of the nature of time-elapse, it almost appeared as if the body were being eaten away by the air itself. Clem Lemon meditated over his decaying friend's corpse, contemplating ubiquitous impermanence—often crying for the same reason.

What resulted, and this according to Halo Kilgore's design, was a time-elapsed presentation of the impermanence of human life, condensed down to the thirty-two minutes and forty-seven seconds of the immortal Pharoah Sanders opus: "The Creator Has a Master Plan."

The movie had no commercial value, and many people who heard of it called it disgusting and potentially illegal. The few people who got to see it, however, and among them were Jane Jefferson and Quentin Hancock, considered it one of the most powerful films they'd ever seen.

By the end of the movie, as the musical sounds wound down to their inevitable conclusion, the body of Halo Kilgore no longer cast a shadow save that of its skeleton—that final white skeleton that could be anybody.

47

AUGUSTUS HERSHEY and Nathan Cameron had become close friends over the course of the previous three years. Well, as close of friends as people like Augustus Hershey and Nathan Cameron could be.

Though Augustus was busy with his dying father and ongoing church affairs, he always tried to find time for his friend Nathan. It was one of the few things he enjoyed outside of his church responsibilities; he and Nathan would spend long hours debating matters of faith and music and whatever else Augustus wished to discuss.

Although Augustus had his suspicions, he never factually learned of the ongoing affair between Nathan and his fiancé.

After all, none of his actions ever showed that he found out. Or perhaps he didn't care.

Pamela Hait would never get to marry her fiancé, because on June sixth of that same year, Augustus Hershey was arrested on the charges of murder, destruction of state property, conspiracy to commit murder, and domestic terrorism.

He and three other Luminarians were tried and convicted for the murders of Dalton Hughes and Marie Delphine. All the materials for rigging explosives, as well as detailed blueprints for the bridge and the location of its structural vulnerabilities, were found in the basement of the church building after law enforcement officers—this time legally and with ID and warrants—raided the Luminarian community.

Augustus Hershey intransigently insisted upon his innocence throughout his arrest, the trial, and his many years in prison. And perhaps he was right when he did so, despite his very real, objective guilt for the murder of the two young lovers. He honestly believed himself to have done good for the good of his soul and the souls of everyone who walked in his faith. He was innocent, you see. He was right, in his heart.

But there is a problem with that explanation. Eleven years into his sentence, Augustus Hershey hung himself in his prison cell and died. The note he left, also hung around his neck, said, "I am already forgiven."

That was the end of his song.

In a moment of desperate weakness, Augustus took his sickly father's advice and kidnapped Jean-Luc to an old shack in the woods, about ten miles south of town. He'd discovered it as a boy while hiking through the forest in search of adventure with a childhood friend.

Nobody was ever convicted of Jean-Luc's murder. Many suspect the murderer was a Luminarian named Allen Ontern, who was one of Manta's more sociopathic citizens. He and Augustus had an argument the morning of the bridge explosion, and Augustus had beaten Ontern bloody and unconscious and never explained himself. Augustus had a long history with Ontern—the two used to tromp around the woods together when they were kids.

NATHAN CAMERON put into practice what he learned throughout his life.

After a long youth of unbridled sexual hedonism afforded him by the fates, fortunate settings, and the nature of his personality and philosophy, Nathan Cameron began to enter a new phase in his life right around the same time he met Victoria Hershey.

Victoria came from a culture vastly different from that of Nathan's upbringing. He saw in this young girl a chance to totally reinvent himself and move in a new direction with his life. He thought maybe he had found the holy water that could sustain his life's vegetation so that never would the roots be dry again. Victoria Hershey, with her remarkable beauty and the controlled intensity burning in her cautious heart, represented a new ideal—something strange and wonderful. Nathan Cameron knew everything but the naturally strange and wonderful, though he did know how to fake it. There are many painters who can recreate the works of the masters, but they can't create masterworks of their own. They have their tricks, but that is all.

For Nathan, all the world is a power struggle, and all things are fair in love and war. And because life is nothing but love and war, all things are permitted.

Like sleeping with your so-called friend's fiancé. Or lying about the trials you went through and the things you were supposed to have seen while being reborn in the sands of Utah, while instead you spent the week visiting old baseball friends in Texas and writing "some bullshit diary" to convince everyone in Manta you were just like they were.

Just like everybody.

48

NATHAN CAMERON is behind the wheel of his white Jeep, and he is heading West.

Alone on this road, with his radio busted and silent, he reflects on a conversation that took place on the banks of the Crondura River, to the north of Manta, a few weeks back.

The sun, in his memory, was orange-red, and it was already down to its mid-belly behind the rocky edge of the horizon. In that light, the ground was dark except for the sparkling orange gash of the moving river at the bottom of the canyon.

In the memory, Augustus Hershey and Nathan Cameron were seated on the hood of Nathan's Jeep CJ-7. They each had a beer and were observing the half-completed bridge and the horizon past the river, where a few Haverbrook houselights were coming to life between the taut power lines in the twilight. Augustus took a heavy swig from his bottle. Nathan thought Augustus looked particularly tense—noticing the large man's overly quick reactions, and the way he couldn't slump against the windshield like Nathan but sat forward with his leg twitching, and the way he kept running his fingers through his hair, as if to pull thoughts or worries out of his head.

For a moment, Augustus stopped twitching, as if he'd reached some difficult conclusion and could now relax and face it rather than dread it.

"Whether you believe it or not," Augustus said, "I know what kind of person you are."

"What's that mean? You okay, man?"

"It's—I need something, Nathan."

"Augustus, you're *The Man* around here. What could I—"

"You're the type of person who can get it, and I need it, and I need your help."

"Dude, what the hell are you talking about?"

"They can't," he said and squeezed his eyes shut, "I can't— That bridge can't stay up. That bridge . . . cannot—"

Nathan's face lit up with understanding. "You want me to talk to those engineers I met when I went fishing in the river that one time?" He smirked knowingly. "I think I could get them to teach me a thing or two about the bridge."

NATHAN CAMERON snaps out of the memory. The wind is flinging his long hair in every direction, and he steps on the accelerator and thinks about what he's leaving behind: a mess. Nathan never meant for Dalton and Marie to die. He didn't realize that Augustus was really that sadistic—never picked up that vibe. He thought Augustus would just blow it up at night or something. Nathan felt a brief but heavy nausea when he saw those two fall in the water like dead toys, and in that moment, inwardly, he completely disengaged from the lives of Victoria and all the Hersheys and everyone in Manta and his life there as he knew it.

He left that night, but not until after seeing Victoria one last time.

Nathan was alone in his room in the Hershey house the evening after Marie and Dalton died. Augustus had disappeared, and everyone was out looking for him, except Victoria, who was mourning with Jane in Dalton's old cabin. As

Nathan ruminated on what to do next, Victoria kept asking herself how this could have happened. How could her brother do that? And how did he know how to dynamite the bridge so effectively? He was the least scientific person she knew. But then her eyes opened wide, and she remembered her boyfriend Nathan telling her about some of the Haverbrook people he'd met—including a few structural engineers.

She raced out of the house, without telling Jane where she was going, and in an instant she appeared in Nathan's room and began slapping him across the face and crying, screaming at him, "HOW COULD YOU DO THAT?" She slapped him and clawed at his face and cut a jagged gash across his cheek with the fingernail of her thumb.

"It was your brother!" Nathan held her down and shouted back.

"I know he did it, but it was *you!*" she screamed. She started crying again.

"Why?" she asked, sobbing. "They were your friends, Nathan. Who *are* you? *What* are you?" She could barely get the words out.

"I didn't know . . . Victoria, I really didn't—"

Victoria wrestled herself out of his grasp and stood over him.

"GET OUT OF HERE!" she screamed and left.

He never saw her again. And neither did anyone else from Manta. Revolted by everything that had happened, Victoria finally followed through on the threat she'd privately held over the Hershey family for years: she abandoned the Luminarian faith.

ONCE AGAIN Nathan shakes away that memory and is back in his Jeep. He's hundreds of miles away from there, and the warmth of the air feels great on his skin. He hits the accelerator again, harder, and rockets forward, guilt-free, his windshield a gleaming reflection of the smoldering sun.

Just ahead, he sees a young man standing on the side of the road wearing a large backpack and holding up the traveler's thumb. The young man is unshaven and looks road-worn, but as Nathan stops he notices an unmistakable, penetrating certainty in the young man's eyes.

"Need a ride?" Nathan says, his Jeep idling throatily.

"Sure, yes sir," says the young man. "I sure could."

"Where you headed?" Nathan asks.

"Anywhere," the young man says. "I want to see everywhere."

"I like that," Nathan says. "Me, too. You found anywhere good yet?"

"Some good, yeah. Seems like they don't often stay too good for too long, though."

"Yeah," Nathan said, indicating the gash across his cheek. "They don't."

"How about you? Looks like you could use a navigator."

"Sure, yes sir," Nathan says with certainty. "I sure could."

EPILOGUE

THE LAST PAGE

The authorities spent a month trying to locate Dalton's family, to send his body back to them, but nobody ever came forward to claim it. Clem, Quentin, and Jane tried, but a confounding bureaucracy would not give them the legal clearance.

He was buried in an unmarked grave in the county cemetery—visited once by Jane and Victoria, before they moved away, and a few times by Clem and Quentin, before they passed away.

And then eventually all that was left of Dalton to the living world were the words he had written.

In his time in Manta, he had filled stacks of notebooks with miles of writing—his own thoughts and his favorite quotations from the books he read. The following is a typed transcript of the final handwritten entry, the last page, containing a size-mixed grid of boxes of text, in the notebooks of the life of Dalton Hughes.

Another day of reading by the big blue lake with the Delphines. On a quiet walk with Marie I can see why Jean-Luc loved this place—we can't look anywhere without seeing what he would consider a beautiful canvas for his marvelous structural ideas. Marie described a few of them to me, and we both sat on the warm grass and pictured them, and they were Jean-Luc, and we cried pathetically.

At night we cloak ourselves in stacks of Marie's favorite poetry and the words of some friends in our despair, Kafka and Kilgore—a good distraction, not only the words but the lives they reveal.

I'm pulling these thoughts out of myself. It's like Marie said earlier, "Jean-Luc is gone, and it feels like we are gone now, too."

What do you think has become of the young and old men? And what do you think has become of the women and children?

They are alive and well somewhere;
The smallest sprout shows there really is no death,
And if ever there was it led forward life, and does not wait at the
end to arrest it,
And ceased the moment life appeared.
—Walt Whitman, from "Song of Myself"

The constant variety of the form it takes, and once, in the midst of it all, the affecting sight of a momentary abatement in its variations.
—Franz Kafka
[Next to this entry, Dalton wrote and circled the name "Nathan."]

I understand hello, but what the hell is goodbye?
—Halo Kilgore

This bridge an old, sinking web,
the trapped scales of a saxophone
struggling to set themselves free.
They will fall one day, sink small ships
passing beneath with the weight accumulated
over years. Carbon dioxide and ice. Crystals
from poisoned towers. Hats and veils from war
widows, crossing for Easter. 1949. 1951. Fragments
of hydrogen bombs, dark from the Pacific. Screams
from jumpers, released from Bellevue, like spiders, returning
the night I was born, to claim prey in midair.
—Jim Carroll, from "New York City Variations"

<u>First draft of possible conclusion to "The Predator Prays":</u>

The church itself is a bear. It is the largest and strongest force in the forest of our experience. In order to survive, the church freely roams its world and devours everything edible in its path. And it will survive, because a bear, both a powerful killer and a shameless scavenger, is an answer.

We awaken as babies horrified in a swirling world of light and dark, hot and cold, motion and stillness, and our great universe of awareness expands and sharpens every day. The more we learn about ourselves and our world, the more questions we meet.

It is a quest for meaning and understanding.

The bear is simply the biggest and easiest answer. The bear devours everything and claims that everything serves its purpose. Good or Bad, the bear goes on, and in fact is powered by both.

Augustus Hershey couldn't shoot the bear.

The bullet he fired would've ripped through his own heart.

About the Author

Daniel Donatelli is the author of the novels *Music Made By Bears* and *Jibba And Jibba*, as well as the sundry collection *Oh, Title!* He was born in Cleveland, Ohio, in 1981.

For more information, please visit www.hhbpublishing.com.

Made in the USA
Lexington, KY
04 March 2012